I0695148

Wrapped Up in Christmas

Mistletoe Falls Series, Book #5

Tara Baisden

Sterling Ridge Press LLC

Copyright

Wrapped Up in Christmas © 2025 by Tara Baisden

All rights reserved. No part of this book may be reproduced, distributed, or transmitted in any form or by any means, including photocopying, recording, or other electronic or mechanical methods, without the prior written permission of the author, except in the case of brief quotations embodied in critical reviews and certain other noncommercial uses permitted by copyright law.

This is a work of fiction. Names, characters, places, and incidents either are the product of the author's imagination or are used fictitiously. Any resemblance to actual persons, living or dead, events, or locales is entirely coincidental.

Cover designed by Sterling Ridge Press LLC

Published by: Sterling Ridge Press, LLC www.sterlingridgepress.com

ISBN: 978-1-966093-40-4 Printed in the United States of America

First Edition: November 2025

For permissions, contact: tara@tarabaisden.com or visit www.tarabaisden.com

Dedication

To everyone who has ever sent a Christmas card to someone who didn't write back, kept believing in a friendship that seemed one-sided, or held onto hope when love felt impossible—this story is for you. To the military families who understand that love isn't measured by presence but by the strength to choose each other across any distance, and to the communities that wrap around returning veterans with the kind of welcome that makes "home" more than just a place on a map. And finally, to every reader who believes that some love stories are worth waiting for, that second chances can be even more beautiful than first ones, and that Christmas miracles happen because grace has a way of wrapping us up in exactly the gifts our hearts need most. May your own story be filled with faithful friends, cozy moments, and the kind of magic that makes every season feel like Christmas morning. With love and warm holiday wishes,

Tara

Contents

Chapter 1

The ladder wobbled slightly as Hallie stretched toward the top shelf, her fingertips just grazing the box of silver snowflake ornaments that had somehow migrated to the back corner during yesterday's rush. Below her, Nina's voice drifted up through the shop's background playlist of gentle instrumental carols.

"I'm telling you, if one more person asks me where we keep the advent calendars, I'm going to start handing out maps."

"They're literally right by the register," Lucy said as she stood near the front window, arranging a miniature village scene complete with tiny ice skaters and a lamppost that actually glowed. "With a giant sign that says 'Advent Calendars Here.'"

Hallie smiled despite the precarious angle of her reach. The box shifted forward an inch, then another, until she could finally grip it properly and ease it down. "Maybe we need a bigger sign."

"Maybe people need to look up from their phones," Nina muttered, but her tone held affection rather than irritation. After managing the shop for three years, she'd perfected the art of gentle exasperation.

Saturday mornings in the Wrapped Up in Christmas Shop always carried a particular energy—that perfect blend of anticipation and routine that made Hallie smile every single time she unlocked the doors. The shop had been open for half an hour, and already the store hummed with activity that would build throughout the day until closing.

She descended the ladder, cradling the ornament box against her hip. The shop stretched around her in all its glittering glory, every corner designed to transport visitors straight into the heart of the holiday season. Twinkling white lights draped across exposed ceiling beams, their glow reflected in hundreds of glass ornaments hanging at varying heights throughout the space. The scent of vanilla and cinnamon drifted from the candle display near the center aisle, where a customer in a burgundy coat was testing different fragrances with the focused intensity of someone on a mission.

Floor-to-ceiling shelves lined the walls, organized by color and theme in a way that looked effortlessly festive but had actually required three full days of careful planning back in September. Red and green dominated one section, silver and gold another, while a third showcased the jewel tones that had become increasingly popular—deep purples, rich teals, and sapphire blues that caught the light like precious gems. Handmade stockings hung from decorative hooks, their embroidered names waiting to be claimed by families creating new traditions. A display of snow globes occupied an entire vintage hutch, each one containing a different miniature world of winter magic.

The front window was Lucy's current domain, and Hallie could see her kneeling on the wide sill, adjusting the position of a tiny sledding hill while humming along to "The First Noel." Her creativity had transformed the space into a scene worthy of a storybook, complete with cotton batting snow and a backdrop painted to look like distant mountains dusted with white.

"Mrs. Henderson wants to know if we can hold three of the large outdoor wreaths for her," Taylor said from behind the counter, phone pressed to her shoulder as she wrapped a set of ceramic angels in tissue paper.

Hallie set the ornament box on the counter beside the register, already mentally calculating inventory. "Tell her yes, but we'll need a deposit since those wreaths are popular. And see if she wants the matching garland for the porch railing."

"Already suggested it." Taylor's grin was triumphant.

This was what Hallie loved most—not just the products or the decorations or even the steady stream of customers, but the rhythm of it all. The way her team moved through the space like a well-rehearsed dance, anticipating needs before they were voiced and solving problems before they became crises. Nina had already restocked the card-making supplies in aisle three, Taylor was working through the phone orders with efficient charm, and Lucy's window display would be finished within the hour, ready to draw in afternoon shoppers with its whimsical appeal.

The bell above the door chimed—not the electronic buzz of modern retail, but an actual brass bell that Hallie's father had installed twenty years ago because he'd insisted a Christmas shop deserved a proper announcement for every arrival. An older couple entered, the woman's face lighting up as she took in the surroundings.

"Oh, Harold, look at this place!"

Harold dutifully looked, his weathered face creasing into a smile.

Hallie moved toward them with a welcoming expression. "Good morning! Welcome to Wrapped Up in Christmas. Is this your first visit?"

"It is," the woman said, already gravitating toward the ornament display. "Our granddaughter just moved to Asheville, and we're driving through on our way to visit. Someone at the diner said we absolutely had to stop here."

"Well, we're glad you did. If you need any help finding something special, just let any of us know."

They wandered deeper into the shop, the woman's delighted exclamations punctuating the background music. Hallie returned to the counter, reaching for the pricing gun to mark the newly retrieved ornaments.

The bell chimed again.

Hallie glanced up, expecting another customer, and instead saw Mark Montgomery pushing through the door with the kind of barely contained energy that made her smile. His silver-touched hair was slightly rumpled, as if he'd run his hands through it repeatedly.

"Hallie." He spotted her immediately, his face breaking into a grin that crinkled the corners of his eyes.

"You look like you just won the lottery. What's going on?" She set down the pricing gun, her attention fully caught by whatever had him practically vibrating with excitement.

"Better than the lottery." Mark said as he approached the counter. "Though I should probably apologize in advance for keeping a secret."

Nina's eyebrows rose. "This sounds interesting."

"Chase is coming home." The words tumbled out with the relief of someone who'd been holding them in too long. "For good, I mean. He's officially done with the Marines, decided not to reenlist, and he's moving back to Mistletoe Falls permanently."

The pricing gun slipped from Hallie's fingers, clattering against the counter. Her pulse kicked up, sudden and sharp, and for a second the shop seemed to tilt slightly before righting itself. "Chase is... he's coming home? To stay?"

"To stay." Mark's grin widened at her reaction. "Liz and I have known for a few weeks that he wasn't reenlisting, but we only found out a few days ago that he was actually planning to move back here instead of settling somewhere else. He wanted it to be a surprise, but I'm terrible at keeping good news to myself, and I figured you'd want to know since..." He gestured vaguely. "Well, since you two were always so close growing up."

Nina moved closer, with interest written across her features.

Mark's attention shifted between them. "Liz and I are throwing him a welcome home dinner at the Community Center this Saturday. Nothing too fancy, just a potluck dinner with family and friends. We'd love for all of you to come."

Sofia appeared from the back room, catching the tail end of the conversation. "Did I hear something about Chase Montgomery?"

"He's moving back to Mistletoe Falls," Nina supplied, her voice carrying the same excitement that was currently making Hallie's thoughts spin. "After twelve years in the Marines."

"I remember him from high school," Sofia said, tilting her head thoughtfully. "Quiet guy, really polite. Always helped Mr. Peterson carry equipment after shop class."

Hallie's mind had already traveled backward, tumbling through memories she hadn't examined in years. Chase, at seventeen, lanky and serious, helping her father unload inventory trucks on summer afternoons. Chase teaching her how to skip stones in the creek behind their houses, patient even when her throws went wildly off course. Chase sitting on her front porch the night before he left for basic training, both of them pretending they weren't sad about the goodbye while mosquitoes buzzed around the porch light.

She'd written him letters that first year. Long, rambling updates about life in Mistletoe Falls, about her college classes, about the shop and her parents, and all the small moments that made up ordinary days. He'd written back for a while, his replies growing shorter and less frequent until they'd stopped altogether. She'd understood—or told herself she understood. Military life was demanding and staying connected to home was probably harder than she could imagine.

But she'd never stopped sending the cards. Every birthday and every Christmas, a handwritten message making its way across whatever distance separated them. She'd never expected a response. The cards had become something else entirely—a way of maintaining a connection that existed whether or not it was acknowledged, a small act of faith that some friendships didn't need constant tending to survive.

And now he was coming home. Not for a visit, but for good.

"Hallie?" Mark's voice held gentle amusement. "You still with us?"

She blinked, pulling herself back to the present. "Sorry, I just... it's been so long. I can't believe he's really moving back."

"Believe it." Mark's expression softened. "He's planning to help out at the toy store while he figures out what's next. Civilian life is a big adjustment after twelve years in the military, so Liz and I figured having him work with us for a while might ease the transition."

"That makes sense. When does he arrive?"

"Sometime this evening. But the dinner's Saturday night, six o'clock at the Community Center. Say you'll come. All of you?" His gaze swept to include Nina, Sofia, and Taylor, who'd been listening with unabashed interest.

"Of course we'll come," Nina said. "Wouldn't miss it."

"Perfect." Mark's entire posture radiated satisfaction. "I should get back to the store before the Saturday crowd hits. Just wanted to make sure you heard the news from me instead of through the town grapevine."

He headed for the door, pausing with his hand on the frame. "I'm so glad my boy is coming home, Hallie. I know he'll be happy to see you again."

The bell chimed his exit, and silence descended on the shop for exactly three seconds before Nina let out a low whistle.

"Well. That was unexpected."

"Chase Montgomery," Sofia mused. "Coming back after all this time. Wonder what made him decide to leave the military."

"Wait, who's Chase Montgomery, and why does everyone look like Christmas came early?" Lucy asked.

"Hallie's childhood best friend," Nina supplied, shooting Hallie a look that held far too much knowing amusement. "And possibly more than that, if senior year was any indication."

"It was a crush," Hallie said firmly, even as heat crept up her neck. "Twelve years ago. Ancient history."

"Ancient history that just made you drop the pricing gun and go completely still for about thirty seconds." Nina's grin was unrepentant. "I know you, Hallie Dawson. You don't react like that to just any news."

"I'm surprised, that's all. We were close, and then he left, and now he's coming back. It's a lot to process."

"Mm-hmm. Well, I think it's exciting. And I definitely think we're all going to that dinner on Saturday."

The older couple approached the counter, arms full of ornaments and ribbon, and Hallie seized the distraction gratefully. She rang up their purchases with her usual attentiveness, wrapped everything carefully in tissue paper, and sent them on their way with genuine wishes for a wonderful visit with their granddaughter.

The morning continued in its progression. More customers arrived, each requiring attention and care. Lucy finished another window display. Taylor fielded phone calls and helped customers. Sofia reorganized the nativity scene collection, grouping them by size and style in a way that made perfect visual sense.

But beneath the routine, beneath the familiar rhythm of work and conversation and the endless small decisions that filled her days, Hallie's thoughts kept circling back to the same place.

Chase Montgomery was coming home.

Not just for a visit, but permanently. He'd be next door at the toy store, working alongside his parents. They'd see each other constantly—at work, at community events, at the grocery store and the bakery, and all the places where Mistletoe Falls' residents inevitably crossed paths.

Twelve years was a long time. People changed. She'd certainly changed—the girl who'd written those early letters with breathless updates about campus life and hometown gossip had grown into a woman who ran a successful business and coordinated the town's largest charitable initiative. Chase had probably changed too, shaped by military service and whatever experiences he'd accumulated in the years since they'd last spoken.

She wondered if he'd thought about her at all during those twelve years, or if their childhood friendship had faded into distant memory.

Part of her was excited. The prospect of seeing an old friend again, of maybe rebuilding a connection that distance and time had eroded, sent anticipation humming through her veins.

But another part, the part she tried not to examine too closely, whispered questions she didn't quite want to answer. Questions about whether the ease of their old friendship would still exist, or if too much time and too much silence had created a gap too wide to cross. About whether she'd built up their connection into something more significant than it had actually been, nostalgia painting over reality with softer colors.

The afternoon crowd arrived right on schedule, and Hallie threw herself into work with renewed focus. There were customers to help, inventory to check, and a call to return about the outdoor decoration order for the town square.

But even as she moved through her tasks, even as she smiled and chatted and made recommendations about which wrapping paper would work best for oddly shaped gifts, a small part of her attention remained fixed on a question she couldn't quite shake.

After twelve years, what would Chase Montgomery have to say to her when they finally stood face-to-face again?

And perhaps more importantly—what would she say to him?

Chapter 2

The truck's headlights carved a path through the deepening twilight as Chase took another curve on Scenic Route 265, his hands steady on the wheel despite the exhaustion that had settled into his bones. The Ford F-150's engine hummed with reliable consistency, the same way it had for the past twelve hours since he'd left Camp Lejeune before dawn. Everything he owned fit in the truck bed beneath a weatherproof tarp—twelve years of military service reduced to a few duffel bags, three boxes of books, a couple of boxes of clothes, his guitar, and a footlocker containing uniforms he'd probably never wear again.

The road climbed higher into the Smoky Mountains with each passing mile; the pavement winding through ancient forests that had stood sentinel over these hills for ages. Chase shifted slightly in his seat, trying to ease the stiffness that had crept into his shoulders somewhere around the Tennessee border. His coffee had gone cold in the cup holder an hour ago, but he'd kept driving, pushed forward by anticipation mixed with nerves.

He hadn't been home for eighteen months. The last visit had been a blur of hospital hallways and worry, seven days spent at his mother's bedside after the accident before duty had called him back to base and another deployment. He'd seen her broken and hurting, surrounded by beeping machines and the antiseptic smell that all hospitals shared. But he hadn't seen her learning to navigate life in a wheelchair. He hadn't witnessed the daily adjustments, the small victories and frustrations that his father mentioned during his calls.

The weight of that absence pressed against his chest as the truck climbed higher.

A weathered sign appeared in the headlights: Mistletoe Falls—5 miles. His grip tightened on the steering wheel. Five miles. Less than ten minutes now, barring any complications. Twenty minutes until he'd see his parents, sleep in his childhood bed, and wake up tomorrow to begin whatever came next.

The uncertainty of that "whatever" had been gnawing at him for weeks. Months, if he was honest with himself. The decision not to reenlist hadn't come easily—twelve years in the Marines had shaped him, given him purpose and structure and a clear understanding of his place in the world. Combat engineering had appealed to both his technical mind and his desire to build things that mattered, to create an infrastructure that protected and served. He'd been good at it. Better than good, if his commendations were any indication.

But somewhere during his last deployment, watching the same dusty landscapes, something had changed. He'd found himself thinking about home more often than he used to. Wondering what his father did on slow Tuesday afternoons at the toy store. Whether his mother had figured out how to manage the household and store duties from her wheelchair, or if she'd accepted help with the tasks that used to be second nature. Whether the old oak tree behind their house still dropped acorns on the garage roof in October, creating that familiar percussion that meant autumn had arrived.

The road curved sharply, and the Snowbell Covered Bridge appeared before him, its timber frame stretched across Mistletoe Creek like a threshold between then and now. Even at the end of October, evergreen garland draped along the bridge's entrance and wrapped around the supporting beams. Small white lights twinkled among the greenery, their glow reflecting off the dark water below.

Chase eased off the gas as the truck entered the covered bridge. The sound of his tires changing from pavement to wooden planks created a hollow echo that resonated in his chest. He'd crossed this bridge countless times growing up—on the school bus, in his father's truck learning to drive, in borrowed cars heading to dates or football games, or just driving because that's what teenagers did when small-town life felt too small.

He'd crossed it one last time at eighteen, heading away from Mistletoe Falls with a one-way ticket to basic training and dreams of adventure that couldn't be contained by mountain valleys and familiar faces.

Now he was crossing it again, heading home for good.

The bridge released him, and the road began its final descent toward town. Within minutes, the forest opened up to reveal the first buildings of Mistletoe Falls proper. Gas lampposts lined the streets, their warm glow spilling onto brick sidewalks that looked exactly as he remembered them. The buildings themselves were unchanged in their essential character—two and three-story structures with their original architectural details preserved, striped awnings furled for the night, large display windows dark except for the security lights that revealed shadowy glimpses of merchandise within.

But it was the Christmas decorations that struck him most forcefully. He'd known intellectually that Mistletoe Falls had fully embraced its identity as Tennessee's year-round Christmas destination. But seeing it in person again, driving through downtown at seven-thirty on an October evening with garland wrapped around every streetlamp and wreaths hanging on every storefront, created a surreal sense of temporal displacement.

It felt like December, even though fall leaves still clung to the trees on the mountainsides and the evening air held the crisp bite of autumn rather than winter's deeper cold.

Chase drove slowly down Mistletoe Lane, taking in details that were simultaneously familiar and strange. The Fireside Diner still occupied its corner location, though a new awning had replaced the faded one he remembered. The building that used to house Miller's Hardware now bore a sign reading "The Reindeer Rack Outfitters"—someone had filled the niche old Mr. Miller left when he retired. The town square came into view, its Victorian gazebo lit from within, the surrounding oak trees strung with lights that would burn every night throughout the year.

How many times had he sat on those benches as a teenager, sharing space with friends who'd scattered to colleges and careers in cities that offered more opportunity than a small mountain town could provide? How many summer evenings had he spent in that gazebo, listening to concert series performances while eating ice cream that melted faster than he could lick it off his fingers?

The memories felt both close and impossibly distant, as if they belonged to someone else entirely.

Chase turned onto a side street, navigating familiar roads that led toward the outskirts of town, where houses spread out with more space between them. His parents' home sat on a quiet residential street lined with mature trees, a modest ranch home with a wide front porch.

Lights glowed in the windows, warm and welcoming, and his father's truck sat in the driveway.

He pulled in behind it, shifted into park and killed the engine. For a moment, Chase sat in the sudden silence, his hands still resting on the steering wheel. This was it. He was home.

The front door opened before he'd made it halfway up the walk, and his father appeared on the porch, his face splitting into a grin.

"Chase! You made it before full dark—I was starting to worry." Mark descended the porch steps with the energy of a much younger man, pulling Chase into an embrace that felt like coming up for air after being underwater too long.

"The drive was smooth. Very little traffic once I got past Asheville." Chase returned the hug, surprised by how much he'd needed it. His father felt solid and real in a way that phone calls could never quite capture.

"Your mother's been watching the window for the past hour. Come on, get inside before she wheels herself out here to drag you in personally."

They climbed the porch steps together, and Chase noticed the wooden ramp that now ran parallel to the stairs, its surface smooth and expertly constructed. His father's handiwork, no doubt. The front door had been widened slightly, he realized as they entered. The threshold was completely level now, with no step to navigate.

"Chase!" His mother's voice carried from the living room, and then she appeared in the doorway—not standing, not walking, but rolling forward in a wheelchair. She stopped and reached her arms out to him, tears streaming down her face.

The sight hit him harder than he'd expected. He'd seen her in the hospital, seen her broken and bruised with machines monitoring her vital signs. But seeing her here, in their home, in a wheelchair that was permanent rather than temporary medical equipment—that made it real in a way his imagination hadn't quite managed.

"Mom." He crossed to her in three strides, kneeling so they were at eye level before pulling her into his arms. She held him tight, one hand gripping the back of his shirt while the other cradled his head like he was still a child who needed comforting.

"My boy. My boy is finally home." Her voice broke on the words, and Chase felt his throat tighten.

They stayed that way for a long moment, and when they finally pulled apart, his mother cupped his face in her hands, studying him with an intensity only a mother could manage.

"You look tired. And thin. Are they not feeding Marines properly these days?"

Chase managed a laugh. "They feed us fine."

"Well, you're home now, and we're gonna put some meat on those bones." She released him, wheeling backward to give him space to stand. "Come into the kitchen. I baked cookies this afternoon—chocolate chip, your favorite—and your father just made coffee."

The kitchen had changed too; he noticed as they moved through the house. The counters had been lowered. A small table had replaced the breakfast bar that used to dominate one wall. But his mother's decorative touches remained—the herbs growing in pots on the windowsill, the collection of vintage tins arranged on top of the refrigerator, the hand-painted "Montgomery Family Kitchen" sign that had hung above the stove for as long as he could remember.

They settled around the dining table, a plate of cookies between them and mugs of coffee that Chase gratefully wrapped his stiff hands around. His mother had questions—dozens of them, flowing one after another with barely a pause for his answers. What was the drive like? How did he feel about leaving the Marines? Had he given any thought to what came next? Was he eating enough vegetables? Getting enough sleep?

His father interjected occasionally with comments about the toy store, about local news, and gossip. Chase listened and responded, feeling some of the tension that had ridden his shoulders for the past twelve hours begin to ease.

This was home. These were his parents. Whatever uncertainty lay ahead, at least he had this foundation to build on.

But exhaustion was catching up with him, making his thoughts fuzzy and his responses slower. When he caught himself nearly nodding off over his third cookie, he pushed back from the table.

"I hate to cut this short, but I need to call it a night. It's been a long day."

"Of course, of course." His mother reached across to pat his hand. "Your room is ready—I changed the sheets this morning."

"What about your things in the truck?" His father glanced toward the front of the house, concern creasing his forehead. "We should at least get them inside."

"I'll unload everything into the garage in the morning. Right now I just need my duffel bag and overnight case. Everything else can wait."

Chase retrieved both bags from the truck, the night air cool against his face after the warmth of the kitchen. The street was quiet, with porch lights glowing on neighboring houses—the peaceful stillness that only existed in small towns after dark. He stood there for a moment, breathing in air that smelled fresh, clean, and like autumn leaves, letting the reality of his return settle into his bones.

Then he headed back inside, said goodnight to his parents, and walked down the hall to his childhood bedroom.

The room was exactly as he'd left it, frozen in time like a museum exhibit of teenage existence. His old football trophies lined one shelf. Band posters that had seemed vitally important at sixteen covered one wall. His bookshelf still held the mix of adventure novels and military history that had fueled his decision to enlist. Even his old desk remained in the corner.

Chase dropped his bags beside the bed and sat down on the mattress, the springs creaking in a way that transported him instantly back to a thousand other nights in this exact spot. He should change into sleep clothes. Brush his teeth. Put his things away. Do all the small rituals that marked the end of a day and the beginning of rest.

Instead, he fell backward onto the bed, not bothering to remove his jeans or the flannel shirt that smelled like twelve hours of highway travel. The ceiling fan turned in slow circles above him, its motor making the same faint clicking sound it had always made on the third rotation.

He'd done it. Left the Marines. Driven home. Walked back into the life he'd abandoned at eighteen with nothing but good intentions and a willingness to figure things out as he went.

But lying here in the darkness, exhaustion pulling him toward sleep, one question surfaced above all the others, clear and unavoidable: Now that he was home, who exactly was he supposed to be?

Chapter 3

Hallie squinted at her laptop screen, her finger hovering over the mouse as she studied the product image of an elaborate music box shaped like a Victorian house. "I don't know, Nina. They're beautiful, but at that price point..."

"But look at the detail." Nina leaned closer from her spot beside the register, where she'd just finished ringing up a customer's purchase. "And we sold out of those carousel ones last year by mid-November. People want something special."

"We sold out because they were twenty dollars cheaper." Hallie scrolled down to check the wholesale cost again, doing quick mental math. "If we order twelve and only sell half, we're stuck with expensive inventory taking up shelf space."

"Order six then."

Hallie chewed her bottom lip, still unconvinced. The Wrapped Up in Christmas Shop was alive with Monday afternoon activity around them—Sofia helping an elderly gentleman select ornaments near the front window, Taylor wrapping purchases at the secondary register, and a handful of customers browsing the aisles with the focused intensity of people on specific missions.

"Fine, six." Hallie added the music boxes to her cart and moved on to the next category. "Now, these nutcrackers—"

"Yes," Nina said immediately.

"I haven't even told you which ones."

"Doesn't matter. Nutcrackers always sell. Order whatever you think makes sense, and let's move on before we're here until midnight."

Hallie grinned despite her indecision. This was their ritual every early November—placing the supplementary orders that would carry them through the busiest shopping season.

"Okay, nutcrackers are a yes. What about these?" She turned the laptop so Nina could see the display of miniature Christmas villages.

"How many pieces?"

"Starter set includes twelve buildings plus accessories. We can order add-ons separately."

Nina tilted her head, considering. "They're cute, but I think we've got enough village options already. That entire section near the snow globes."

The brass bell above the door chimed, and Hallie turned automatically toward the entrance, her professional greeting already forming. "Welcome to Wrapped Up in—"

The words died on her tongue.

Chase Montgomery stood just inside the doorway, one hand still on the door handle, wearing jeans and a dark green flannel shirt. His hair was slightly damp, as if he'd recently showered, and he held something in his other hand—a thick bundle of cards and envelopes bound together with a rubber band.

For a second, maybe two, Hallie forgot how to breathe. Forgot that she was perched on a stool at the counter with her laptop open, with Nina standing right beside her and customers moving through the shop. The world narrowed to just Chase, standing there with that crooked grin she remembered from a thousand teenage memories, except now it sat on a face that belonged to a man rather than a boy.

Twelve years had changed him. Broadened his shoulders, added definition to arms that had been wiry rather than muscular when he left. There was confidence in the way he carried himself now, a steadiness that came from experience and discipline. But his eyes—those were the same. Deep blue and warm, crinkling slightly at the corners when he smiled.

"Hey, Hallie."

His voice was deeper than she remembered, rougher somehow, but the familiarity of hearing him say her name made something in her chest crack wide open.

She tried to respond and nearly fell off her stool instead, catching herself on the counter edge with graceless urgency. "Chase. I—you're—" She pressed a hand to her sternum, trying to slow her racing pulse. "You're here."

"I am." He moved further into the shop, and she noticed how he seemed to fill the space differently than customers—not taking up more room exactly, but commanding attention in a way that made her hyperaware of every movement he made. "Hope it's okay that I just showed up. I probably should have called first."

"No, it's—I'm just—" Hallie slid off the stool, grateful when her legs held steady beneath her. "It's good to see you. Really good."

Nina made a small sound beside her that might have been amusement or encouragement, but Hallie didn't dare look away from Chase long enough to check.

He held up the bundle in his hand, and now she could see what it was—cards and letters, dozens of them, their edges worn from handling. "You kept writing," he said, and there was something in his voice that made her throat tight. "Even when I didn't."

The brass bell chimed again as another customer entered, but Hallie barely registered it. All she could focus on was Chase and the way her composure was crumbling like sand.

"I can't believe you kept them."

"Of course I kept them." He looked down at the bundle, his thumb brushing across the top card. "There were a lot of nights when I'd pull these out and read through them. Made deployment feel less..." He paused, searching for the word. "Lonely, I guess."

Something broke loose in Hallie's chest—joy and relief. She hurried around the counter and closed the distance between them.

"Chase." His name came out on a half-laugh, half-sob as she threw her arms around him, hugging him with enough force to make him stagger back a step.

"Whoa." But he was laughing too, steadying himself while returning the embrace with one arm, the other still holding her cards. "Guess you're happy to see me."

"Happy doesn't even begin to cover it." She pulled back just enough to look at him, aware that tears were threatening and not particularly caring. "I've missed you so much."

"Missed you too." His grin widened. "Even if I was terrible at showing it."

Nina appeared at Hallie's shoulder, and Chase's attention shifted to include her. "Nina Barlow. No way."

"Way." Nina pulled him into a hug of her own once Hallie stepped back. "Welcome home, Montgomery. About time you got back here."

"It's good to be back. You're working here now?"

"Managing, actually." Nina gestured around the shop with obvious pride. "Hallie runs the show, but I keep things organized."

"You definitely keep me sane," Hallie corrected, using the moment to swipe at her eyes and try to compose herself. But composure felt impossible when Chase was standing three feet away, real and solid and somehow even more handsome than the boy she'd known.

The years had carved away his boyish softness, replacing it with defined features that drew her gaze despite her best intentions—the strong line of his jaw, the way his flannel shirt fit across shoulders that looked like they could handle any burden, and the calloused hands that spoke of work and service. This wasn't the eighteen-year-old who'd left for basic training with nervous excitement in his eyes. This was a man who'd spent years becoming someone new while somehow remaining himself.

And she was staring. Definitely staring.

Hallie forced her attention back to his face, finding him watching her with an expression she couldn't quite read. If he'd noticed her assessment, he gave no sign. Instead, he glanced around the shop, taking in the twinkling lights and elaborate displays with the focused observation that suggested he was cataloging details.

"The store looks amazing. Better than I remember."

"Thanks. I've made some changes over the years." Hallie said as she tucked a loose strand of hair behind her ear. "Added more inventory, expanded the holiday decoration section. And Operation Christmas Cheer has kind of taken over the basement."

"Operation Christmas Cheer?"

"It's Hallie's baby," Nina supplied. "Gift baskets for local residents, toy drives, food collections—she basically runs a Christmas charity-type program for the whole town now."

Chase's expression shifted to something warmer, prouder some-how. "That sounds exactly like something you'd do."

Heat crept up Hallie's neck. "It just grew organically. Started with a few baskets for shut-ins and kind of spiraled from there."

"That's incredible, Hallie. Really."

A customer approached the counter with a question about wrapping paper, and Nina moved to help them while Sofia appeared from the storage room with a box of replenishments. She stopped short when she saw Chase, recognition dawning on her features.

"Chase Montgomery? Is that really you?"

"Sofia." He offered her a friendly smile. "Good to see you again."

"You too! Welcome home." She shifted the box to one hip. "I'd hug you, but my hands are kind of full; just give me a minute."

She continued toward the front display, leaving Hallie and Chase in a small pocket of relative privacy near the counter. The shop's activity continued around them—customers browsing, Nina processing pur-chases, Taylor restocking shelves—but Hallie felt oddly isolated from it all, as if she and Chase existed in their own separate bubble.

He shifted his weight, glancing around again with what looked like uncertainty. "This probably isn't the best time. You're clearly busy, and I'm kind of making myself the center of attention here."

"You're not—" Hallie started, but he was right. Several customers were casting curious glances their way, and she could see Mrs. Williams two aisles over pretending to examine ornaments while obviously eavesdropping.

"I was actually hoping we could grab lunch," Chase continued. "Catch up a little without..." He gestured vaguely at the surrounding shop. "Would you want to? I mean, if you have time. If not, I totally understand."

"Yes." The word came out too quickly, too eagerly, but Hallie didn't care. "I'd love that. I just need to—" She looked back at Nina, who was already waving her away.

"Go. I've got this. Taylor, Sofia, and I can handle the afternoon rush."

"Are you sure?"

"Positive. You've been here since seven this morning, anyway. Take a break."

Hallie grabbed her purse from beneath the counter, her hands slightly unsteady as she pulled out her phone to check the time. Just after one o'clock.

"The Fireside Diner, okay?" Chase asked as they headed toward the door. "Unless it's changed completely since I left."

"It's exactly the same. Carter and Michelle are still running it."

"Perfect."

The brass bell chimed their exit, and Hallie stepped out onto the sidewalk into the crisp November afternoon. Chase fell into step beside her, close enough that their arms nearly brushed, and Hallie tried to ignore how aware she was of his presence.

"I really missed you, you know. Even when I was terrible at staying in touch."

"I've missed you too. I'm so glad you're home."

"Me too."

Two simple words, but the way he said them—quiet and sincere—made Hallie wonder if coming home meant more to him than just returning to familiar places.

And as they turned the corner toward the diner, she found herself wondering something else entirely: if twelve years had been long enough to turn her teenage crush into something she could safely ignore, or if seeing him again had just proven that some feelings didn't fade as easily as she'd convinced herself they had.

Chapter 4

Chase held the door open, the warm air from inside the Fireside Diner rushing out. Hallie ducked under his arm with a quick smile of thanks, and he followed her into the familiar interior that somehow smelled exactly as it had twelve years ago—coffee, bacon grease, and something indefinably comforting that belonged to small-town restaurants everywhere.

"Hallie Dawson!" Michelle Bentley's voice carried across the diner from where she stood behind the hostess stand, her face lighting up with genuine pleasure. Then her gaze shifted to Chase, and her expression transformed into delighted surprise. "Chase Montgomery? Well, I'll be. Look what the mountain wind blew in."

"Hi, Michelle." Chase accepted her enthusiastic hug, remembering how she'd always snuck him extra fries when he'd come here after football practice.

"When did you get back? Your mama didn't say anything about you visiting when she was in last week."

"Just got in Saturday night. I'm back for good this time."

"For good?" Michelle's eyebrows rose toward her carefully styled gray hair. "Well, that's the best news I've heard all week. You two want a booth?"

"That'd be perfect," Hallie said, already moving toward the back corner booth that had always been their spot in high school. Some habits, Chase realized, ran deeper than conscious thought.

The diner had changed little. Red vinyl booths still lined both walls, their surfaces worn smooth by decades of use but meticulously maintained. The black-and-white checkered floor showed its age in places where the pattern had faded, but it was spotlessly clean. Framed photographs of Mistletoe Falls through the decades covered the wood-paneled walls, including one from 2012 that showed the high school football team—Chase spotted his younger self in the back row, trying to look serious.

"Sweet tea?" Michelle asked as they slid onto opposite sides of the booth.

"Please," Hallie said.

"Coffee for me. Black."

"Some things never change." Michelle winked at them before heading toward the kitchen. "I'll give the two of you a minute to look at the menu."

Chase picked up the laminated menu out of habit, though he probably could have recited it from memory. "Do they still make that chicken-fried steak special on Mondays?"

"Every single Monday without fail." Hallie hadn't even opened her menu. "Your mom and dad still come for dinner here every Monday as well."

"Really?"

"Yep. I join them sometimes."

Chase shook his head, marveling at the continuity. In the Marines, he'd rarely stayed anywhere long enough to see the slow progression of daily life that marked a genuine community. Everything had been temporary, transitional, always with an eye toward the next deployment or assignment.

Michelle returned with their drinks. "Know what you want, or need more time? Wait... let me see if I remember your favorite Chase... the Monday special, and you, Hallie... a turkey club."

"You remembered," Chase said.

"Fruit instead of fries, please," Hallie said with a grin.

"Some things never change. Coming right up." Michelle scribbled on her pad and disappeared again.

Chase wrapped his hands around the coffee mug, appreciating its warmth. "You know, I forgot how everyone here knows everyone else's business. It's like the whole town has a shared memory bank."

Hallie laughed, stirring sugar into her already-sweet tea. "Oh, just wait. By dinner tonight, half the town will know you're back and that we had lunch together. By tomorrow, Mrs. Dillard will probably have us engaged."

"Mrs. Dillard is still the town gossip?"

"Some positions are appointed for life, apparently." She leaned back against the booth, and Chase studied her face. The afternoon light from the window brought out gold highlights in her blonde hair that he didn't remember from high school. Or maybe he'd just never noticed. "So tell me about the Marines. Your parents shared bits and pieces over the years, but I want to hear it from you."

He took a sip of coffee, organizing his thoughts. "It was good. Hard sometimes, but good. The structure suited me—always knowing what was expected, what the mission was. I did many deployments, mostly construction and infrastructure work. Combat engineering."

"Building things or blowing them up?"

"Both, depending on the day." He grinned at her expression. "Mostly building them, though. Schools, wells, and bridges. Things that would last after we left."

"Your dad mentioned you were in Afghanistan?"

"Twice. Iraq once. Spent some time in Germany too, which was nice. Have you traveled much?"

"A little. I went to Charleston for college, but you knew that already. I got my business degree. I stayed there after graduating for a few years. I took a few trips to Atlanta for trade shows and to Nashville for vendor meetings. Nothing as exotic as Germany."

"What brought you back here instead of staying in Charleston?"

"Homesickness, honestly. And the feeling that I was meant to be doing something more personal than managing some corporate chain store." She paused, taking a sip of her tea. "Plus, Dad needed help with the shop. Mom was deep into her writing by then and—"

She stopped abruptly, something flickering across her face before she smoothed it away with a bright smile. "Anyway, I came back, and it was the right choice. I can't imagine living anywhere else now."

Michelle appeared with their food, setting down Chase's chicken fried steak—enormous and drowning in white gravy—and Hallie's club sandwich with a colorful array of fresh fruit.

"This looks exactly as I remembered," Chase said, cutting into the steak. The first bite was pure comfort—crispy coating, tender meat, and gravy that probably violated several health codes with its richness. "Oh man, I missed this."

"The food in the Marines wasn't good?"

"It was fine. Functional. But it wasn't this." He gestured with his fork. "This is good ole comfort food."

Hallie picked up a triangle of her sandwich, and Chase noticed how she still ate the corners first, saving the middle for last. "Do you remember when we came here after prom our senior year?"

"I do. I remember all of us having the time of our lives in here... We had more fun here than at prom itself," Chase smiled at the memory.

"You had that terrible rented tux that was too short in the arms."

"You had that blue dress that made you look like you were heading to a country club instead of a high school dance."

"It was powder blue, thank you very much, and I thought I was very sophisticated." She threw a grape at him, which he caught reflexively. "Besides, you're one to talk. Didn't you try to highlight your hair that year?"

"We agreed never to speak of that."

"No, you asked me never to speak of it. I made no such promise."

They fell into the easy rhythm of shared memories—the time they'd gotten lost hiking and ended up missing the homecoming game, the summer they'd tried to build a raft to float down Mistletoe Creek and ended up soaking wet and grounded for a week, the way she'd helped him study for his Spanish finals even though she was taking French.

"It's strange," Chase said, working his way through the massive portion of food. "Being back, I mean. Everything looks the same but feels different. Like I'm wearing clothes that don't quite fit anymore. In the Marines, everything had a purpose, a clear objective. Wake up at this time, complete these tasks, and achieve this mission. Now I wake up and think... what am I supposed to do today? Who am I supposed to be?"

"That must be jarring."

"It is. Even little things, like not having to be anywhere at a specific time. This morning I woke up at five-thirty out of habit, then realized I had nowhere to be, nothing urgent to accomplish." He shrugged, trying to make light of it. "So I went for a run, then helped Dad organize some inventory at the store. Trying to find new rhythms, I guess."

"Your parents must be thrilled to have you home."

"They are. Though living with them again is... an adjustment." He smiled ruefully. "I'm thirty years old and sleeping in my childhood bedroom, looking at posters of bands that broke up a decade ago."

"Planning to get your own place?"

"Actually, yeah. The apartment above the toy store has been empty for a while. Dad's been using it mostly for storage. I figure I'll clean it out this week, do some basic repairs and painting. If I can make it livable, I'll move in next week."

Hallie brightened. "I live above my store too! We'll be neighbors again."

"Just like the old days, except instead of riding bikes between our houses, we can walk twenty feet and compare notes on retail management."

"And dealing with tourists asking why everything's Christmas-themed in July."

"Do you get that a lot?"

"You have no idea. Last summer, a woman asked me, in complete seriousness, if we knew Christmas was in December." Hallie's impression of the tourist's confused expression made him laugh hard enough that other diners glanced their way. "I told her we'd made note of it."

Michelle refilled Chase's coffee without being asked, patting his shoulder as she passed. The afternoon crowd was thinning, leaving them in relative privacy.

"Your parents have kept me pretty well informed about your travels over the years," Hallie said. "They're so proud of you, Chase. Every time you got promoted or received a commendation, your dad would come into the store to tell me about it."

"They mentioned you a lot in their letters too. Mom and Dad think highly of you."

"They've always felt like family to me. Especially after—" She stopped, a flicker of something crossing her features. "They're wonderful people."

Chase wanted to ask about that hesitation, the words she kept swallowing back, but something told him to let it be.

"I should probably head back," Hallie said eventually, glancing at her phone. "Monday afternoons can get busy."

Chase signaled Michelle for the check, but she waved him off.

"Already taken care of," she called out. "Welcome home present from Carter and me."

"Michelle, you don't have to—"

"I don't have to do anything. But I'm doing it anyway. You two get out of here."

They slid out of the booth, and Chase found himself reluctant to end this. It had been so easy, sitting here with Hallie, as if the twelve years between them had compressed down to nothing. She still laughed at his terrible jokes, still called him out when he was being ridiculous, and still had that way of tilting her head when she was really listening.

Outside, the air had turned crisp. As they walked back toward their shops, Chase found himself hyperaware of how close she was.

"I'm working at Mom and Dad's store for the rest of the day," he said as they approached her store. "Need to get caught up on inventory and procedures if I'm going to be useful. Dad's going to show me how things work now."

"Sounds like you have a busy afternoon ahead of you." Hallie said as she turned to face him fully. "This was nice catching up."

"Yeah, it was. Maybe we could do it again sometime?"

"I'd like that. Welcome home, Chase. I'm really glad you're back."

She smiled at him once more, then disappeared into her shop, the brass bell chiming her entrance. Chase stood there for a moment, hands in his pockets, watching through the window as she greeted Nina and Sofia.

Then he turned and headed next door to Bells & Whistles, his mind full of Hallie's laugh and the way she'd looked at him across the diner table.

Which was a dangerous thing to think about someone who'd been nothing but a good friend for most of his life. He'd been back less than forty-eight hours, and already Hallie Dawson was making him question everything he thought he knew about what he wanted from this second chance at civilian life.

Chapter 5

Hallie clicked through the supplier's website, her cursor hovering over the quantity field for hand-blown glass snowflake ornaments. Twenty dozen or thirty? She'd already been through this particular decision three times in the past hour, but her mind kept drifting to thoughts about Chase.

Twenty dozen. She typed the number, then immediately deleted it. The memory of Chase catching that grape she'd thrown surfaced unbidden, his reflexes sharp from military training. The way his flannel shirt had stretched across his shoulders when he'd reached for his coffee.

"Get it together, Dawson," she muttered, forcing her attention back to the screen. Thirty dozen. They'd sold out of the snowflakes last year by December tenth. Better to have too many than disappoint customers.

The sound of footsteps in the storage area pulled her from her internal debate. Nina appeared in the doorway, the day's cash deposit bag tucked under one arm and exhaustion written across her features.

"Tell me you're not still agonizing over that ornament order." Nina crossed to the safe built into the wall, spinning the combination with practiced ease. The heavy door swung open with its familiar creak, and she deposited the bank bag inside before securing it again.

"I'm being thorough."

"You're overthinking." Nina dropped into the worn leather chair across from Hallie's desk, kicking off her flats with a grateful sigh. "You've been staring at that same screen since four o'clock. What's it going to be?"

"Thirty dozen snowflakes, twenty dozen icicles, and forty dozen of those little wooden reindeer that everyone went crazy for last year."

"Good. Order extra while you're at it. We both know you'll second-guess yourself tomorrow and wish you'd gotten more." Nina stretched her arms above her head, her auburn hair escaping from its ponytail. "The afternoon rush was brutal. That family from Nashville bought six hundred dollars worth of decorations. Said they wanted to recreate our window display in their living room."

"Lucy will be thrilled. She spent hours on that village scene."

"Speaking of which, she asked if she could come in early tomorrow to start on the Thanksgiving transition display. I told her yes."

Hallie added five dozen to each ornament order and hit submit before she could change her mind again. The confirmation screen loaded slowly, giving her time to notice how Nina was studying her with that expression that meant an interrogation was coming.

"So," Nina said, drawing out the word. "Are we going to talk about it, or are you going to pretend that having lunch with Chase Montgomery was just a normal Monday afternoon occurrence?"

"It was nice catching up with an old friend."

"Nice." Nina's tone could have dried paint. "You rushed out of here like the building was on fire, and you came back with your cheeks flushed and that little smile you get when you're trying not to look too happy. But sure, let's go with nice."

Hallie closed her laptop, buying time by organizing the papers on her desk. Order forms in one pile, invoices in another, vendor catalogs stacked by date. "It really was a pleasant lunch. We talked about his time in the Marines, my taking over the shop, and normal catching-up things."

"Hallie Rose Dawson, you are the worst liar I've ever met." Nina leaned forward, elbows on knees. "This is me you're talking to. The person who held your hair back when you got food poisoning at the county fair. Who helped you practice your valedictorian speech seventeen times? The person who knows you had his high school photo hidden in your jewelry box senior year."

Heat crept up Hallie's neck. "That was twelve years ago."

"And yet here you are, organizing papers that don't need organizing and avoiding eye contact like you're guilty of something." Nina's expression softened. "Come on. Tell me about lunch. The real version."

Hallie surrendered, sinking back into her desk chair. "He's different. Broader, more solid. Like he's grown into himself, if that makes sense. But also the same—still makes terrible jokes, still loves straight black coffee, still does that thing where he runs his hand through his hair when he's thinking."

"You noticed his hair habits?"

"I notice everyone's habits. It's a character trait, not a sign of anything."

"Right. And the fact that you haven't stopped fidgeting with that pen means nothing."

Hallie looked down at her hands, where she was indeed clicking the pen repeatedly. She set it down deliberately. "He kept all my cards, Nina. Every birthday card, every Christmas card. Who does that?"

Nina's expression shifted to something gentler. "Oh, honey."

"You heard him say he'd read them during deployments." The words tumbled out now, released from wherever she'd been holding them since lunch. "And he looked at me like—I don't know—like he was really seeing me. Not just childhood friend Hallie, but actual me."

"That's because the actual you is pretty amazing."

"Stop."

"I'm serious. You run a successful business, coordinate charity work for the entire town, and somehow still remember every customer's grandkid's name. Chase Montgomery would be lucky to—"

"We're just friends." Hallie's voice came out sharper than intended. "That's all we were before, and that's all we'll be now."

Nina studied her for a long moment. "You sure about that? Because from where I'm sitting, it looks like those old feelings are stirring back up. And before you deny it, remember that I was there senior year. I saw how you looked at him when you thought no one was watching."

"That was a teenage crush. Ancient history."

"Mmm-hmm. And the fact that you're death-gripping that armrest right now is because you're totally over it."

Hallie forced her fingers to relax. "It doesn't matter what I felt then or what I might feel now. I'm taking a break from dating, remember? After Daniel—"

She stopped, the name still carrying weight six months after he'd stood in her apartment above the shop and explained, with lawyer-like precision, why their relationship no longer worked for him. How she was wonderful but not quite right. How he'd tried to love her the way she deserved but simply couldn't.

"Daniel was an idiot," Nina said firmly.

"Daniel was honest. He didn't love me anymore. End of story."

"Daniel was a self-absorbed attorney who wanted a trophy fiancée to impress his law partners, not a real partner. You dodged a bullet."

"I got my heart broken."

"You got freed from a mediocre relationship with a man who thought your charity work was 'cute' and suggested you should maybe tone down the enthusiasm because it wasn't sophisticated enough for his firm's parties."

Hallie rubbed her temples. "Can we please not rehash this?"

"Fine. But don't let what happened with that pretentious suit determine what happens with Chase."

"Nothing is happening with Chase. We're friends who are reconnecting after years apart. That's it."

"He's moved back permanently. He'll be working next door."

"Which makes friendship even more important. We'll be seeing each other constantly. The last thing I need is to complicate that by developing feelings that he doesn't reciprocate."

Nina made a sound that might have been a snort. "Have you considered that maybe he does reciprocate? The man kept your cards for twelve years, Hallie. That's not nothing."

"He kept them as reminders of home, not me."

"You're impossible." Nina stood, slipping her shoes back on. "But fine, live in denial. Just know that I saw how he looked at you today. That wasn't the look of someone who sees just a childhood friend."

"Nina—"

"I'm going home." She paused at the door. "Just promise me something?"

"What?"

"Don't close yourself off to possibilities because one guy was too stupid to recognize what he had. Chase Montgomery isn't Daniel

Whitaker. And thirty-year-old Chase definitely isn't eighteen-year-old Chase."

"I know that."

"Do you? Because from where I'm standing, you're so busy protecting yourself that you might miss something good."

Nina left before she could respond, her footsteps fading through the storage room and out the back entrance. The silence that followed felt heavier than it should, filled with questions Hallie didn't want to examine.

She opened her laptop again, determined to focus on work. There were vendor emails to answer, schedules to confirm, and a preliminary budget for next week's Operation Christmas Cheer food drive to review. Normal, manageable tasks that didn't require emotional excavation.

But Nina's words echoed in the quiet office. The way Chase had looked at her—she'd noticed it too, of course. The intensity in his blue eyes. The way he'd stood on the sidewalk after lunch, hands in his pockets, looking like he wanted to say something more.

She thought about Daniel, about the precise way he'd dismantled their relationship like a contract negotiation. How he'd scheduled the breakup conversation for a Tuesday evening because it was "least disruptive to both their schedules." How he'd never once lost his composure while her world crumbled around her.

Her phone buzzed with a text from Lucy: "The window display is going to be AMAZING tomorrow! Victorian Christmas meets harvest celebration! See ya in the morning."

Hallie smiled despite her churning thoughts. This was what mattered—her business, her team, her community work. She'd built something solid here, something that belonged entirely to her. She didn't need romance complicating that. Didn't need to risk the kind of devastating loss that came from believing someone would stay.

Her mother had loved her father completely, and his death had broken her so thoroughly she'd fled to Florida rather than face the memories. Daniel had claimed to love her, then walked away when it became inconvenient.

No, friendship with Chase was enough. It had to be enough.

Chapter 6

Chase stared at the laptop screen, trying to decipher the inventory management system that had apparently replaced the handwritten ledgers he remembered from his teenage years. A green notification popped up in the corner: "Order #4782 from Burlington, Vermont—Expedited Shipping Required." Before he could click on it, two more orders appeared in quick succession.

"The notifications can be overwhelming at first," his mother said from beside him, maneuvering her wheelchair closer to the counter with practiced ease. "But you'll get used to the rhythm. Wednesday afternoons are always busy online. And be prepared because the weekends are even busier."

"How do you keep track of it all?" Chase minimized the inventory window to reveal the order processing screen, where a queue of twelve purchases waited for attention. Wooden trains, educational puzzles, a collector's edition dollhouse, three sets of building blocks—the variety alone made his head spin.

"Practice and good systems." Liz reached across him to click on the first order, her movements confident despite the angle required from her chair. "This one's a regular customer—Mrs. Clark from Vermont. Orders from us every month for her grandchildren. She always wants the packages wrapped."

The bell above the door chimed, and Chase looked up to see a harried-looking father enter with twin boys who immediately scattered in opposite directions, one heading for the train sets while the other made a beeline for the sports equipment.

"I've got them," Mark said, already moving to intercept the more adventurous twin before he could scale the bicycle display. "Chase, can you handle the register for a few minutes?"

Chase abandoned the laptop, grateful for a task he understood as a woman approached with an armful of board games. Chase began scanning barcodes, making small talk about whether they were gifts or family purchases. Behind her, a line formed—three more customers clutching various toys, their faces showing the patient resignation of weekday afternoon shoppers.

As he worked through the transactions, Chase found himself really seeing the store for the first time since his return. Not just glancing around with nostalgia-clouded eyes, but truly observing what his parents had built.

The space seemed to have doubled since his memories of it. The main floor sprawled in organized chaos that somehow made perfect sense—educational toys flowing naturally into creative play areas, then to classic games, and finally to the showcase section where his father's handcrafted wooden pieces gleamed under spotlights. The ceiling, which he remembered as basic acoustic tiles, now featured exposed beams painted in primary colors with model airplanes and kites suspended at varying heights, creating a sense of whimsy that made children's eyes go wide the moment they entered.

Every detail showed intentional care. The sample toys available for testing. The reading corner with beanbags and picture books. The accessible pathways were wide enough for his mother's wheelchair—and strollers, and families walking side by side.

"Your parents have quite an operation here," the last customer in line commented, an older man purchasing a wooden rocking horse that Mark had crafted. "Been coming here for forty years, since my own kids were small. Never seen it looking better."

"Thank you," Chase said, carefully wrapping the rocking horse in protective paper. "They've worked hard to keep it special."

"Shows in everything. That online store too—my daughter in California orders from there regularly. Says this is the only place she trusts for quality toys that'll last."

After the man left, Chase returned to the laptop, where the order count had climbed to seventeen. His mother had wheeled herself to the puzzle section to help a customer, her voice carrying across the store as she explained the developmental benefits of different difficulty levels. His father was on his knees beside the train display, showing the twins how to connect magnetic cars while their father looked on with visible relief.

Chase clicked through to the business dashboard, and his breath caught at the numbers. Daily sales figures dwarfed what he remembered from his youth. Customer reviews scrolling past—hundreds of them, averaging 4.9 stars. Repeat customer rate of sixty-three percent. Geographic distribution included all fifty states and several international orders.

"Impressive, isn't it?" Mark said as he stood beside Chase. "Your mother insisted we go digital five years ago. I fought it at first—thought we'd lose the personal touch. But she was right. We've reached families we never could have otherwise."

"This is incredible, Dad. You've really expanded. It's hard to wrap my head around."

Mark's expression shifted, a shadow crossing his features. "We've been blessed. Though I won't lie—the past year and a half since your mother's accident has been rough. There were days I wondered if we'd have to close."

Chase felt the familiar twist of guilt in his chest. "I should have been here."

"You were serving your country. We understood that." Mark's hand landed on Chase's shoulder, solid and reassuring. "Besides, the community stepped up. Hallie especially—that girl organized volunteer schedules, arranged meal deliveries, and even helped run the register during the Christmas rush when we were overwhelmed."

"Really?"

His mother had returned, navigating her chair behind the counter with the fluid grace of long practice. "She saved us, Chase, literally. I don't know what we would have done without her."

The bell chimed again, and the afternoon rush began in earnest. For the next two hours, Chase was swept into the rhythm of retail—answering questions, processing sales, restocking shelves that emptied as quickly as they could fill them. He watched his parents work in seamless coordination, Mark handling the physical tasks that required height or strength, Liz managing customer questions with encyclopedic knowledge of their inventory.

They moved around each other like dancers who'd been partners for decades, which of course they had been. Thirty-three years of marriage had created an unspoken communication system—a glance from

Liz sending Mark to retrieve something from storage, a subtle gesture from Mark alerting Liz to a customer who needed special attention.

Between customers, Chase studied them more closely. The way his father's hand would brush his mother's shoulder as he passed. How she would tilt her face up to him with a smile. The quiet "thank you, love" when he brought her a glass of water without being asked. The way they still looked at each other—like teenagers with a secret.

The memory of his ex-wife Janice surfaced. They'd never had that easy synchronization, even in the beginning. Their relationship had been built on shared service, mutual respect, and the logical compatibility of two Marines who understood the demands of military life. But watching his parents now, Chase recognized what had been missing—that ineffable something that transformed a partnership into true unity.

Janice had been right to end things. They'd been trying to force something that should have flowed naturally, checking boxes on a relationship checklist rather than building something organic and real. The divorce had been painful but not devastating, disappointing but not surprising. They'd both known, perhaps from the beginning, that they were better suited as friends than spouses.

"Chase?" His mother's voice pulled him from his thoughts. "Could you help Mrs. Mackenzie? She's looking for something in the wooden toy section."

He found Mrs. Mackenzie examining the handcrafted trains; her weathered hands gentle on the smooth wood. "My grandson loves trains," she explained. "But I want something that will last, something special. Not the plastic nonsense that breaks in a week."

Chase lifted one of his father's newest creations—a complete set with an engine, three cars, and a caboose, each piece detailed down to tiny wooden wheels that actually turned. "Dad made this one. See the way the cars connect with these magnets? Strong enough to hold but easy for small hands to manage."

"Your father made this?" Mrs. Mackenzie's eyes brightened. "Oh, I remember when you were just a boy, following him around the workshop. Are you planning to take over the family business?"

"I'm... just helping out while I figure out what's next in my life."

After she left with the train set wrapped in festive paper, Chase stood among the wooden toys his father had crafted with patient hands and decades of skill. Each piece represented hours of work—selecting the wood, cutting, sanding, painting, finishing. Creating something tangible and lasting in a world increasingly dominated by screens and disposable entertainment.

Was this his future? Learning the business systems, mastering inventory management, and eventually taking over so his parents could retire? He could picture it—years stretching ahead filled with Christmas rushes and quiet January afternoons, customer birthday purchases and back-to-school shopping seasons for the best learning toys available for little minds. Watching other people's children grow up through their toy purchases, becoming as much a fixture of Mistletoe Falls as the town square gazebo.

The thought didn't fill him with dread, exactly. But it didn't ignite any passion either. It felt like putting on a suit that almost fit—comfortable enough, appropriate certainly, but not quite right in ways he couldn't articulate.

"Getting overwhelmed?" His father appeared at his elbow, voice gentle with understanding.

"Just thinking."

"About?"

Chase gestured at the surrounding store. "All of this. What you and Mom have built. What happens next for me?"

"You don't have to decide anything today, son. Or this week. Or even this month." Mark picked up one of the wooden alphabet blocks from a nearby display, turning it over in his hands. "When I came back from the Marines, it took me two years to figure out what I wanted. We opened the store almost by accident—your mom's father was selling the building, we needed income, and I'd always been good with my hands."

"And it became your life's work."

"It became one part of my life." Mark set down the block, his gaze finding Liz across the store. "The work matters, yes. But what matters more is who you build it with. Your mother and I—we could have sold insurance or run a restaurant or taught school. The business is just the framework. The life we built inside it—that's what counts."

"How did you know, though? That Mom was the right person to build it with?"

Mark's smile carried decades of accumulated wisdom. "I didn't at first. We figured it out together, one day at a time. Made mistakes, had arguments, and wondered if we were crazy more than once. But we kept choosing each other, kept choosing to try again each day. Eventually, it wasn't a choice anymore. It just was."

The bell chimed, and Chase watched his mother greet the new customer with genuine warmth despite the fatigue visible in the set of her shoulders. His father moved to help, and their hands touched briefly as he passed—a momentary connection that spoke of countless such moments, accumulated over years into something unbreakable.

Chase wanted that. Not necessarily the toy store, though he could learn to love it. Not even Mistletoe Falls, though the town was growing on him again. But that connection, that certainty of partnership, that quiet confidence of being exactly where you belonged with exactly who you were meant to be with.

The laptop chimed with another order notification, and Chase returned to the screen, adding it to the processing queue. As he worked through the technical details of shipping and inventory, his mind kept circling back to the same question: If the business was just the framework, as his father said, then what kind of life was he supposed to build inside whatever framework he chose?

And perhaps more unsettling—with whom was he supposed to build it with?

Chapter 7

Chase stared at the laptop screen, trying to decipher the inventory management system that had apparently replaced the handwritten ledgers he remembered from his teenage years. A green notification popped up in the corner: "Order #4782 from Burlington, Vermont—Expedited Shipping Required." Before he could click on it, two more orders appeared in quick succession.

"The notifications can be overwhelming at first," his mother said from beside him, maneuvering her wheelchair closer to the counter with practiced ease. "But you'll get used to the rhythm. Wednesday afternoons are always busy online. And be prepared because the weekends are even busier."

"How do you keep track of it all?" Chase minimized the inventory window to reveal the order processing screen, where a queue of twelve purchases waited for attention. Wooden trains, educational puzzles, a collector's edition dollhouse, three sets of building blocks—the variety alone made his head spin.

"Practice and good systems." Liz reached across him to click on the first order, her movements confident despite the angle required from her chair. "This one's a regular customer—Mrs. Clark from Vermont. Orders from us every month for her grandchildren. She always wants the packages wrapped."

The bell above the door chimed, and Chase looked up to see a harried-looking father enter with twin boys who immediately scattered in opposite directions, one heading for the train sets while the other made a beeline for the sports equipment.

"I've got them," Mark said, already moving to intercept the more adventurous twin before he could scale the bicycle display. "Chase, can you handle the register for a few minutes?"

Chase abandoned the laptop, grateful for a task he understood as a woman approached with an armful of board games. Chase began scanning barcodes, making small talk about whether they were gifts or family purchases. Behind her, a line formed—three more customers clutching various toys, their faces showing the patient resignation of weekday afternoon shoppers.

As he worked through the transactions, Chase found himself really seeing the store for the first time since his return. Not just glancing around with nostalgia-clouded eyes, but truly observing what his parents had built.

The space seemed to have doubled since his memories of it. The main floor sprawled in organized chaos that somehow made perfect sense—educational toys flowing naturally into creative play areas, then to classic games, and finally to the showcase section where his father's handcrafted wooden pieces gleamed under spotlights. The ceiling, which he remembered as basic acoustic tiles, now featured exposed beams painted in primary colors with model airplanes and kites suspended at varying heights, creating a sense of whimsy that made children's eyes go wide the moment they entered.

Every detail showed intentional care. The sample toys available for testing. The reading corner with beanbags and picture books. The accessible pathways were wide enough for his mother's wheelchair—and strollers, and families walking side by side.

"Your parents have quite an operation here," the last customer in line commented, an older man purchasing a wooden rocking horse that Mark had crafted. "Been coming here for forty years, since my own kids were small. Never seen it looking better."

"Thank you," Chase said, carefully wrapping the rocking horse in protective paper. "They've worked hard to keep it special."

"Shows in everything. That online store too—my daughter in California orders from there regularly. Says this is the only place she trusts for quality toys that'll last."

After the man left, Chase returned to the laptop, where the order count had climbed to seventeen. His mother had wheeled herself to the puzzle section to help a customer, her voice carrying across the store as she explained the developmental benefits of different difficulty levels. His father was on his knees beside the train display, showing the twins how to connect magnetic cars while their father looked on with visible relief.

Chase clicked through to the business dashboard, and his breath caught at the numbers. Daily sales figures dwarfed what he remembered from his youth. Customer reviews scrolling past—hundreds of them, averaging 4.9 stars. Repeat customer rate of sixty-three percent. Geographic distribution included all fifty states and several international orders.

"Impressive, isn't it?" Mark said as he stood beside Chase. "Your mother insisted we go digital five years ago. I fought it at first—thought we'd lose the personal touch. But she was right. We've reached families we never could have otherwise."

"This is incredible, Dad. You've really expanded. It's hard to wrap my head around."

Mark's expression shifted, a shadow crossing his features. "We've been blessed. Though I won't lie—the past year and a half since your mother's accident has been rough. There were days I wondered if we'd have to close."

Chase felt the familiar twist of guilt in his chest. "I should have been here."

"You were serving your country. We understood that." Mark's hand landed on Chase's shoulder, solid and reassuring. "Besides, the community stepped up. Hallie especially—that girl organized volunteer schedules, arranged meal deliveries, and even helped run the register during the Christmas rush when we were overwhelmed."

"Really?"

His mother had returned, navigating her chair behind the counter with the fluid grace of long practice. "She saved us, Chase, literally. I don't know what we would have done without her."

The bell chimed again, and the afternoon rush began in earnest. For the next two hours, Chase was swept into the rhythm of retail—answering questions, processing sales, restocking shelves that emptied as quickly as they could fill them. He watched his parents work in seamless coordination, Mark handling the physical tasks that required height or strength, Liz managing customer questions with encyclopedic knowledge of their inventory.

They moved around each other like dancers who'd been partners for decades, which of course they had been. Thirty-three years of marriage had created an unspoken communication system—a glance from

Liz sending Mark to retrieve something from storage, a subtle gesture from Mark alerting Liz to a customer who needed special attention.

Between customers, Chase studied them more closely. The way his father's hand would brush his mother's shoulder as he passed. How she would tilt her face up to him with a smile. The quiet "thank you, love" when he brought her a glass of water without being asked. The way they still looked at each other—like teenagers with a secret.

The memory of his ex-wife Janice surfaced. They'd never had that easy synchronization, even in the beginning. Their relationship had been built on shared service, mutual respect, and the logical compatibility of two Marines who understood the demands of military life. But watching his parents now, Chase recognized what had been missing—that ineffable something that transformed a partnership into true unity.

Janice had been right to end things. They'd been trying to force something that should have flowed naturally, checking boxes on a relationship checklist rather than building something organic and real. The divorce had been painful but not devastating, disappointing but not surprising. They'd both known, perhaps from the beginning, that they were better suited as friends than spouses.

"Chase?" His mother's voice pulled him from his thoughts. "Could you help Mrs. Mackenzie? She's looking for something in the wooden toy section."

He found Mrs. Mackenzie examining the handcrafted trains; her weathered hands gentle on the smooth wood. "My grandson loves trains," she explained. "But I want something that will last, something special. Not the plastic nonsense that breaks in a week."

Chase lifted one of his father's newest creations—a complete set with an engine, three cars, and a caboose, each piece detailed down to tiny wooden wheels that actually turned. "Dad made this one. See the way the cars connect with these magnets? Strong enough to hold but easy for small hands to manage."

"Your father made this?" Mrs. Mackenzie's eyes brightened. "Oh, I remember when you were just a boy, following him around the workshop. Are you planning to take over the family business?"

"I'm... just helping out while I figure out what's next in my life."

After she left with the train set wrapped in festive paper, Chase stood among the wooden toys his father had crafted with patient hands and decades of skill. Each piece represented hours of work—selecting the wood, cutting, sanding, painting, finishing. Creating something tangible and lasting in a world increasingly dominated by screens and disposable entertainment.

Was this his future? Learning the business systems, mastering inventory management, and eventually taking over so his parents could retire? He could picture it—years stretching ahead filled with Christmas rushes and quiet January afternoons, customer birthday purchases and back-to-school shopping seasons for the best learning toys available for little minds. Watching other people's children grow up through their toy purchases, becoming as much a fixture of Mistletoe Falls as the town square gazebo.

The thought didn't fill him with dread, exactly. But it didn't ignite any passion either. It felt like putting on a suit that almost fit—comfortable enough, appropriate certainly, but not quite right in ways he couldn't articulate.

"Getting overwhelmed?" His father appeared at his elbow, voice gentle with understanding.

"Just thinking."

"About?"

Chase gestured at the surrounding store. "All of this. What you and Mom have built. What happens next for me?"

"You don't have to decide anything today, son. Or this week. Or even this month." Mark picked up one of the wooden alphabet blocks from a nearby display, turning it over in his hands. "When I came back from the Marines, it took me two years to figure out what I wanted. We opened the store almost by accident—your mom's father was selling the building, we needed income, and I'd always been good with my hands."

"And it became your life's work."

"It became one part of my life." Mark set down the block, his gaze finding Liz across the store. "The work matters, yes. But what matters more is who you build it with. Your mother and I—we could have sold insurance or run a restaurant or taught school. The business is just the framework. The life we built inside it—that's what counts."

"How did you know, though? That Mom was the right person to build it with?"

Mark's smile carried decades of accumulated wisdom. "I didn't at first. We figured it out together, one day at a time. Made mistakes, had arguments, and wondered if we were crazy more than once. But we kept choosing each other, kept choosing to try again each day. Eventually, it wasn't a choice anymore. It just was."

The bell chimed, and Chase watched his mother greet the new customer with genuine warmth despite the fatigue visible in the set of her shoulders. His father moved to help, and their hands touched briefly as he passed—a momentary connection that spoke of countless such moments, accumulated over years into something unbreakable.

Chase wanted that. Not necessarily the toy store, though he could learn to love it. Not even Mistletoe Falls, though the town was growing on him again. But that connection, that certainty of partnership, that quiet confidence of being exactly where you belonged with exactly who you were meant to be with.

The laptop chimed with another order notification, and Chase returned to the screen, adding it to the processing queue. As he worked through the technical details of shipping and inventory, his mind kept circling back to the same question: If the business was just the framework, as his father said, then what kind of life was he supposed to build inside whatever framework he chose?

And perhaps more unsettling—with whom was he supposed to build it with?

Chapter 8

Chase pulled his truck into the Community Center parking lot, scanning for an empty space among the unexpected sea of vehicles. "Popular potluck tonight," he said, finally spotting an opening near the back.

"Potlucks usually draw a crowd." Hallie adjusted her scarf, a deep green that brought out the gold flecks in her hazel eyes. She'd dressed casually in jeans and a cream sweater, but somehow she made simple look elegant.

"I didn't realize half the town came to these things." He maneuvered the truck into the space, noting the overflow parking along the street.

They climbed out, and Chase came around to walk beside her toward the building. The restored 1920s structure glowed warmly against the darkening November sky, light spilling from the tall arched windows. He could hear voices and laughter from inside, the sound of a community gathering in full swing.

"So who usually comes to these?" He held the main door for her, juggling the pie in his other hand.

"Oh, you know. The usual suspects. Mrs. Williams and her book club, the Bentleys from the diner, various families." Hallie seemed focused on the inner doors to the main hall, walking with purpose. "Pretty much anyone who just wants to enjoy an evening of good home-cooked food and socializing."

"Sounds like my kind of people."

She reached for the hall doorknob, then paused. "Ready?"

"For a potluck? I think I can handle—"

The door swung open to reveal a room packed with what looked like the entire population of Mistletoe Falls. "WELCOME HOME!" The collective shout hit him like a physical force.

Chase froze, his brain struggling to process the scene. Hundreds of faces, all smiling. A massive banner stretched across the far wall: "Welcome Home, Chase Montgomery." Tables groaned under the weight of enough food to feed an army. Photos of him—in uniform, as a child, at high school graduation—decorated every available surface.

"What—" He couldn't form words.

His parents emerged from the crowd, his mother rolling forward with tears streaming down her face while his father followed with the biggest grin Chase had ever seen.

"Surprise, son." His father pulled him into a hug that nearly knocked the pie from his hands. "The whole town wanted to welcome you home properly."

"We've been planning this for over a week," his mother added, reaching up to squeeze his hand. "Everyone insisted on helping."

Chase looked back at Hallie, who stood just inside the door with an expression of careful innocence. "You knew about this?"

"I knew about it for only a few days. Your mom needed someone to get you here without suspecting... that's my only involvement."

"And it worked perfectly!" Liz beamed at Hallie before turning back to Chase. "Now come on, everyone wants to say hello."

What followed was a blur of handshakes, hugs, and welcome-home wishes. Chase found himself passed from person to person like a cherished artifact, each one sharing a memory or expressing pride in his service. His high school English teacher, Mrs. Crawford, told him she still used his essay on military history as an example for current students. Mr. Paulson, who looked exactly the same despite being ninety-two, recalled teaching Chase to fish in Mistletoe Creek when he was seven.

The warmth of it all threatened to overwhelm him. He'd spent twelve years in the structured environment of the military, where emotion was controlled and measured. This outpouring of genuine affection from people who'd known him since childhood—it was almost too much.

"Chase Montgomery, as I live and breathe!"

He turned to find Mayor Hayes approaching with hand extended. The mayor had aged well, his silver hair lending him distinction rather than frailty.

"Mayor Hayes, good to see you."

"Roger, please. You're not a kid anymore." The mayor guided him toward the front of the room, where a microphone waited. "I hope you don't mind, but I'd like to say a few words."

Before Chase could protest, Roger had the microphone and was calling for attention. The room quieted, and Chase stood alone beside the mayor, desperately wishing for the anonymity of a crowd.

"Friends, neighbors, family," Roger began, his voice carrying easily through the space. "We're here tonight to welcome home one of our own. Chase Montgomery left us as a boy of eighteen, eager to serve his country. He returns to us as a man who has done exactly that, with honor and distinction."

Chase stared at a spot on the far wall, military bearing the only thing keeping him upright under the weight of so many eyes.

"In twelve years of service as a Marine Combat Engineer, Chase built schools and infrastructure in places most of us can't imagine. He served multiple combat deployments, earning commendations for leadership and technical excellence. But more than his service record, what speaks to his character is that he chose to come home—to family, to community, to the place that shaped him."

Applause erupted, and Chase felt heat climb his neck. He caught Hallie's eye across the room where she sat with her employees, and she offered him a small, understanding smile that somehow made the attention bearable.

"We're proud of you, son," Roger concluded, clapping him on the shoulder. "Welcome home."

The applause continued as Chase made his way through the crowd, accepting congratulations with what he hoped looked like grace rather than discomfort. Finally, the attention shifted to the food tables, and he could breathe again.

The spread was overwhelming—casseroles and salads, roasted meats and vegetarian options, breads and rolls. The dessert table alone could have fed a battalion: pies, cakes, cookies, and what looked like every grandmother in town had contributed their signature sweet.

Chase loaded his plate with familiar comfort foods—Mrs. Adam's mac and cheese that he'd dreamed about during MRE dinners, the Bentleys' famous fried chicken, green bean casserole that looked exactly like his grandmother's recipe. Around him, the community fell into the peaceful rhythm of a shared meal, with conversation flowing between tables, children darting between chairs, and elderly couples holding court at the front of the room.

"Chase Montgomery!"

He turned to find Luke Harper standing behind him, broader than in high school but with the same simple grin that had gotten them both in trouble more than once.

"Luke?" Chase set down his plate to accept the back-slapping hug his old friend offered. "Man, it's been forever."

"Twelve years, give or take." Luke stepped back, assessing him with obvious approval. "Military life agreed with you. You look like you could bench press a truck."

"You're not doing so bad yourself. Still in town?"

"Never left. Took over my uncle's old store when he retired. Turned it into The Reindeer Rack, right down from your parents' place."

"That's yours? I saw it the other day—it looks impressive."

"It pays the bills and keeps me in fishing gear." Luke grabbed a plate and started loading it. "We need to catch up. Grab dinner or coffee when you're settled."

"I'd like that."

They found seats at one of the tables, and Chase listened as Luke filled him in on twelve years of Mistletoe Falls developments—who'd married, who'd moved away, who'd surprised everyone by staying. It was comfortable and strange simultaneously, this easy slide back into friendship that distance and time hadn't eroded.

Between bites, Chase found his gaze drifting to Hallie's table. She was laughing at something Nina had said, her entire face lit with genuine amusement. Sofia was gesturing animatedly about something while Taylor and Lucy listened with rapt attention.

"She turned out pretty great, didn't she?" Luke followed his gaze with knowing amusement.

"Who?"

"Right. Play dumb. That'll work." Luke took a sip of his sweet tea. "Hallie Dawson. The one and only girl you spent half of your high school years hanging out with but never dated."

"She was one of my best friends."

"I always wondered why you two never got together."

"Like I said, we were just friends. She was my next-door neighbor, that's all."

Luke's expression grew more serious. "She's had a rough few years. She lost her dad; her mom took off for Florida without looking back, broken engagement about six months back. But she keeps that shop running and takes care of half the town through her charity work."

Chase processed this information, adding it to the pieces he'd been gathering since his return. The hesitations in conversation, the things she didn't say, the way she deflected when topics turned too personal—it was starting to make sense the more puzzle pieces he gathered.

"She seems happy though," he said, watching her help Lucy clean up a spilled drink.

"She's good at seeming a lot of things." Luke stood to get seconds. "Just saying."

As Luke walked away, Chase continued to watch Hallie. She must have felt his gaze because she looked up, catching his eye across the crowded room. For a moment, they just looked at each other, some wordless communication passing between them that he couldn't quite define.

Then someone called his name, another well-wisher wanting to welcome him home, and the moment broke.

The evening continued in waves of conversation and connection. Chase talked to teachers and coaches, business owners and retirees, young families who'd moved to town since he'd left and older residents who remembered his grandparents. Each interaction wove another thread in the fabric of belonging he'd forgotten existed.

But through it all, he remained aware of Hallie. The way she moved through the room with effortless grace, chatting with everyone. She belonged here in a way that went deeper than mere residence. She was part of the foundation that held the community together.

"You did good, Mom," he said when he finally made it back to his parents' table. "This is... overwhelming, but in the best way."

"I think it turned out nice," Liz said simply.

Chase looked around the room—at the decorations, the photos collected from dozens of sources, and the sheer number of people who'd given up their Saturday night to welcome him home. His throat tightened with emotion.

These people had known him as a child, watched him grow, celebrated when he'd enlisted, and kept faith that he'd return. They'd supported his parents through difficult times, especially after his mother's accident. They'd maintained his place in the community even when he'd been absent from it.

This wasn't just a welcome-home dinner. It was an affirmation that he belonged, that twelve years and thousands of miles hadn't severed the roots that connected him to this place and these people.

Chase caught Hallie's eye again across the room. She was helping an elderly woman with her coat, but she paused to smile at him—warm and genuine and somehow exactly what he needed.

Maybe coming home wasn't about figuring out what came next. Maybe it was about recognizing what had been waiting all along.

Chapter 9

Hallie stared at the chaos of Chase's shopping list, which he'd scrawled on a scrap piece of paper in handwriting that looked like it had survived a windstorm. "Okay, we need a strategy here. If we just wander randomly, we'll be here until midnight."

Chase peered over her shoulder at the crumpled paper, standing close enough that she caught the scent of laundry detergent and something woodsy that might have been aftershave. "It's just shopping. How complicated can it be?"

"Famous last words." She pulled a pen from her purse and started reorganizing his list by store section, grouping linens with bath items, kitchen supplies with pantry staples. Her handwriting formed neat columns in the margin, each category numbered for efficiency.

"Are you making a battle plan for the cereal aisle?"

She looked up to find him watching her with barely contained amusement, one eyebrow raised in a way that had always meant he was about to tease her mercilessly.

"I'm creating an efficient shopping route so we don't backtrack seventeen times." She kept writing, but felt heat creep up her neck. "There's a difference."

"If you say so, General Dawson."

Hallie stopped mid-word, the pen hovering above the paper. Was she doing it again? Taking over, organizing, micro-managing every detail because staying busy meant not thinking too hard about how aware she was of his presence beside her? She glanced at the list, at her careful reorganization of his simple scrawl, and recognized the pattern Nina had called her out on more than once.

"You're right." She folded the paper and handed it back to him. "Your list, your system. I'll just... follow your lead."

He grinned at her. "I didn't mean you had to stop. I was just giving you a hard time."

"No, I'm over-managing." She grabbed a shopping cart from the corral. "Let's just shop and see what happens."

"Now that's a philosophy I can work with." He snagged his own cart, falling into step beside her.

The store stretched before them in overwhelming abundance—row after row of products under fluorescent lights that made everything look slightly too bright. A tinny version of "Silver Bells" played through the overhead speakers, and the Sunday afternoon crowd moved through the aisles with the purposeful determination of people trying to accomplish weekend errands before Monday arrived.

Chase stopped just inside the entrance, taking it all in with an expression Hallie couldn't quite read. "It's bigger than I remember."

"They expanded four years ago. Added the grocery section and outdoor living." She watched him scan the store as if he were memorizing exits and entry points. "You okay?"

"Yeah, just…" He shook his head, offering a rueful smile. "The commissary was never like this. Everything there was organized for efficiency, not consumer choice. This is like stepping into a different universe."

"Welcome to civilian shopping. It only gets worse from here."

They started in the home goods section, where towers of towels rose in every conceivable color. Hallie pulled two sets from the display—one navy blue, one slate gray—and held them up for inspection.

Chase barely glanced at them. "They both dry water, right?"

"That's your criteria? Functional towels?" She shook the navy set at him. "Color affects mood, Chase. You're going to see these every single day. Navy is calming, professional. Gray is neutral, goes with everything." She returned the navy set and selected a second gray option, this one slightly darker. "See? Different grays create different atmospheres."

"I cannot tell those apart."

"One is slate, one is charcoal."

"Those are the same thing."

She looked at him to see if he was serious, found him fighting a grin, and swatted his arm with the darker towel. "You're messing with me."

"Little bit." He took both sets from her, examining them with exaggerated concentration. "Okay, explain the mood difference between slate and charcoal."

"Slate is lighter, more modern. Charcoal is richer, cozier."

"And which one will dry me after a shower?"

"Both, but—" She caught herself about to launch into a detailed explanation of thread count and absorbency and made herself stop. "You know what? Get whichever one you want. Or get both. Live dangerously."

He tossed both sets into his cart. "Problem solved."

They moved through the bath section, accumulating a shower curtain and a bath mat, hand soap and toilet paper in quantities that made Chase mutter something about supply logistics. Hallie grabbed cleaning supplies—spray bottles and sponges, floor cleaner and glass cleaner—while Chase studied dish soap options like they held the secrets of the universe.

"Do I need antibacterial or is regular fine?"

"Antibacterial if you're concerned about germs. Regular if you're not."

"That's not helpful."

"Neither is standing here for five minutes staring at soap." She plucked a bottle of antibacterial from the shelf and dropped it in his cart. "Next category."

The kitchen aisle presented new challenges. Chase picked up a spatula that bent when he tested it against his palm, and Hallie immediately confiscated it, replacing it with a heat-resistant silicone version.

"This one won't melt in your pan," she explained, adding a matching spoon and slotted spatula to his cart.

"I wasn't planning to melt it."

"Everyone plans not to melt their spatulas. It happens anyway." She surveyed his cart, mentally cataloging what else he needed. "Measuring cups, mixing bowls, cutting board, knife set—"

"Hallie."

She looked up to find him watching her with patient amusement.

"I appreciate the help, but you're doing that thing again where you take over."

"I'm just—" She stopped, recognizing the truth in his words. "Sorry. Old habits."

"Don't apologize. I like your caring enough to have opinions about my spatulas." He picked up a wooden spoon, testing its weight. "But maybe let me make some calls? I need to learn this stuff."

"Right, okay." She stepped back, forcing herself to browse rather than direct. "Your kitchen, your choice."

"Though I reserve the right to ask for advice."

"Granted."

He moved through the kitchen section with methodical attention, selecting items with the same focus she'd watched him apply to everything. A can opener that felt solid in his hand. A set of mixing bowls that nested efficiently. Measuring cups that seemed straightforward enough. But when he reached for a flimsy-looking pot, Hallie couldn't help herself.

"That's going to warp the first time you use it."

"How can you tell?"

"The bottom's too thin. See?" She tapped it, producing a tinny sound. "You want something heavier." She found a better option two shelves up. "This will last for years."

Chase compared them both, then nodded and exchanged them. "Good catch."

"I've learned a few things from watching cooking shows."

"You cook?"

"Sometimes. When I have time and energy, which isn't often... but I love to cook." She picked up a cast-iron skillet, surprised by its weight. "This is heavy."

"Perfect." Chase set the other two skillets aside and took it from her hands like it weighed nothing and added it to his cart. "Every kitchen needs cast iron."

"You planning on cooking with that or defending the apartment?"

"Multi-purpose tool. Marines believe in efficiency." He lifted it experimentally, giving it a testing swing that made Hallie duck.

"Put that down before you take someone out."

"I have excellent control."

"Famous last words." But she was laughing, imagining him accidentally wielding cookware like weapons. "What are you going to make in a cast-iron skillet, anyway?"

"I don't know. Eggs? Meat?" He set it carefully in the cart. "I'll figure it out."

They continued gathering essentials—plates and bowls, glasses and mugs, silverware that wouldn't bend. Hallie pointed out items he hadn't considered: pot holders, dish towels, a colander for draining pasta. Chase added them without argument, his cart filling rapidly.

She led him back to the cookware section and picked up a cheerful red nonstick pan set, the handles bright as candy apples. "These would be perfect for everyday cooking."

Chase gave them a skeptical look. "They look like they came out of Santa's workshop."

"Exactly! Christmas cheer while you scramble eggs."

"I was thinking more... tactical black... like the cast iron pan."

She imagined his apartment outfitted entirely in black and gray, like a military operation. "Your kitchen would look like a stealth mission if I left you alone in here."

"And that's a problem because?"

"Because you don't live in a bunker anymore." She put the red pans in his cart before he could protest. "Trust me. A little color won't hurt. And you need more than just a cast-iron pan."

"If you say so." But he was smiling, and Hallie realized she'd won this negotiation.

They moved to the bedding section, where pillows rose in pyramids of varying firmness. Chase grabbed one labeled "medium firm" and tested it with clinical precision, pressing his palm into the center.

"How do you even know which one's right?"

"You try them out." Hallie showed him by taking a pillow from the display and putting it behind her head, closing her eyes briefly. "See? Too soft."

Chase grabbed the firmest option available and mimicked her position, lying back against a shelf display with the pillow behind his head and his eyes closed. "This one's good."

"You can't nap in home goods."

"You'd be surprised what Marines can do under pressure. I can sleep anywhere." But he opened his eyes and grinned at her, and something about the combination of his relaxed posture and the mischief in his expression made her feel suddenly warm.

She swatted his arm lightly, trying to regain her composure. "Come on. We've got more areas of the store to cover."

He tossed two firm pillows into her cart, and they moved on.

The grocery section tested their efficiency. Hallie automatically reached for her favorite holiday blend coffee, the bag decorated with snowflakes and promising notes of cinnamon and cocoa. Chase grabbed the largest container of plain roast he could find; its industrial label promised nothing but caffeine.

"That stuff could strip paint," she said, eyeing his choice.

"Good. Means it's working."

"You'll never sleep."

"I don't sleep much anyway." He added the coffee to his cart, then paused, looking at her selection. "What's in the holiday blend?"

"Cinnamon, nutmeg, vanilla notes. It's fantastic."

He took it from her hands, studied the description, then added it to his cart alongside his paint-stripping variety. "I'll try it. Maybe it'll convert me."

"Or you'll hate it and stick with your industrial strength."

"Either way, I've got options."

They moved through the aisles, Chase tossing items in with the enthusiasm of someone who'd been deprived of shopping choices for too long. Cereal—three different kinds. Pasta and jarred sauce. Canned soup and crackers. Peanut butter, jelly, bread. Practical staples that suggested a man who planned to survive rather than thrive in his kitchen.

But then they hit the snack aisle, and something changed. Cookies appeared in his cart—chocolate chip, oatmeal raisin, sandwich cookies with cream filling. Candy bars in variety packs. Little chocolate cakes wrapped in crinkly packages. Bags of gummy bears and sour candies.

Hallie watched the pile grow with increasing amusement. "You planning on opening a dessert buffet?"

"You said I needed basics." He added a bag of marshmallows to the collection, completely unbothered. "Sugar's basic."

"Sugar's not a food group."

"It should be."

She'd forgotten about his legendary sweet tooth, how he used to demolish entire sleeves of cookies after school and still be hungry moments later. The memory surfaced with startling clarity—Chase at seventeen, sitting on her kitchen counter stealing cookies from the jar while her mother pretended to scold him.

"You're going to give yourself a sugar coma."

"I'll risk it." He surveyed his collection with satisfaction. "Besides, I work out. Balances out."

"That's not how nutrition works."

"It's how my nutrition works." He grinned at her completely unrepentant, and Hallie smiled despite her better judgment. How he stayed in shape while apparently living on sugar and good intentions was one of life's great mysteries.

She reached past him to grab hot chocolate mix—the kind with tiny marshmallows already included. "Since you're stocking up on essentials."

Chase took the container from her hands, reading the label. "You remembered."

"Your lifelong marshmallow obsession? Hard to forget the man who put seven huge marshmallows in one mug and called it hydration."

"It was hydration. Hot chocolate with flavor enhancement."

"It was diabetes in a cup."

But inside, beneath the teasing, Hallie was aware of how easily she remembered these details about him. Small things she thought she'd forgotten, surfacing like they'd been waiting just beneath consciousness. The way he took his coffee straight and black as night. His sweet tooth. How he'd always chosen the cookie jar over actual dinner.

They moved through produce, where Chase looked completely lost among the vegetables, then to paper goods where he grabbed enough paper towels and napkins to supply a small battalion. The carts grew heavier, more unwieldy, loaded with the accumulated necessities of building a home from nothing.

Near the cleaning supplies, an elderly woman was stretching for a bottle of floor cleaner on the top shelf, her fingers just missing the edge. Before Hallie could move to help, Chase was already there, reaching up to grab it with ease.

"Here you go, ma'am."

"Oh, thank you, dear. These stores keep putting things higher and higher." She accepted the bottle with a grateful smile. "So kind of you."

"No problem at all."

He returned to his cart as if nothing had happened, but Hallie had watched the entire exchange. The natural kindness, unprompted and unthinking. The respect in how he'd addressed the woman.

Something tugged at her chest—an awareness she immediately tried to suppress. Good people helped strangers in stores. It meant nothing. She focused on the cart, on the list, on anything except the warmth spreading through her.

They rounded another corner and nearly collided with Mrs. Dillard, who took one look at them—both pushing carts, shopping together on a Sunday afternoon—and her face lit up like she'd witnessed a proposal.

"Hallie! Chase Montgomery! Don't you two make the cutest couple, shopping together like newlyweds setting up house?"

Hallie felt heat flood her face. "Oh, we're not—we're just—Chase needs supplies for his apartment, and I'm helping."

"Such a sweet girl, helping out." Mrs. Dillard patted Hallie's arm with grandmotherly affection. "And Chase, your mother must be thrilled to have you home. The whole town's been talking about your welcome dinner."

"It was very generous," Chase said smoothly.

"Well, you two have fun with your shopping." Mrs. Dillard winked—actually winked—before pushing her cart away, leaving them in awkward silence.

"I'm sorry about that," Hallie said finally, gripping her cart handle. "She means well, but she's still the town's unofficial gossip central."

"I remember." Chase seemed entirely unbothered, already moving forward. "By tomorrow, half of Mistletoe Falls will know we were shopping together."

"Probably."

"Could be worse. At least she called us cute."

Hallie wasn't sure how to respond to that, so she focused on navigating toward the home fragrance section. Chase followed, looking skeptical as they approached walls of candles and diffusers.

"Every home needs a comforting scent," she explained, selecting several options and holding them up for his inspection. "Otherwise, it just smells like... nothing. Or worse, like cleaning products and paint."

"I didn't realize smell was that important."

"It affects mood, memory, how you feel in a space." She handed him a candle labeled Mountain Pine. "Try this one."

He removed the lid and sniffed cautiously, then his expression softened. "Smells like home."

"Exactly. That's what you want—something that makes your space feel welcoming." She added it to his cart before he could decide against it. "Trust me on this."

"I'm starting to think I should trust you with everything. You clearly know what you're doing."

"Years of retail experience."

They passed through the tool section, which proved to be a mistake. Chase stopped to examine a drill set, his attention caught like a child in a toy store.

"I don't actually need this today," he admitted, still looking at the display.

"Then we keep moving."

"But if I'm doing renovations—"

"Chase." She grabbed his cart and started pushing it forward. "Tools are a rabbit hole. We still have other things to look for."

He followed reluctantly, casting one last look at the drill sets. "This is censorship."

"This is efficiency. You can come back for tools next weekend or something."

"Promise?"

"Yes, I promise I'll bring you back to the tool section. Now come on."

By the time they reached the checkout lanes, both carts overflowed with purchases. Chase started unloading items onto the conveyor belt, and Hallie helped, creating a system—linens here, kitchen supplies there, groceries at the end.

The total climbed with each scanned item, and Hallie watched Chase's expression remain carefully neutral. This had to be costing more than he'd expected, outfitting an entire apartment from scratch. But he just pulled out his card when the cashier announced the final amount, swiping it without comment.

They loaded everything into the truck bed, Chase organizing boxes and bags with military precision while Hallie handed items up to him. The afternoon had shifted toward evening, the November air carrying the promise of chilly nights ahead. Her fingers felt stiff by the time they'd finished, and she rubbed them for warmth.

"You in a rush to get home?" He asked, closing the tailgate.

Hallie checked her phone—just past four o'clock. "Not particularly. Why?"

"I still need furniture. Couch, table, dresser, bed frame—all the big stuff. Thought maybe..." He paused, looking almost uncertain. "Would you want to help with that too? I know it's asking a lot."

She should probably say no. She'd already spent hours with him. But the afternoon had been easy, comfortable in ways she hadn't expected. And the thought of going home to her empty apartment while Chase faced furniture shopping alone felt wrong.

"I'll help. This ought to be interesting."

"Interesting is one word for it."

As they climbed back into the truck, Hallie glanced at his profile—the strong line of his jaw, the way his hands rested easily on the steering wheel, the contentment in his expression—and wondered exactly when "just friends" had started feeling like such an enormous lie.

Chapter 10

Twelve years in the Marines, and this was what made Chase nervous—a warehouse full of furniture.

The store stretched before him like an obstacle course designed by someone who thought interior decorating was a competitive sport. Sectionals in every color imaginable. Dining sets that could seat anywhere from four to fourteen people. Bedroom suites with more pieces than he knew what to do with. The overhead lighting made everything gleam with showroom perfection, and the smell of new furniture—a combination of leather, fabric treatment, and wood polish—hit him the moment they walked through the entrance.

Hallie was already three steps ahead, talking to a saleswoman in a navy blazer whose name tag read "Sandra." They were comparing fabric swatches, discussing something about durability and stain resistance, while Chase stood there trying to remember why he'd thought this was a good idea.

"Mr. Montgomery?" Sandra approached with a tablet and a smile that suggested she sensed commission potential. "Hallie tells me you're furnishing an entire apartment from scratch. That's exciting! Let's start with your vision. What kind of aesthetic are you going for?"

Vision.

Aesthetic.

Chase glanced at Hallie, who looked entirely comfortable with these words, then back at Sandra. "Functional?"

"He means comfortable and durable," Hallie translated smoothly. "Something that will last but doesn't require a PhD in maintenance."

"Perfect. And color scheme?"

Chase gestured vaguely at the surrounding store. "Clean?"

Hallie laughed, the sound bright and unguarded. "That's not a color."

"Then... the kind that hides dirt?" He was aware he sounded ridiculous, but furniture shopping hadn't been covered in any training manual he'd ever studied. "No white. No cream."

"Practical," Sandra said, typing notes into her tablet. "I can work with that. Let's start with the living room and go from there."

She led them into a maze of furniture arrangements, each one staged like a magazine spread. Chase followed, noting emergency exits out of habit, while Hallie examined pieces with the focus of someone evaluating strategic assets.

The first sofa Sandra showed them looked comfortable enough—deep cushions, soft fabric in a muted gray. Chase sat down and immediately sank so far into the cushions that standing up again required genuine effort.

"Too soft," he announced, extracting himself with less grace than he'd like.

"That's our cloud collection," Sandra explained. "Very popular with people who want that sink-in feeling."

"I want a couch, not a marshmallow."

Hallie bit back a smile. "Try this one."

The second sofa felt like sitting on concrete. Chase shifted, trying to find any give in the cushions, and found none. "Are we sure this isn't just a wooden bench with fabric stretched over it?"

"That's our contemporary line. Very firm support."

"Very uncomfortable. Is there something between quicksand and concrete?"

"You need something that's comfortable but supportive," Hallie said, moving to a different section. "Like this one."

She gestured to a leather sofa in rich brown, the kind of leather that looked like it would age well rather than crack. Chase sat, and this time the cushions held him without swallowing him. The back provided support without feeling rigid. He could picture actually sitting here to watch a game or read without constantly adjusting position.

"This works."

"It's very... brown," Hallie observed, her head tilted slightly.

"Brown's a color."

"Technically, yes."

"And it hides dirt."

"Also true." She ran her hand across the armrest, testing the leather. "It's good quality. Should last you years."

"Sandra, this couch will work."

Sandra was already typing information into her tablet. "Excellent choice. This is one of our bestsellers. Now, do you want a matching loveseat or are you thinking recliners?"

"Recliners," Chase said immediately.

They moved to the recliner section, where the options multiplied exponentially. Power recliners with USB ports. Massage functions. Heat settings. Cup holders built into the armrests. Chase stared at a model that appeared to have more buttons than his truck's dashboard.

"I just want a chair that reclines," he said, studying the control panel with suspicion. "Not one that could double as a spaceship."

"This model is very popular," Sandra began, but Hallie was already shaking her head.

"Too complicated. Show us something simpler."

She led them to a different display—a recliner with clean lines and solid construction. No power controls, no unnecessary features. Just a lever on the side and comfortable padding. Chase tried it out, pulling the lever and feeling the footrest extend smoothly.

"This is more my speed."

"It suits you," Hallie said, and something in her tone made him glance up.

"I'll take two," he told Sandra.

The bedroom section loomed ahead, and Chase felt his confidence waver again. Bed frames in metal and wood, headboards upholstered and carved, footboards that matched or contrasted. Sandra started explaining construction methods and warranty coverage, but Chase watched Hallie instead.

She moved through the space with calm assurance, touching fabrics, checking drawer construction, asking questions about materials that he wouldn't have thought to consider. She was in her element here, making sense of choices that overwhelmed him.

Maybe he should just stand here and nod occasionally.

"What about this one?" Hallie gestured to a set in dark wood—simple lines, sturdy construction, drawers that opened smoothly when she tested them.

"It's nice," Chase said, because it was, though he couldn't have articulated what made it better than the dozens of other sets they'd passed.

"The craftsmanship is excellent," Sandra added. "Solid wood throughout, not veneer. This will last decades with proper care."

"And a mattress?" Hallie turned to Sandra. "What do you recommend?"

"We have several options. Memory foam is very popular—it contours to your body and remembers your preferred sleeping position."

Chase's eyes narrowed. "Why would I want a bed that remembers things? That sounds suspicious."

Hallie doubled over laughing, one hand pressed to her stomach. "You might be the only person I know who can make shopping for a mattress sound like a security threat."

"I'm just saying, I don't need my furniture collecting data on me."

"It's not collecting data," Sandra said patiently, though her lips twitched with amusement. "It's just responsive foam. But we also have traditional innerspring and hybrid options if you prefer."

Chase ended up choosing a hybrid—some combination of foam and springs that the salesperson promised would provide the best of both worlds. He wasn't entirely convinced, but Hallie nodded approval, which somehow made the decision feel more solid.

They moved to the dining furniture, where Chase immediately gravitated toward a wooden table—solid oak, according to Sandra, with thick legs and a surface that looked like it could withstand daily use without complaint. Four matching chairs surrounded it, their seats cushioned but not fussy.

Hallie ran her hand along the tabletop, her fingers tracing the grain. "This is beautiful work. Feels like something that could hold a lot of wonderful memories."

The softness of her voice caught him off guard. She wasn't just evaluating furniture anymore—she was imagining a life lived around it. Meals shared, conversations held, the accumulation of ordinary moments that transformed a house into a home.

Chase looked away before she could catch him staring, focusing on Sandra's tablet instead. "Yeah, I'll take this one."

"Excellent. Now, do you need any accent pieces? Lamps, decorative items, throw pillows?"

"No," Chase said at the same time Hallie said, "Yes."

They looked at each other.

"You need some personality in your home," Hallie explained. "Otherwise, it's just going to look like a furniture showroom."

"What's wrong with that?"

"Everything." She was already moving toward a display of decorative items, and Chase followed with resignation.

She held up a throw pillow embroidered with reindeer wearing scarves. "This would be perfect for your couch."

"If I buy that, I'll have to turn in my man card."

"You'll have to accept that your living room needs personality."

"Didn't realize my furniture would have self-esteem issues." But he was fighting a grin now, because her enthusiasm was infectious even when directed at ridiculous decorative pillows.

She grabbed three pillows—the reindeer one, another in solid tan, and a third with a subtle geometric pattern. "These will balance each other out. Trust me."

"Do I have a choice?"

"Not really." She added them to Sandra's growing list before he could protest further.

They moved through the lighting section, where Chase picked the plainest lamp he could find—simple base, beige shade, the kind of thing that would fade into the background. Hallie made a face.

"What's wrong with this one?"

"Nothing if you want your apartment to look like a hotel room." She selected a different option—brushed metal base, drum shade that would cast warm light. "This one has character."

He examined it, turning it to check the build quality. The metal felt solid, substantial. "It's nice."

"Nice enough to replace your boring choice?"

"I wasn't aware lamp shopping had become a negotiation."

"Everything's a negotiation." She handed the lamp to Sandra. "Add three of these, please—two tabletops and one floor-standing model."

By the time they'd finished, Sandra's tablet held a list that made Chase's head spin. She walked them through delivery options, explaining how everything would arrive within a week and offering assembly services for an additional fee.

"I can handle assembly," Chase said. He'd built infrastructure in war zones; he could manage furniture.

"Perfect. Let me get this totaled for you."

While Sandra disappeared to process everything, Chase and Hallie stood in the middle of the showroom surrounded by furniture. The overhead lights hummed faintly. Somewhere in the distance, another salesperson was explaining sectional configurations to a young couple.

"Thank you," Chase said. "For all of this. I would have walked out with the first brown couch I saw and called it done."

"You're welcome. Though I have to say, your complete terror of decorative pillows was entertaining."

"They're unnecessary."

"They're comforting."

"That's what the couch is for."

She shook her head, but she was smiling. "You have a lot to learn about civilian living."

"Apparently." He looked around the showroom again, at the carefully staged rooms that promised comfort and belonging. "It's strange, you know? In the Marines, everything was provided. Barracks, gear, even meals. I never had to think about whether my furniture had personality. Now I'm supposed to have opinions about lamps."

"Is it overwhelming?"

"Yeah. But also..." He paused, trying to find the right words. "It's good. Different, but good. Like I'm actually building something that's mine."

Sandra returned with a printed invoice and a timeline for delivery. Chase signed the paperwork, authorized the payment, and accepted the receipt that confirmed he'd just spent more on furniture than he had on anything in his adult life besides his truck.

Chapter 11

Chase pushed through the back entrance of Bells & Whistles, balancing his travel mug of coffee in one hand while he shut the door behind him with the other. Voices drifted from the office at the rear of the building, and he headed in that direction, his boots echoing against the polished hardwood floor.

His parents were already at work. Mark stood at the filing cabinet near the window, pulling folders from one of the upper drawers, while Liz sat at the desk, sorting through what looked like vendor invoices. She'd spread papers across every available surface, organizing them into piles only she could decipher.

"Morning," Chase said.

Both turned at his voice, and his mother's face brightened like he'd brought sunshine with him.

"Chase! Good morning, sweetheart. How was your first night in the apartment? Did you sleep okay?"

Chase took a long drink of his coffee, considering his answer. "Wasn't too bad. But I can't wait until my furniture gets delivered. That old bed of mine is killing my back."

His mother's eyebrows shot up. "You went furniture shopping already? I didn't realize you'd done that."

"Over the weekend." Chase set his mug on the corner of the desk that wasn't buried in paperwork. "Hallie helped me pick everything out."

"Hallie did?" His father glanced up from the filing cabinet, a slight smile tugging at his mouth. "That was nice of her."

"More like lifesaving." Chase leaned against the wall, folding his arms. "You should have seen me at the furniture store. I walked in thinking I could just point at things and be done in an hour. Turned out furniture shopping is a whole different kind of warfare."

Liz laughed. "Oh, I wish I could have been there to see that. Tell me everything. How did it go?"

Chase launched into the story. He told them about the big-box retail store first, how Hallie had systematically worked through everything he needed. Towels that matched. Dish soap that actually smelled decent. A shower curtain that wasn't prison-issue beige.

"She made me buy a candle," he admitted, shaking his head. "Said my apartment would smell like nothing if I didn't. I thought she was exaggerating until she made me smell one called Mountain Pine, and I promise you, it smelled exactly like the woods behind your house."

"She has a good eye for those details," Liz said, wheeling over to retrieve a folder from the lower file drawer. "That's why her shop does so well. She understands people want more than just products—they want the feeling that goes with them."

"Then we went to the furniture store, and I thought that would be straightforward." Chase rubbed the back of his neck, remembering his bewilderment. "Turns out there are approximately seven thousand types of couches, and they all look the same until you sit on them. The first one I tried swallowed me whole. Second, one felt like sitting on concrete."

Mark chuckled, pulling more files from the cabinet and stacking them in the desk corner. "Let me guess—Hallie found you the perfect middle ground?"

"She did." Chase picked up his coffee again. "Brown leather. Comfortable but not ridiculous. Two recliners that don't require an engineering degree to operate. The salesperson kept trying to sell me power recliners with massage functions and USB ports, and I just wanted a chair that went back when I pulled the lever."

"That sounds exactly like you," his mother said.

"The best part was the bedroom furniture." Chase grinned, remembering Hallie's reaction. "The salesperson started explaining this memory foam mattress, saying it would remember my preferred sleeping position. I asked why I'd want my furniture collecting data on me. Hallie about died laughing."

His mother pressed a hand to her mouth, her shoulders shaking with silent laughter. Even his father was grinning now, setting aside his filing work to give Chase his full attention.

"Anyway, she saved me from buying the most boring furniture known to man. She had an opinion about everything. I told her I didn't need personality in my furniture, and she informed me that was exactly why I needed her help."

"She's not wrong," Liz said, still smiling. "Left to your own devices, you probably would have bought everything in the same shade of brown."

"Hey, brown is practical."

"Brown is boring." His mother reached for another stack of papers, stretching slightly to grab them from the far corner of the desk. The movement made her wince—just barely, but Chase caught it.

He moved before thinking about it, crossing the small space and taking the papers from her hands. "Here. Let me get that."

"I've got it, Chase. I'm fine."

"I know you've got it. But I'm standing right here, so you might as well let me help." He handed her the papers, then looked at the filing system his father had been working on. The cabinet had five drawers, and the upper three were completely out of his mother's reach.

His mother followed his gaze. "Your father's been meaning to reorganize things."

Chase walked over to the filing cabinet, studying the labels on each drawer.

"Chase, really, we'll get it figured out—"

"Mom." He turned to face her, keeping his voice gentle but firm. "I'm here now. Let me help make things easier. Please."

For a moment, she looked like she might argue. The Montgomery family trait—stubborn independence—was alive and well in his mother. But then her shoulders relaxed slightly, and she nodded.

"The vendor files," she said quietly. "And the correspondence folders. I use those most days."

Chase and his father spent the next twenty minutes reorganizing the filing system, moving frequently used files to lower drawers while relocating older archives to the upper sections. His mother directed them, her organizational preferences clear and sensible, and Chase made mental notes about other adjustments they could make. Lower shelves for commonly used supplies. A different desk height, maybe, or at least a better arrangement of what sat on top of it.

As they worked and talked, Chase began to understand exactly how much his parents had been managing alone. The filing cabinet was just the beginning. Business correspondence, vendor invoices, customer orders, maintenance issues—his father had been handling all of it while simultaneously caring for his mother and running the customer service side of the store.

"Dad," Chase said, sliding the last drawer closed, "what kind of maintenance issues have you been dealing with?"

Mark waved a hand dismissively. "Oh, the usual. Leaky faucet in the bathroom, some loose floorboards near the toy train display, the back door sticks in humid weather. Nothing I can't handle."

"When's the last time you had a day off?"

His father paused, thinking. "I don't know. A few weeks, maybe? We're closed on Sundays, but there's always something that needs doing in here."

Chase looked at his mother, who'd gone back to sorting invoices. She worked with steady efficiency, but he could see the way she shifted in her chair every few minutes, adjusting her position. The accident had taken so much from her—mobility, independence, the ease she'd once had moving through her own space. And she'd been managing it all with the same grace she'd brought to everything else in life, never complaining, never asking for help unless absolutely necessary.

Guilt twisted through him. He should have been here. Should have visited more often, or at least called more regularly, to understand the full scope of what they were dealing with.

"I want to take on more," he said abruptly. "Maintenance, inventory management, whatever you need. You shouldn't be handling all of this alone, Dad. You either, Mom."

"Chase, you're already helping plenty—"

"I mean it. Make me a list. Everything that needs fixing, updating, or improving." He met his father's eyes, trying to communicate the sincerity of the offer. "I'm good with my hands, I've got the time, and you need help. Let me actually be useful."

His father studied him for a long moment, then nodded slowly. "All right. I'll make you that list."

Chase turned back to the desk, intending to ask his mother what else they could reorganize, when his attention caught on the bulletin board mounted on the wall above her workspace. It displayed the usual mix of community announcements, upcoming events, and business cards from vendors. But one item stood out—a handmade card with elegant calligraphy that he recognized immediately.

The handwriting was Hallie's. He'd seen it on enough of his own cards he'd received from her to know the distinctive style—graceful letters with just enough flourish to feel personal without being fussy.

He stepped closer, reading the message inside the card.

Dear Liz,

Thinking of you today and sending love. I know the hard days come and go, and I wanted you to know you're not facing them alone. I'm here whenever you need me—whether that's for grocery runs, a listening ear, or just sitting together over coffee.

You're stronger than you know, and I'm lucky to have you in my life.

With love always, Hallie

Chase stared at the card, something warm and complicated expanding in his chest. "When did Hallie give you this?"

His mother looked up from her paperwork, following his gaze to the bulletin board. "Oh, that one? Maybe three months after the accident? I hadn't been home but a few days, and I was having a rough day. Everything felt overwhelming." She smiled softly. "Hallie showed up with groceries and that card. Told me she'd put me on her weekly check-in list, and I wasn't allowed to argue about it."

"Weekly check-ins?"

"Mm-hmm. She called or stopped by the house regularly. Sometimes she brought meals. Sometimes she brought baskets filled with little pick me up items... thoughtful things that made me happy. Sometimes she just dropped by, and we'd talk for hours over coffee or bake cookies or make dinner together. Other times she just asked for the grocery list for the week and then took off and did our shopping for us." His mother's voice carried deep affection. "She's been a lifeline this past year and a half, Chase. Especially in those first few months after I came home from the hospital. More than she probably realizes."

Chase kept looking at the card, at the careful attention Hallie had put into every word.

His father joined the conversation, setting down the last of the files he'd been reorganizing. "You know about Operation Christmas Cheer, right? The program Hallie runs during the holiday season every year?"

"She mentioned it last week." Chase turned away from the bulletin board, leaning against the desk. "But I don't really know what it involves."

"It's remarkable, that's what it is." Mark pulled the desk chair over and sat down with a slight groan. "Hallie coordinates the whole thing from the basement of her shop. Toy drives, food drives, gift baskets for the veterans living at the veterans' home and shut-ins, Christmas baskets for the retirement community. She's everywhere during the holidays, making sure no one in Mistletoe Falls gets forgotten."

Liz nodded, adding her own observations. "She organizes the toy donation program. We donate through the store every year. Hallie matches donated items with specific children in need, making sure each gift feels personal rather than generic."

"She does the same with the food drives," Mark continued. "Collects donations, organizes them into baskets or boxes, delivers everything to families who need it. And not just food—she includes personal care items, cleaning supplies, things people might actually need."

Chase absorbed this information. She wasn't just running a business—she was running a full-scale ministry that served the entire community.

"The veterans' home especially loves her," his mother added. "She makes baskets for every one that lives there, personalizes them based on individual interests and needs. She must spend hours putting them together."

"How does she manage all this and run her store?" Chase asked.

"Her employees help," Mark said. "They all volunteer their time—Lucy, Nina, Taylor, Sofia. Hallie couldn't do it alone, though she'd probably try if they let her." He rubbed his chin thoughtfully. "The entire operation is impressive. She coordinates volunteers from all over town as well when delivery time comes around. She processes donations and keeps detailed records of who needs what. It takes serious organizational skills and dedication."

Chase thought about Hallie as he'd seen her this past week—cheerful, energetic, and always ready with a smile or a joke. He'd known she was kind. That much had been obvious since childhood. But this went beyond kindness.

"You should volunteer," his mother said suddenly, breaking into his thoughts. "For Operation Christmas Cheer, I mean."

Chase looked at her, surprised. "You think Hallie would want help?"

"I think Hallie needs help more than she'd ever admit." Liz set down her pen, giving him her full attention. "She runs herself ragged every Christmas season between her store and her program. Having another pair of hands, especially someone with your organizational skills and work ethic, would be a blessing to her. Plus, it would give you a chance to contribute to the community in a meaningful way. Help you get back into the rhythm of civilian life."

The suggestion appealed to Chase more than he wanted to examine too closely. The idea of working alongside Hallie felt right.

"Yeah," he said slowly. "Yeah, I think I'll ask her about that."

His mother smiled. "Good. I think the two of you would work well together."

Chase stood there looking at that handmade card on the bulletin board and wondered when exactly his childhood friend had become someone he couldn't stop thinking about.

When had shopping for household supplies with her become the best part of his weekend? When had making her laugh start to feel like an accomplishment worth celebrating?

He didn't have an answer to those questions, but he realized he wanted to know more about her. Not just as his childhood friend or his parents' neighbor or the helpful woman who'd made his apartment shopping bearable. He wanted to understand what drove her, what made her laugh, and what dreams she carried beneath that bright exterior.

Chapter 12

Hallie's desk was a battlefield of paperwork—employee schedules spread across one corner, her calendar of upcoming events occupying another, and somewhere underneath it all, the budget spreadsheet she'd been avoiding. She picked up her coffee mug, took a sip that had gone lukewarm twenty minutes ago, and went back to scribbling names into time slots on the master schedule for the upcoming Christmas season.

Lucy, Wednesday through Saturday, ten to six. Nina, Tuesday through Saturday, nine to seven. Taylor, Monday through Friday, afternoons and evenings. Sofia, Mondays through Friday plus Saturday mornings when Lucy needed time off.

And now two new hires—Missy Harvey and Grace Rogers—who'd both impressed her during interviews last week with their genuine enthusiasm and prior retail experience. Missy could work mornings and afternoons Tuesday through Friday. Grace was available Monday through Saturday, afternoons and evenings. The extra coverage would be a lifesaver during the Christmas season when the store became a madhouse and Operation Christmas Cheer demanded increasing amounts of her attention.

Hallie cross-referenced her schedule against the calendar she'd marked up with Operation Christmas Cheer events. The toy drive delivery on November 27th. Food basket assembly sessions scheduled. The Letters to Santa Booth in December. Delivery days for the veterans' home and independent living facility. Coordination meetings with community volunteers who helped with distribution.

The logistics made her head spin, but this was the work that mattered. This was why she got up every morning and pushed through exhaustion when December hit and sleep became a luxury she couldn't quite afford.

A knock on her open office door pulled her attention up from the schedule.

Chase stood in the doorway, one shoulder leaning against the frame, wearing jeans and a navy blue henley that made his eyes look impossibly blue. His expression carried warmth and what looked like nervous energy—like a man on a mission.

Surprise shot through her, followed immediately by that traitorous flutter in her chest that she'd been trying to ignore all week.

"Chase. Hi." She set down her pen, suddenly conscious of how messy her office must look—papers everywhere, empty coffee mugs on the desk corner, her cardigan hanging crooked on the back of her chair. "What are you doing here?"

"Am I interrupting?" He straightened from the doorframe. "Nina told me you were back here and said to come on through."

"No, that's fine." Hallie gestured at the paperwork explosion on her desk. "Just wrestling with schedules and trying to make sure I haven't accidentally double-booked myself. What's up? Do you need more help shopping for stuff for your apartment?"

His mouth curved into a slight smile that did unhelpful things to her pulse. "No, I think you got me pretty well set up. Furniture arrives Thursday, and I've got enough food to last me a week or so."

"So what brings you by?" She tried for casual, but her voice came out a little too bright.

He stepped further into the office, his hands sliding into his pockets. "I've been learning about Operation Christmas Cheer. From my parents. They told me about everything you do—the toy drives, the food baskets, the veterans' home, all of it."

"They did?"

"Yeah. And I'd like to help. If you need volunteers."

For a second, she just stared at him, processing words that didn't quite make sense. Chase wanted to volunteer for Operation Christmas Cheer. Chase, who was juggling apartment renovations and learning his parents' business and adjusting to civilian life.

"You want to help?"

"If you'll have me." His expression turned earnest and sincere. "I want to feel useful, you know?"

Hallie opened her mouth, closed it, and tried again. "Chase, that's—that's really kind of you. But do you really have time? Between working on your apartment and helping your parents at the store, you're already stretched pretty thin, I imagine."

"I'll make time. I've spent the last twelve years following orders and completing missions. Now I get to choose what I do with my time, and I choose this. If you'll let me."

The words settled around her like snowfall, soft and transformative. He was choosing this. Choosing to spend his free time on the work that consumed her every November and December. Choosing to step into the chaos and exhaustion and endless coordination that made Operation Christmas Cheer possible.

Hallie's instinct was to protect herself—to maintain the careful friends-only boundary she'd been reminding herself of since his return. Friends. Just friends. Nothing more complicated than that. But Operation Christmas Cheer wasn't about her heart or her fear or her determination to keep Chase safely in the friend category.

Operation Christmas Cheer was bigger than her comfort zone.

"Okay," she heard herself say. "Let me show you what you'd be getting into."

She stood and led him out of the office. They moved through the storage area where extra inventory lined metal shelving units, past boxes of ribbon and gift wrap and decorative items that would rotate onto the sales floor as current displays sold through. The familiar path felt different with Chase following her, his presence making her aware of every detail in a way she rarely noticed.

At the back of the storage area, a sturdy wooden staircase descended to the basement. Hallie flicked on the lights as she started down, the steps creaking under her weight in a comforting rhythm she'd memorized over years of daily trips.

The basement spread before them, transformed from a simple storage space into a workshop of holiday miracles. Exposed brick walls and concrete floors gave the space an industrial feel, but Hallie had softened it with strings of warm white lights and colorful banners that read "Operation Christmas Cheer" in her own hand-lettered calligraphy.

She watched Chase's expression as he took it all in, cataloging his reaction.

His eyes widened slightly, scanning the inventory. Long folding tables formed work stations throughout the space—one section dedicated to gift wrapping with rolls of paper in every pattern imaginable, another focused on food basket assembly with donated canned goods sorted by type, a third covered in craft supplies for making the personalized cards and decorative touches that went into every delivery.

Donation boxes lined one wall, each labeled clearly. "Toys—Ages 0-5," "Toys—Ages 6-10," "Toys—Ages 11-15," "Winter Clothing," "Personal Care Items," "Books and DVDs." The boxes overflowed already, and they were only a week into November.

Against another wall, completed gift baskets waited for delivery, each one wrapped in cellophane and tied with elaborate bows. Clipboards hung above them, displaying detailed resident information—names, addresses or room numbers for those living at the veteran's home and the independent living facility, and special notes about preferences or needs.

Coordination lists covered a bulletin board near the stairs—volunteer schedules, delivery routes, donation goals, and families served. The sheer scope of the operation was visible on every color-coded chart and at every carefully organized station.

"Wow," Chase said. "This is incredible."

"It's a lot, I know. Probably looks like chaos to anyone who isn't used to it."

He moved closer to one worktable, examining the sorting system. "Tell me more about what you do down here."

She walked him through it, explaining each station's purpose. "Donations come in through multiple channels. We have collection boxes set up around town—businesses, churches, the community center. People drop off toys, food, clothing, whatever they want to contribute. Some folks bring things directly here. We also coordinate with other organizations—the school district does a toy drive, the churches handle food collections. And then I do several special events and accept donations during those."

Chase nodded. "And then you sort everything?"

"Sort, categorize, match to recipients." Hallie gestured to the detailed lists on her clipboard station. "I maintain a database of families who need support. Some are referred by social services, others by teachers or church leaders. I verify each referral, make sure we're reaching people who actually need help rather than people trying to game the system."

"That's smart." He moved to the food basket area, studying the way items were organized. "I'm guessing you've got some kind of quality control process?"

"Everything gets inspected. No expired food, no broken toys, nothing that would make someone feel like they're getting leftovers." Pride colored her voice. "Every recipient deserves dignity. These aren't charity cases—they're neighbors going through hard times or people who just need some holiday cheer in their lives and to be reminded that they have not been forgotten."

Chase picked up one of the handmade cards from the crafting station, reading the message inside. His expression softened. "You write these yourself?"

"Most of them. My employees help with some—Nina, Sofia, Lucy, Taylor—they all volunteer their time down here. Community volunteers help with the heavy lifting stuff, like delivery, event setup and even running some events alongside me, but my team handles the personal touches."

"Tell me about the veterans' home deliveries."

"That's one of my favorite parts. We make personalized baskets for each resident based on their interests and service history. If someone served in the Navy, we include maritime-themed items. If they love gardening, we add seed packets and gardening magazines. It takes research, but it makes them feel seen."

"That's really special, Hallie."

"They deserve it." She moved to the station where completed veterans' home baskets waited. "These men and women served their country. The least we can do is make sure they're remembered at Christmas."

He studied the baskets with renewed attention, and Hallie realized his military background made this particular aspect of Operation Christmas Cheer resonate differently for him than it might for others.

"The independent living facility gets similar treatment," she continued. "Personalized baskets delivered before Christmas. Books, puzzles, craft supplies, comfort items—whatever brings joy to each resident specifically."

"And the toy drive?" Chase moved to the donation boxes overflowing with stuffed animals and board games.

"We collect toys from mid-September through mid-December. Match them with specific children based on age, gender, and interest. We try to include at least one special item each child has been wanting, plus practical things like clothes and school supplies." Hallie pulled out her clipboard with the current recipient list. "This year we're serving forty-seven families with a total of one hundred and thirty-two children."

Chase studied the list, his eyebrows rising. "That's a lot of coordination."

"It's why I need help." The admission came easier than expected. "I've got my core team, but we can always use another pair of hands. Especially someone with organizational skills and—" She paused, choosing her words carefully. "—someone who understands logistics and efficiency."

"Military training has its uses." He glanced at her, something warm in his expression. "What can I do to help?"

"Anything you'd like," she said honestly. "Sort donations, assemble baskets, coordinate deliveries, help at fundraising events. It's all important, and there's never enough time or hands to do it all."

Chase's mouth curved into a slight smile. "I'm good at following orders. Point me where you need me, and I'll show up."

Warmth spread through Hallie's chest, followed immediately by anxiety. This was exactly what she'd been trying to avoid—Chase becoming more integrated into her life, spending more time with her, making it harder to maintain the safe boundaries she'd promised herself.

But Operation Christmas Cheer wasn't about her comfort. It was about serving people who needed help. And if Chase genuinely wanted to contribute, she couldn't turn him away just because his presence made her heart do complicated things.

"I have one condition," she said, straightening her shoulders and meeting his eyes directly. "No quitting halfway. If you commit to this, I need to know you're in for the duration. Operation Christmas Cheer runs through Christmas Day, and I can't have volunteers disappearing when I've built schedules around their availability."

Chase nodded and smiled. "I get it. You need people you can count on. People who'll actually show up when they say they will."

"Exactly."

"I give you my word, Hallie. You can count on me." He extended his hand. "Shake on it?"

Hallie looked at his outstretched hand, hesitating for just a heartbeat. This was a simple handshake. A volunteer agreement. Nothing more complicated than that.

His grip was warm and solid, his calloused palm against hers creating friction that had nothing to do with the actual handshake and everything to do with the man holding her hand.

Their eyes met and held, and for a suspended moment, the basement fell away. Just her and Chase, hands clasped, something unspoken but undeniable hanging between them like tinsel catching light.

Hallie pulled her hand back first, her pulse hammering. "Good. Welcome to Operation Christmas Cheer."

Chase's smile widened. "Thanks for letting me help."

"Don't thank me until you've spent four hours wrapping toys in this cold basement while Christmas music plays on repeat. You might regret your generous offer."

"I doubt that." He glanced around the basement again, taking in the operation's scope with what looked like anticipation rather than intimidation. "When do I start?"

"We're making wreaths and assembling baskets for the veterans' home and independent living residents this Wednesday evening. Nina and Sofia will be here helping. You could join us if you're free?"

"What time?"

"Around six? That gives me time to close the store, grab dinner, and change into comfortable clothes."

"I'll be here." Chase's grin turned slightly mischievous. "Should I bring anything? Tools? Snacks?"

"Just yourself and a willingness to accept direction from women who know what they're doing."

"Following directions from competent leadership? That I can handle."

They stood there in the basement surrounded by the physical evidence of Hallie's mission—donations waiting to be sorted, baskets waiting to be delivered, and lists waiting to be checked off. Somewhere above them, the shop's muffled sounds filtered through—customer conversations, the register chiming, and Nina's laugh.

Chase was looking at her with an expression she couldn't quite name. Something soft and admiring and impossibly complicated.

"This really is incredible, Hallie. What you've built here. The lives you're touching. It matters."

The words wrapped around her like a blanket, warm and comforting and terrifying all at once. Chase seeing this part of her—understanding the work that consumed her every holiday season, recognizing its value—felt more intimate than any physical touch. This was her heart laid bare in organized donation boxes and carefully crafted gift baskets.

And she'd just invited him to become part of it.

"Thanks. That means a lot."

They climbed back up the stairs, emerging into the storage area. The transition from basement workshop to retail storage room felt jarring, like returning from another world.

Chase paused at the door leading to the sales floor. "I'll let you get back to work. I'm sure you've got a million things to do."

"Always."

"See you Wednesday, then." He offered that slight smile again, the one that made dimples appear in his cheeks. "Six o'clock. I'll bring my best wreath-making attitude."

"I'll hold you to that."

He left, and Hallie stood in the storage area.

She'd just agreed to work with Chase. Wednesday evening in her basement making wreaths. Future volunteer sessions sorting toys and assembling baskets. Hours spent side by side pursuing the mission that mattered most to her. Hours spent pretending her heart didn't race every time he smiled. Hours spent maintaining boundaries that felt more impossible every day.

Hallie pressed her palm to her chest, feeling her heart hammer beneath her ribs.

This was either the best decision she'd made all year or the biggest mistake.

Chapter 13

Chase's apartment door clicked shut behind him, double checking he'd locked the door before turning toward the metal staircase. Six o'clock on a Wednesday evening, and instead of collapsing on his bed after a full day at the toy store, he was heading to his first official Operation Christmas Cheer volunteer session.

His boots clanged on the stairs as he descended into the alley, the November air cool against his face. Movement caught his attention—Hallie emerging from her own apartment, her steps light and quick as she reached the bottom landing.

Their eyes met, and Chase grinned. "Hey, neighbor."

She laughed, the sound bright and genuine. "Hey yourself."

He crossed the alley toward her, taking in her appearance. She wore black leggings and an oversized cream-colored sweatshirt that hung off one shoulder, revealing the strap of a red tank top underneath. Her hair was pulled back in a loose ponytail, and she'd traded her usual work flats for fuzzy socks and slip-on house shoes.

Cute. The word materialized in his brain before he could stop it.

Since when did he notice what Hallie wore? Since when did "cute" become part of his vocabulary?

"You ready for some Christmas magic?" she asked, her eyes sparkling with anticipation.

Chase fell into step beside her as they walked toward the back entrance of her store. "After you, sergeant."

She shot him an amused glance. "Sergeant? I've been promoted?"

"You're running this operation. Seemed appropriate."

"Fair enough." She pulled open the door, and they stepped into the storage area.

As they descended the basement stairs, Chase heard voices rising to meet them. Laughter, bright and infectious. The murmur of conversation. Christmas music playing softly.

Nina stood at one of the long folding tables, her hair pulled into a messy bun, arranging evergreen branches into circular forms. Sofia worked at an adjacent station, hot glue gun in hand, attaching red ribbon to a wreath.

Both women looked up as Chase and Hallie reached the bottom step.

"He came!" Sofia set down her glue gun, her face breaking into a welcoming smile.

"Welcome to the madness, Chase," Nina said.

"Thanks for having me." Chase surveyed the workspace, taking in the scope of tonight's project. Wreaths in various states of completion covered one table. Another held baskets of different sizes, surrounded by boxes of items waiting to be arranged—personal care products, books, DVDs, small comfort items wrapped in tissue paper. A third table displayed craft supplies that made his military training feel completely inadequate—spools of ribbon in every color, glitter in multiple shades, artificial berries, pinecones, and bells that probably served some decorative purpose he didn't understand.

"So what do you want to do, Chase?" Hallie moved to the wreath station, picking up one of the evergreen forms and looking at Nina's work. "Wreaths or baskets?"

Chase looked between the options, weighing his choices. The wreaths looked simpler—circular forms with greenery attached, then decorated with bows and ornamental additions. The baskets seemed more complex, requiring aesthetic judgment about arrangement and presentation.

"I'll try wreaths."

"Good choice," Sofia said. "Come over here and I'll show you what we're doing."

Chase joined her at the wreath station while Hallie moved to the basket area, pulling supplies closer and settling into her work with practiced ease. Nina stayed at her spot, already back to securing evergreen branches to wire forms.

Sofia held up a completed wreath. "These are for the veterans' home and the independent living facility. Small enough to hang on individual doors, but substantial enough to feel special. We start with these wire forms, and we attach evergreen branches using floral wire. Once the greenery is secure, we add the fun stuff. Ribbons, bells, whatever feels right for each one."

"Got it." Chase said as he picked up a wire form. "And we're making how many?"

"We need twelve more for the veterans' home, another twenty for the independent living facility," Hallie called from the basket station.

"What's the timeline?"

"We need the ones for the independent living facility done tonight," Nina said, cutting a length of evergreen branch with pruning shears.

"Then the wreaths that go to the veteran's home we still have time to make."

"Sounds good." Chase selected a bundle of evergreen branches from the supply box, studying how Nina had attached hers to the wire form. The process looked straightforward—wrap the branch around the frame, secure with thin wire, repeat until the circle was full.

He got to work, and for the first ten minutes, the basement settled into comfortable productivity. Christmas music played softly in the background—something classical with bells and strings. The scent of cinnamon came from the candle burning on a shelf near the stairs.

Chase wrapped his second branch around the form, secured it, and reached for another. His hands worked while his mind processed the environment—the simple conversation between the women, the obvious affection they shared, and the way they moved around each other with familiarity that came from years of working together.

"Coffee's fresh if anyone wants some," Nina announced, gesturing toward a small coffee station Chase hadn't noticed earlier. A coffeemaker sat on a folding table near the wall, surrounded by mismatched mugs and containers of cream and sugar.

"I need caffeine after the day I've had. The twins had a competition to see who could make the biggest mess in the kitchen while I was helping Levi with dinner prep earlier," Sofia said.

"Who won?" Hallie asked, wrapping tissue paper around something delicate before placing it carefully in a basket.

"Everyone lost." Sofia poured herself coffee, adding generous amounts of cream. "There was flour everywhere."

"How old are your twins?" he asked.

"Ten, Mitchell and Maya. They're at that age where everything is either hilarious or a catastrophe, with zero middle ground." She returned to her station with her coffee, picking up the hot glue gun again. "Last week, Mitchell. decided to 'improve' his sister's science project by adding glow-in-the-dark paint to her model volcano. Without asking first."

Nina snorted with laughter. "How'd that go over?"

"About as well as you'd expect. Maya screamed. Mitchell defended his artistic vision, and I had to explain to their teacher why the volcano now looked like something from a sci-fi movie."

Chase grinned, imagining the chaos. "Did the glow paint at least work?"

"Surprisingly well. The teacher gave Maya bonus points for creativity." Sofia attached a red bow to her current wreath, positioning it just right before securing it with glue. "I made Mitchell apologize for not asking permission first. Creative vision doesn't excuse a lack of communication."

"Words to live by," Hallie said.

He finished his first wreath—a full circle of evergreen secured to the wire form—and moved to the decoration station where spools of ribbon waited in neat rows. Red, gold, silver, burgundy, navy blue. He selected red, figuring it was classic and hard to mess up, and began fashioning a bow.

His first attempt came out lopsided. The second one looked slightly better but still uneven. By the third try, he'd managed something that resembled an actual bow rather than a wadded mess of ribbon.

"Not bad," Nina said, glancing over at his work. "Though if you loop it one more time, you'll get better volume."

Chase followed her suggestion, and the resulting bow looked fuller, more polished. "Thanks."

"No problem. Ribbon's tricky until you get the feel for it."

He attached the bow to his wreath, then reached for the box of decorative elements. Small pinecones, artificial berries, and tiny bells that jingled when he picked them up. He studied Sofia's completed wreaths, noting how she'd clustered decorations rather than spacing them evenly around the circle.

Made sense.

He selected a few pinecones and some berries, arranging them near his bow in what he hoped was a pleasing cluster. Then he reached for the hot glue gun.

"Careful with that," Hallie warned from the basket station. "Hot glue has a mind of its own."

"I handled explosives in the Marines. I think I can manage a glue gun."

Famous last words.

Chase squeezed the trigger, applying glue to the back of a pinecone. Too much glue came out, creating a blob that immediately started dripping. He tried to press the pinecone against the wreath quickly, but the excess glue spread everywhere—his fingers, the evergreen branches, the ribbon he'd just attached.

"Ah—" He lifted his hand, and a string of glue stretched between his fingers and the wreath like some kind of craft-supply spider web.

"Hold still." Hallie appeared at his elbow, hand wipes already in her grip. "Let me help before you glue yourself to the wreath."

She took his hand, her fingers cool against his, and began carefully wiping away the adhesive. Her touch was gentle, methodical, and Chase became acutely aware of how close she was standing. Close enough that he could smell her perfume—something floral and light. Close enough to see the small scar on her left eyebrow he'd never noticed before.

"How did you manage to get glue on your wrist?" she asked, her tone caught between amusement and exasperation.

"Talent."

"That's one word for it." But she was smiling as she cleaned his wrist, then moved to his other hand. "There. Crisis averted."

"Thanks." He flexed his fingers experimentally, relieved to find them no longer sticky. "Maybe I should stay away from the glue."

"Probably wise," Sofia agreed. "We don't need you creating modern art installations when we're going for traditional Christmas charm."

Chase returned to his wreath, this time skipping the glue and using the thin wire to attach his decorative elements. Slower, but definitely safer. He worked methodically, securing pinecones and berries while listening to the conversation flowing around him.

"So what's everyone's favorite Christmas memory from growing up?" Nina asked, starting a new wreath form.

Sofia answered first. "My abuela's tamales. Every Christmas Eve, the whole family would gather in her kitchen and help make hundreds of them. The house would smell incredible, and we'd all be laughing and telling stories while we worked. Those are some of my best memories."

"That sounds wonderful," Hallie said. "Food memories are the best because they engage all your senses. You don't just remember what happened—you remember how it felt, how it smelled, and how it tasted."

"What about you?" Sofia asked. "What's your favorite Christmas memory?"

Hallie was quiet for a moment, and Chase glanced over to find her carefully arranging items in a basket, her expression distant. "My dad's Christmas light traditions. Every year on the first Saturday of December, he'd spend the entire day putting up elaborate light displays on our house. He'd make it into this big production—playing Christmas music and letting me hand him supplies. He made me feel like I was his official assistant, like the whole thing wouldn't work without me."

"That's a great memory," Nina said

"Yeah." Hallie placed a small wrapped item in her basket, adjusting its position. "I still put up lights every year on the first Saturday of December. It's my way of keeping that tradition alive."

"Chase, what about you? What's your favorite Christmas memory?" Sofia asked.

He considered the question while attaching another pinecone to his wreath. "Christmas Eve pancakes for dinner. My mom made them every year—chocolate chip pancakes shaped like Christmas trees. And my dad would read 'The Night Before Christmas' after we finished eating."

"That's adorable," Sofia said.

The conversation moved on, and Chase relaxed into the rhythm of it. These women were easy to be around, their humor genuine and their acceptance uncomplicated. They teased each other freely, and they included him without making him feel like an outsider or treating him like a novelty.

"Okay, new question," Nina announced. "Christmas decorating fails. Who's got one?"

"Oh, I have a good one." Sofia set down her glue gun. "The year we got our first cat, Mischief. We put up the tree, decorated it beautifully, and went to bed feeling very accomplished. Woke up the next morning to find Mischief had knocked the tree over. There were ornaments everywhere, the tree flat on the floor, and the cat sitting in the branches looking incredibly proud of herself."

Chase laughed, picturing the scene. "What did you do?"

"Took a photo while we all laughed hysterically. Then we had to completely redecorate. We learned real fast how to stabilize the tree stand so she couldn't knock the tree over and wired every ornament to the tree so she couldn't bat them off."

"I hot-glued an entire wreath to my dining table once," Nina admitted. "I was working on a craft project, got distracted by a phone call, and wasn't paying attention to how much glue I was using and everything I had attached... well, that glue dripped down between the branches right onto my table. When I finally noticed and tried to move the wreath, half the table varnish came with it."

"Please tell me you took pictures," Sofia said.

"But of course... I had to document that crafting failure for sure."

Chase grinned. "In the Marines, we decorated with duct tape and determination."

All three women turned to look at him, and then they burst into laughter.

"That's the most Marine answer possible," Sofia managed between giggles.

"It worked. We'd rig up whatever we could find—MRE boxes shaped into trees, glow sticks for lights, spent ammunition casings as ornaments if we were feeling creative."

"That's actually kind of sweet," Hallie said. "Making something festive out of nothing. Decorating even in difficult circumstances."

"We did what we could." He attached his bow to the wreath, then stood back to evaluate his work. Not perfect, but respectable.

More conversation flowed—debating favorite winter comfort foods. Hallie defended soup with passionate intensity while Nina argued for chili and Sofia made a compelling case for her abuela's posole.

Sofia asked about the care packages he'd received overseas, and Chase told her about one of his mother's cookie shipments that arrived as cookie powder. "We sprinkled it on everything like seasoning. Oatmeal, coffee, whatever we had. Figured the thought counted more than the execution."

"That's actually brilliant," Nina said. "Cookie crumble—it could be a trend."

"Don't give the bakeries in town any ideas."

They moved on to favorite Christmas movies, which sparked good-natured debate. Hallie defended "White Christmas" with the fervor of someone protecting a national treasure. Sofia loved "Elf" for its childlike joy. Nina claimed "Die Hard" counted as a Christmas movie and refused to be swayed by opposing arguments.

Chase stayed quiet during most of the debate, focusing on his third wreath while listening to them articulate their positions with impressive passion.

"What about you, Chase?" Hallie asked. "What's your favorite Christmas movie?"

"It's a Wonderful Life."

The basement went quiet. All three women stopped what they were doing to look at him.

"Really?" Sofia asked.

"Yeah." Chase positioned berries on his wreath, not meeting anyone's eyes. "There's something about good ole George Bailey—how he thinks his life doesn't matter, how he's stuck in a town he wanted to escape, how he gives up his dreams to take care of other people. And then he gets shown how much his presence mattered all along, how many lives he touched just by being decent and showing up." He paused, adjusting a pinecone. "Hits harder than I'd like to admit."

When he finally glanced up, Hallie was watching him with an expression he couldn't quite read.

"I love that."

Chase cleared his throat, suddenly uncomfortable with the emotion hanging in the air.

"What's the most creative Christmas you ever had overseas?" Nina asked, and he mentally thanked her for the subject change.

"My last deployment, our unit made a tree out of stacked water bottles and glow sticks. The chaplain held an improvised service in the mess tent. I played guitar, we sang carols off-key, and the cooks made something that was supposed to be turkey but tasted more like seasoned cardboard." He smiled at the memory. "But it was Christmas. We made it work."

"Awww, I love that," Sofia said. "Creating joy in the middle of difficulty."

The conversation moved naturally from there to the worst gifts ever received. Sofia's was a vacuum cleaner from her husband the first year they were married. Chase's was a terrible fruitcake sent by a well-meaning stranger oversees during a deployment. Hallie's anonymous snow globe mystery gift that had been left outside her door one year that featured a Santa in swim trunks and sandals still puzzled her years later.

Through it all, Chase watched Hallie work. She moved between stations effortlessly, checking on everyone's progress. She asked Sofia about her twins' Santa wishlists. She noticed when Nina's smile didn't quite reach her eyes and asked gentle questions about the guy she was dating—a conversation that revealed Nina was planning to end things because the connection wasn't there.

Hallie was a natural leader—not because she demanded authority, but because people wanted to follow her. She made everyone feel necessary, appreciated, and part of something important.

And she did it all while maintaining a work pace that would exhaust most people. She'd assembled four baskets in the time it took Chase to complete three wreaths. Her hands moved with ease, and she never lost a beat even while talking, selecting items, arranging them, and tucking in personalized cards she'd handwritten earlier.

Chase finished his fourth wreath. He stepped back to survey his evening's production. Not bad for someone who'd started the night wondering if he could actually create something that looked at least halfway decent.

He glanced at the clock mounted on the basement wall and was shocked to discover three hours had passed.

"I should head home," Sofia announced, echoing his thoughts. "Levi is handling the twins' bedtime routine, but if I don't get back soon, they'll convince him to let them stay up watching movies."

"Yeah, let's call it a night," Hallie agreed, surveying their collective work with satisfaction. "We got a lot done. Fifteen wreaths completed, thirteen baskets assembled. That's fantastic progress."

They cleaned up their stations, putting away supplies and organizing completed projects for the next session. Chase helped Nina carry finished wreaths to a storage area while Sofia rinsed out coffee mugs at the small sink in the corner.

As they climbed the stairs back to the main level, Sofia turned to Hallie. "Is it okay if I bring the twins to the Santa on Ice event Saturday? Levi has a work thing and can't watch them."

"Of course. Bring them."

"What's the Santa on Ice event?" Chase asked.

All three women turned to look at him with expressions that suggested he'd just asked what Christmas was.

"It's one of our biggest fundraisers," Hallie explained as they reached the storage area. "Out at Frost Hollow Lake. They set up a huge seasonal ice skating rink during the fall before the lake freezes naturally. Kids can skate with Santa, Mrs. Claus, and the elves. We set up donation tents, take pictures, and the Peppermint Patty Snack

Shack donates a portion of their proceeds to Operation Christmas Cheer."

"It's magical," Sofia added, her eyes bright. "The whole place is lit up with torches, Christmas music plays over the speakers, and everyone's in this amazing holiday spirit. People are incredibly generous during that event."

"For every donation, people get a coupon for free ice skating later in the season," Nina said.

Chase's interest sharpened. "What time?"

"Six to nine Saturday night," Hallie said, watching him with curious hope. "You're welcome to come. We can always use extra volunteers."

"Count me in."

"Great." Hallie's smile brightened her entire face. "Meet us under the donation tent around six?"

"I'll be there."

They said their goodbyes at the back door—Sofia heading to her car parked on the street, Nina climbing into her vehicle in the small lot behind the stores. Chase and Hallie stood in the alley.

"Thanks for tonight," Hallie said, hugging her arms against the chill. "You did great for your first session."

"Even with the glue incident?"

"Especially with the glue incident. It's a rite of passage." Her eyes sparkled with amusement. "Everyone has a craft failure of some kind. You got yours out of the way early."

"Always efficient."

She laughed, the sound soft in the quiet alley. "See you Saturday, then?"

"Saturday," he confirmed.

She climbed her stairs while he climbed his, their footsteps echoing off the building walls in mismatched rhythm. As he unlocked his apartment door, he glanced over at her as she unlocked hers.

"Goodnight, Hallie," he called.

"Night, Chase," she said

He grinned as he watched her step into her apartment and close the door.

Chapter 14

The donation tent was alive with activity as Hallie accepted a grocery bag filled with canned goods from Mrs. Harbinger, who'd driven all the way from Gatlinburg specifically for the Santa on Ice event. Behind Hallie, Nina processed monetary donations while Sofia organized physical items into labeled boxes—toys, personal care products, winter clothing, and food items.

"This is wonderful, Mrs. Harbinger," Hallie said. "Thank you so much for coming out tonight."

"Wouldn't miss it, dear. Operation Christmas Cheer has helped so many people, and I want to be a part of it," she said as she patted Hallie's hand.

Frost Hollow Lake stretched beyond the rink—dark and unfrozen, waiting for deeper cold to transform its surface into natural ice. But tonight, the huge seasonal ice skating rink buzzed with activity. Children shrieked with laughter as they wobbled across the ice, parents skated hand-in-hand, and Mrs. Claus glided gracefully among them all, her red velvet costume swirling around her.

Christmas music drifted from speakers mounted around the property—instrumental versions of classics that created a festive atmosphere. The Peppermint Patty Snack Shack glowed invitingly between the rink and the lake, its outdoor seating area packed with families warming themselves around fire pits while enjoying hot chocolate and snacks.

Next to the donation tent, the Santa photo booth did steady business. A professional photographer worked efficiently, capturing images of children perched on Santa's lap against a backdrop of Christmas decorations. The line stretched twenty deep—parents clutching excited toddlers, and older children trying to maintain cool sophistication while clearly thrilled to see the big man in red.

Hallie wore her warmest coat—a navy blue parka that hit mid-thigh—over jeans and boots. A cream-colored scarf wrapped around her neck, and her knit gloves kept her fingers functional despite the temperature that had dropped into the low forties as evening settled over the mountains.

Movement caught her attention as Chase emerged from the crowd near the snack shack, weaving between families as he walked toward the donation tent. He wore a dark green coat over a gray henley, jeans, and hiking boots that looked built for mountain terrain. No gloves yet, but she noticed a pair sticking out of his jacket pocket.

Her pulse did something unhelpful. She ignored it.

Chase ducked into the tent. "Sorry I'm late. Had to help Dad with a last-minute toy store crisis. A customer's grandson wanted a specific action figure, and we had to search the entire inventory room."

"Did you find it?" Sofia asked, sorting donated books into age-appropriate piles.

"Eventually." Chase scanned the organized chaos of their operation. "What can I do to help?"

Hallie opened her mouth to assign him a task, but Nina beat her to it.

"Actually, you can convince Hallie to take a break and go ice skating." Nina gestured at the rink beyond the tent. "She's been here since five helping with setup, and she needs to actually enjoy this event instead of just working it."

"I'm fine," Hallie protested. "There's still so much to do—"

"We've got it covered," Sofia interrupted, her tone brooking no argument. "Seriously, Hallie. Go skate. Have fun. That's an order from your employees."

Hallie looked between them, recognizing the stubborn determination on both faces. When Nina and Sofia agreed on something, resistance was futile.

"Chase?" She turned to him, and grinned. "Wanna go ice skating?"

His face lit up. "You better believe it."

They walked toward the Peppermint Patty Snack Shack, navigating through crowds of families and couples. The mountain air bit at Hallie's cheeks, sharp and clean, carrying the scent of wood smoke from the fire pits and hot chocolate from the snack shack.

Inside the snack shack, warmth enveloped them immediately. A wood-burning stove crackled in the corner, surrounded by vintage skating memorabilia and Christmas decorations that created a cozy atmosphere. They approached the rental counter, where a teenager worked at the register.

"Hallie! You finally taking a break?" Jake grinned at her. "What size skates?"

"Seven and a half."

"I'm a twelve," Chase added.

Jake disappeared into the back room, returning moments later with two pairs of well-maintained skates. "Have fun out there. The ice is in great condition tonight."

They carried their skates to the benches positioned at the rink's edge. Hallie sat down, unlaced her boots, and slipped them off. The cold immediately penetrated her wool socks, and she hurried to pull on the first skate, lacing it snugly around her ankle.

Muscle memory kicked in—the familiar weight of blades and the specific tightness needed for ankle support. She'd spent countless Friday nights here as a teenager, skating with friends until the rink closed.

Chase finished lacing his skates and stood, testing his balance. "It's been a while since I've done this."

"How long?"

"Probably not since high school. We didn't have many ice-skating opportunities while I was in the Marines."

Hallie laughed, standing carefully and finding her center of gravity.

They stepped onto the ice.

The first glide felt like coming home. Hallie's blades cut smoothly across the surface, her body remembering the rhythm even a few years had passed since she'd skated regularly. Beside her, Chase moved with similar confidence—not flashy or showy, just fluid and balanced. Natural.

They circled the rink slowly, warming up, reacquainting themselves with the feel of ice beneath their blades. Around them, children squealed, Mrs. Claus called out encouragement, and parents offered steadying hands to wobbling beginners. But Hallie focused on Chase, watching how he moved, noting the ease with which he navigated the ice.

"You're not rusty at all," she observed.

"Neither are you." He glanced over, and in the torchlight his eyes looked impossibly blue.

They picked up speed gradually, falling into rhythm. Their movements synchronized naturally—when she leaned into a turn, he matched it. When he adjusted his stride, she followed instinctively. Years collapsed, and suddenly they were eighteen again, racing each other around Frost Hollow Lake on Friday nights when the entire world felt full of possibility.

"Remember the skating competition?" Chase asked.

Hallie grinned. "Senior year. You convinced me to enter with you even though I swore I wasn't coordinated enough."

"You were plenty coordinated. You just needed confidence."

"We came in third."

"We should have won." Chase's mock indignation made her laugh. "That couple from Knoxville had nothing on our routine."

"Their lifts were more impressive."

"Only because you wouldn't let me throw you in the air."

"Because I valued my life." But she was laughing now, remembering the hours they'd spent practicing, the way Chase had patiently taught her the more complex moves, his steady presence making her brave enough to try things that terrified her.

They'd been inseparable back then. Best friends who did everything together—ice skating on winter nights, hiking mountain trails in summer, studying for tests while eating pizza in his parents' kitchen. She'd loved him even then, though she'd never found the courage to say it. Too afraid of ruining their friendship. Too certain, he didn't see her that way.

And then he'd left for the Marines, and she'd buried those feelings.

"Bet you can't still do a spin," Chase challenged, pulling her from memory.

"Bet I can." Hallie pushed off, building speed, then lifted one foot and turned. Once, twice, three rotations before she stuck the landing with only minor wobbling.

Chase attempted to copy her, his execution slightly less graceful. His arms flailed for balance, and he nearly collided with a teenager before correcting course. Laughter burst from Hallie—pure and unguarded.

"Okay, you win that one," he admitted, skating back to her side.

"I win most things."

"That's not how I remember it."

"Then your memory needs work."

They fell into comfortable banter, trading playful insults while they skated. Hallie spun again, just to show off, and this time when she came out of it, Chase was there—hand extended, catching hers mid-turn to steady her momentum.

His grip was warm even through their gloves. Firm. Secure.

They glided forward together, hands clasped.

Chase spun her unexpectedly, a move from their old competition routine. She laughed in surprise, turning under his arm before he pulled her back beside him. They picked up speed, skating faster now, their breath coming quicker as they wove around other skaters.

"Figure eights?" Chase suggested.

"You remember how?"

"I remember everything."

They moved into formation, skating wide sweeping figure eights that brought them closer each time the loops crossed. Hallie's heart hammered—from exertion, from joy, and from the terrifying realization that this felt exactly like it had when she was a senior in high school and hopelessly in love with him.

Except now they were adults, and her feelings were more complicated.

Chase lifted one foot in mock fancy style—some ridiculous move he'd made up years ago that always made her laugh. He wobbled dramatically, careening toward the railing before catching himself at the last second with exaggerated relief.

"Smooth," Hallie called, skating past him.

"I meant to do that."

"Sure you did."

He caught up easily, matching her pace. Then he moved in front of her, skating backward while taking both her hands. Leading her the way he used to during their teenage skating sessions.

"Show off," she said.

"Just proving I haven't completely lost it." His expression turned more serious, though warmth lingered in his eyes. "This is nice, Hallie. Being here with you. Feels like old times."

Old times. When everything had been simple. When friendship had been enough because she'd convinced herself it had to be.

But it had never been enough. Not really.

They skated side by side after that, sometimes bumping shoulders lightly, joking about who was more out of practice. Christmas music shifted to something instrumental and gentle—bells and strings creating an atmosphere that transformed the rink into something magical. The torches flickered, casting moving shadows across the ice. Above them, stars emerged as full darkness settled over the mountains.

Hallie felt young again. Free in a way she hadn't felt in years.

She noticed how Chase still read her movements effortlessly—adjusting his speed when she slowed, turning when she turned, always exactly where she needed him to be. Like they'd been skating together yesterday instead of twelve years ago.

"You getting tired?" he asked after they'd completed another wide loop.

"Maybe a little." Her cheeks burned from the cold and exertion, and her legs were starting to feel the workout. "One more lap?"

"One more."

They skated a final circuit, slower this time, both catching their breath. When they reached the benches, they carefully stepped off the ice and sat down.

Chase leaned back against the bench, his breathing slightly elevated. "That was fun."

"Yeah." Hallie unwound her scarf slightly, suddenly too warm despite the cold air. "I'd forgotten how much I loved skating."

"We should do it again. Once the lake freezes."

"I'd like that," she said.

They sat watching other skaters glide past. Children chased each other, couples held hands, and families created memories.

Chase turned to look at her. "You haven't changed a bit."

She smiled. "Neither have you."

It wasn't entirely true—they'd both changed in countless ways. But at the core of who they'd been, the essential connection that had bound them together as teenagers, that remained. Solid. Real. Undeniable.

Hallie glanced at her phone, noting the time with reluctance. "I should get back to the donation tent. It's been over an hour."

"I'll help." Chase started unlacing his skates. "That's why I'm here, right?"

They returned their rental skates to the snack shack and walked back toward the donation area. The event showed no signs of slowing—families still arrived, the photo booth line remained long, and donations continued flowing into the tent.

As they approached, Hallie felt the evening's joy transforming into something more complex. The skating had cracked something open inside her—some protective wall she'd built to keep her heart safe.

"What are your plans tomorrow?" She asked.

"Nothing, actually. It's Saturday, and somehow I got lucky and have the day off. Why?"

"I'm delivering gift baskets to the Independent Living Retirement Home tomorrow afternoon. Want to help?"

"Absolutely."

Relief and anxiety swirled together in her stomach. "Great. We'll take my SUV. I have all the baskets loaded already. Meet me around one tomorrow afternoon?"

They reached the donation tent entrance, and Chase caught her elbow gently before she could duck inside. When she turned to face him, his expression carried determination and something else she couldn't quite name.

"I'll help tomorrow on one condition," he said.

"What condition?"

"Come over to my place tomorrow evening. We'll order pizza and watch a movie. Just like old times."

Just like old times. Except everything felt different now. Charged with possibility and danger.

Hallie's heart hammered against her ribs. She should say no. Should maintain the friends-only boundary.

But when she looked at his face—open and hopeful and so achingly handsome—she couldn't form the word.

"Okay," she heard herself say. "Pizza and a movie. Tomorrow night."

"It's a date."

"Not a date," she corrected.

He glanced at her and grinned. "Not a date, Miss Dawson. Just two old friends having pizza and watching a movie."

Hallie watched him as he joined Nina and Sofia and began helping them sort donations.

Calm it down a bit, Hallie. Breathe, she thought. *Just friends... nothing more. That's all this could ever be.*

Chapter 15

Hallie knocked on apartment 2B, balancing the gift basket carefully in her arms while Chase stood beside her holding two more. They'd already delivered three baskets in the past twenty minutes—brief interactions filled with grateful smiles, warm thank-yous, and the particular joy that came from watching people light up at unexpected kindness.

The Independent Living Retirement Home felt more like a mountain inn than any institutional facility. Warm wood floors gleamed beneath their feet, floral curtains framed cheerful windows, and the scent of fresh coffee and something cinnamon-spiced drifted from the common dining room down the hall. The building's craftsman-style architecture created an atmosphere of home rather than healthcare, exactly as the residents deserved.

Footsteps approached from inside the apartment, slow but steady. The door opened to reveal a woman in her early seventies with silver hair styled in a neat bob, wire-rimmed glasses perched on her nose, and eyes that widened with recognition and delight.

"Hallie Dawson? And—" The woman's hand flew to her chest. "Chase Montgomery? Is that really you?"

Hallie's face split into a genuine grin. Their senior year English teacher looked exactly the same, just with more silver in her hair and deeper laugh lines around her eyes. "Hi Mrs. Whitmore. We're delivering Operation Christmas Cheer baskets today."

"Well, for heaven's sake." Mrs. Whitmore stepped back, pulling the door wider. "Come in, come in! Don't just stand in the hallway like strangers."

"We don't want to intrude," Chase said. "We've got several more baskets to deliver—"

"Nonsense. You'll come in and visit properly." Mrs. Whitmore's tone carried the same gentle authority that had commanded respect in her classroom. "I haven't had decent company in days, and I certainly haven't seen either of you in far too long. Besides, I just made apple pie this morning, and it's criminal to eat it alone."

Hallie glanced at Chase, finding him already looking at her with raised eyebrows that clearly asked, your call. The remaining baskets could wait. Mrs. Whitmore had always been one of her favorite teachers—the kind who actually cared about her students as people rather than just test scores.

"We'd love to," Hallie said. "But only if you're sure we're not interrupting."

"The only thing you're interrupting is my attempt to finish a crossword puzzle that's been defeating me all morning." Mrs. Whitmore ushered them inside. "I could use the distraction."

The apartment was small but immaculately kept, reflecting its occupant's personality in every detail. Built-in bookshelves lined one wall, packed with worn paperbacks and hardcovers organized by author. A cozy reading chair sat near the window overlooking the mountains, with a knitted afghan draped across its arm. Photos covered another wall—black and white images of people from different eras, color photographs of what looked like family gatherings, and several pictures of what must be her late husband.

"Sit, sit." Mrs. Whitmore gestured toward a small sofa upholstered in blue floral fabric. "Let me get coffee and pie. You both drink coffee, I assume?"

"Yes, ma'am," Chase said.

Mrs. Whitmore disappeared into her kitchenette, and Hallie heard the sounds of plates being retrieved, forks clinking, mugs being filled. She took the opportunity to study the apartment more closely, noting the care with which everything had been arranged. This wasn't just a place Mrs. Whitmore lived—this was a home she'd created from memories and meaningful objects.

Her gaze landed on a wedding photograph displayed prominently on the mantle above the gas fireplace. A young couple stared back at her, impossibly young, dressed in early 1970s wedding attire. The bride wore a simple white dress with long sleeves, her dark hair styled in soft waves. The groom stood tall beside her in a suit, his hand at her waist, both of them beaming with the kind of joy that only comes from believing the future holds nothing but good things.

"That was taken fifty-two years ago," Mrs. Whitmore said, returning with a tray laden with generous slices of pie and steaming mugs. "Hard to believe sometimes. Feels like yesterday and a lifetime ago simultaneously."

She set the tray on the coffee table, handing out plates and mugs with practiced efficiency.

"This pie looks amazing," Hallie said. "Thank you so much."

"My pleasure. Luther always said my apple pie was the reason he proposed." Mrs. Whitmore said as she settled into her reading chair.

"Of course, I like to think my sparkling personality had something to do with it too."

Chase took a bite of the pie and made an appreciative sound. "This is incredible, Mrs. Whitmore."

"I haven't lost my touch yet." She smiled. "Though I don't bake as often as I used to. Seems silly to make a whole pie when you're eating alone."

Something in the way she said it—matter-of-fact rather than self-pitying—made Hallie's chest tighten. Mrs. Whitmore had always been surrounded by students, her classroom full of energy and conversation. Living alone after decades of marriage and years of teaching must feel impossibly quiet.

"How long have you lived here? It's been a couple of years now, right?" Hallie asked.

"Three years this January. After Luther passed, I tried staying in our house for a while, but it was too much space and too many memories." Mrs. Whitmore sipped her coffee. "This place is perfect for me. I have my independence, but there's community when I want it. The staff is wonderful, and the other residents are good people. I get lonely now and then, but that's life at this age. You learn to find contentment in your own company while treasuring the moments when others share it." She gestured at them with her fork. "Which is why I'm so delighted you two stopped by. Tell me everything. What are you both doing with your lives?"

Hallie launched into a summary of the shop and Operation Christmas Cheer, explaining how the program had grown over the years. Mrs. Whitmore listened with genuine interest, asking thoughtful questions.

"That doesn't surprise me one bit," Mrs. Whitmore said when Hallie finished. "You always had that special quality of caring too much about everyone except yourself. Even in high school, you were the one making sure everyone felt included, remembering birthdays, organizing study groups." She paused, her expression turning gently shrewd. "Though I always wished you'd learned to advocate for your own needs as passionately as you advocated for others."

Heat crept up Hallie's neck. Some observations hit too close to home, even years later.

"And you, Chase?" Mrs. Whitmore turned her attention to him. "I heard through the grapevine that you'd come home from the Marines recently. Are you settling back into civilian life?"

"Getting there." Chase set down his empty plate. "It's been an adjustment. But I'm helping my parents with their toy store, volunteering with Operation Christmas Cheer, and figuring out what comes next."

"Married? Children?"

Chase's expression shifted—something closed off, became carefully neutral. "Divorced. No children."

"I'm sorry to hear that."

"It was a long time ago." Chase reached for his coffee mug, and Hallie noticed the slight tension in his shoulders. "Things didn't work out."

Then, before Mrs. Whitmore could respond, he redirected smoothly. "Is that your husband in all these photos?"

Mrs. Whitmore followed his gesture to the wall of photographs, and her face softened. "It is. Luther taught history at the high school for thirty years."

"Mr. Whitmore was my freshman year history teacher," Chase said. "He made the Civil War actually interesting, which I didn't think was possible."

"He had a gift for that." Mrs. Whitmore rose from her chair and walked to the photo wall, touching one frame gently. "This was taken during our honeymoon in the Smoky Mountains. We were so young—twenty-three and twenty-four. Thought we had all the time in the world."

Hallie joined her at the wall, studying the photograph. The couple stood at an overlook, mountains stretching behind them, both wind-blown and laughing.

"You waited six years to get married?" Hallie asked, doing quick math based on the wedding photo date.

"We did. Luther served in Korea, and then we were both finishing college. Money was tight, timing was complicated." Mrs. Whitmore smiled at the memory. "My mother kept insisting we should wait until we were 'established.' But Luther finally said we'd been waiting long enough, that established was overrated, and we should just start our lives together already."

She turned back to face them, and something in her expression made Hallie pay closer attention.

"I'm glad we didn't wait longer," Mrs. Whitmore continued. "We had many wonderful years together. But it wasn't enough. I remember thinking we'd travel more later, when we had time. We'd visit all those places we talked about—Ireland, Scotland, New England in the fall. But later kept becoming even later, and then suddenly there wasn't any later left."

The apartment fell quiet except for the distant sound of a television from another unit and the muffled conversation of residents passing in the hallway.

"I'm not telling you this to be maudlin," Mrs. Whitmore said, her voice gentle but clear. "I'm telling you because you're both at an age where it's easy to think you have endless time. That you can put off the important things while you handle the urgent things. But life doesn't work that way."

Hallie's throat tightened. She thought about all the years she'd spent building her business, throwing herself into Operation Christmas Cheer, telling herself she was too busy for anything else.

"The gift baskets are lovely," Mrs. Whitmore said, returning to her chair and picking up her coffee. "But the greatest gift you can give someone is your time and attention. Your actual presence in their life, not just your good intentions."

Chase shifted slightly on the sofa, and when Hallie glanced at him, she found him studying his hands. Something in his posture suggested Mrs. Whitmore's words had landed as heavily with him as they had with her.

"Now," Mrs. Whitmore said, her tone lightening deliberately, "tell me about the skating event last night. I heard it was quite successful."

Hallie grabbed the subject change gratefully, describing the turnout and donations. Gradually the conversation shifted to easier topics—memories of high school, updates about former classmates, and stories about the town's changes over the years.

But Hallie remained hyperaware of Chase beside her on the sofa. Close enough that she could feel the warmth radiating from him. Close enough to notice how he leaned forward when he was engaged in conversation, how he laughed at Mrs. Whitmore's dry humor, and how he asked follow-up questions that showed he was genuinely listening rather than just being polite.

She watched him examine her bookshelf and ask about her favorite authors, then promise to loan her a military memoir he thought she'd enjoy. She watched him be kind in ways that cost him nothing but meant everything.

This was who Chase had become. Not the eighteen-year-old who'd left for the Marines with more bravado than wisdom. And Hallie was running out of reasons to keep her heart guarded.

"I should let you two finish your deliveries," Mrs. Whitmore said eventually, glancing at the clock on her mantel. "You've been kind to humor an old woman's need for company."

"It's not humor." Chase stood, collecting empty plates and carrying them to the kitchenette before Mrs. Whitmore could protest. "We enjoyed visiting you. And I mean what I said about that book—I'll drop it by next week."

"I'll hold you to that." Mrs. Whitmore walked them to the door, pausing before opening it.

"Take care of yourselves," she added, pulling them each into brief hugs. "And don't wait too long for whatever it is you're both waiting for."

They stepped into the hallway, and the apartment door closed softly behind them. Hallie stood there for a moment, trying to collect herself.

"She seems happy here," Chase said.

"But lonely." Hallie's voice came out thick.

"Yeah, I noticed that too."

They finished the remaining deliveries. Each interaction followed a similar pattern—surprise at receiving the basket, appreciation for the personalized touches, and genuine warmth toward both of them.

As they walked through the retirement home's common area toward the exit. A few residents sat in the lounge area near the fireplace, reading or chatting quietly. Classical music played softly from hidden speakers.

Outside, the November air bit at Hallie's face, sharp and clean after the building's warmth. They walked to her car in the parking lot. Chase held the driver's side door for her, then rounded to the passenger's side.

Hallie started the engine, letting it warm while they sat in the enclosed space. The heater began pushing cold air that would eventually turn warm, and the silence between them felt weighted with everything neither of them was saying.

"That was nice," Chase said finally. "The visit with Mrs. Whitmore especially... she reminded me why I came home."

"What do you mean?"

"Connection. Community. People who remember who you were and care about who you're becoming." He turned to look at her, and his expression was open in a way that made her chest ache. "People like you."

The words hung between them—simple, honest, loaded with implications that terrified her.

"Chase—"

"I know." He held up a hand, stopping whatever protest she'd been forming. "I'm not trying to make things complicated. I just wanted you to know that being here, doing this work with you, spending time with people like Mrs. Whitmore—it matters. You matter."

Hallie wanted to say something equally honest. She wanted to tell him that having him back in Mistletoe Falls had awakened parts of her she'd thought were safely buried. That watching him with his parents, with her employees, with lonely retired teachers made her remember why she'd fallen for him in the first place.

But the words stuck, trapped behind years of self-protection and fear.

"We should head to your place," she managed instead. "Pizza and a movie, right?"

If Chase noticed the deflection, he didn't call her on it. "Right. You still like pepperoni?"

"Always."

He grinned, and some of the tension dissipated. "Some things don't change. I'll call in the order and set up delivery now."

Hallie pulled out of the parking lot and headed toward downtown, toward Hollyberry Lane, toward Chase's apartment where they'd spend the evening pretending this was just two old friends reconnecting over pizza.

But as she drove through Mistletoe Falls' familiar streets, Hallie couldn't shake Mrs. Whitmore's words.

Don't wait too long for whatever it is you're waiting for.

The problem was, Hallie wasn't sure she was waiting anymore.

She was just trying not to fall.

Chapter 16

Hallie raised her hand to knock on Chase's apartment door, then paused. Her fuzzy-socked feet in her slip-on shoes felt ridiculous suddenly, and she second-guessed the oversized sweatshirt she'd changed into. Too casual? Too comfortable?

She knocked before she could overthink it further.

The door opened almost immediately, and Chase's smile erased her nervous spiral. He'd changed too—dark jeans and a navy henley.

"Hey. Perfect timing. The pizza should be here in about twenty minutes," he said.

"I'm not too early?" She stepped inside as he moved back to give her room.

"Are you kidding? I've just been sitting here reading." He gestured around the apartment. "What do you think about the furniture?"

The transformation from a few days ago was remarkable. The cream walls provided the perfect backdrop for the furniture they'd chosen together. The brown leather couch sat against the main wall, positioned to face the mounted television, with the two matching recliners flanking it at comfortable angles. The coffee table she'd talked him into—solid wood with clean lines—anchored the seating area.

"Chase, this looks so good." Hallie walked further into the living room, taking in the details. The floor lamp stood beside one recliner, and the throw pillows added warmth to the leather couch.

"Thanks," he said as he moved back into the kitchen area, which opened to the living space.

She followed him, noting the dish rack beside the sink holding the practical plates and bowls they'd selected. Through the open bedroom door, she glimpsed the simple oak bed frame and matching dresser.

"It feels like you," she said. The space reflected the same quiet competence Chase brought to everything—organized without being sterile, comfortable without being cluttered. "How does it feel having your own place?"

"Strange. Good." He opened the refrigerator and pulled out two bottles of water. "I keep expecting someone to tell me it's time to move out, or that I'm needed somewhere else. But this is mine. For as long as I want it."

He'd spent years living in temporary quarters, always ready to pack up and relocate at a moment's notice? Hallie couldn't imagine a life like that.

"I'm glad you moved back here," she said.

His gaze held hers for a second, something unspoken passing between them before a knock at the door broke the moment.

"That'll be dinner." Chase set the water bottles on the counter and headed for the door.

She busied herself grabbing napkins from the package on the counter while Chase handled the delivery. The scent of pepperoni and melted cheese filled the apartment as he brought the pizza box to the coffee table in the living room.

She settled onto the couch, tucking her legs beneath her.

He opened the box, and the steam rose, making her stomach growl.

They served themselves slices, and Chase grabbed the remote to navigate through streaming options. The casual domesticity of it all—sharing pizza, debating what to watch, sitting close enough that she could smell his aftershave—felt both natural and dangerous. This was exactly the kind of comfortable intimacy that could make her forget why she needed boundaries.

"How about this one?" He'd stopped on a romantic comedy she'd mentioned enjoying during their furniture shopping trip.

"You don't have to watch a rom com just because I'm here."

"I offered, didn't I?" He hit play before she could protest further.

The opening credits rolled, showing a busy New York street scene with a collision between the two leads. Hallie bit into her pizza, aware of Chase settling back onto the couch cushions, his arm stretched along the back behind her shoulders.

Twenty minutes in, the female lead delivered a monologue about fate and timing that made Hallie wince.

"Do people actually talk like this?" Chase asked, his tone genuinely confused.

"Only in movies." She wiped her fingers on a napkin. "Real people don't give speeches about destiny in the middle of coffee shops."

"Thank goodness. I was worried I'd been doing civilian life wrong."

She laughed, watching him try to follow the increasingly convoluted plot. His brow furrowed slightly as the male lead made a grand gesture involving a flash mob.

"You look so serious," she teased. "It's just a silly movie."

"I'm trying to understand the logic. Why would anyone think public humiliation is romantic?"

"It's not supposed to be logical. It's supposed to be grand and sweeping and make you feel something."

"I feel confused."

"You're impossible." But she was smiling, enjoying his running commentary more than the actual film.

As the movie progressed, they fell into easier conversation, talking during scenes and sometimes ignoring the screen altogether. Chase asked about her shop, and she described the complicated relationship she had with the business her father had built.

"Sometimes I wonder if I kept it because I loved it, or because I was afraid of disappointing him," she admitted. "Even though he's gone."

"Can it be both?"

"Maybe." She considered it. "I do love it. But those first few years after he died, I think I was just going through the motions. Trying to prove I could handle it."

"Sounds like you handled it remarkably well."

The compliment made her smile. On screen, the couple was having their inevitable third-act conflict, but Hallie was more interested in the man beside her.

"Is it strange?" she asked. "Being back here? Having an apartment next door to me, kind of like when we were growing up?"

"Strange and different." He was quiet for a moment, seeming to search for the right words. "But a good different. It's quieter than I expected."

"Quiet's not so bad when it feels like home."

"I've slept in a hundred different bunks," he said, his voice low. "Hotels, barracks, tents in the desert. But I never really had a place that was mine until now. Somewhere I chose. Somewhere I wanted to be."

He was quiet after that, his eyes on the television screen but clearly somewhere else. That stillness—the way he seemed comfortable with silence—made her curious about the parts of his life she didn't know.

She hesitated, then turned slightly to face him. "Can I ask you something a little personal?"

"Sure."

"Earlier today, when Mrs. Whitmore asked about your marriage, you seemed uncomfortable. I know it happened—your mom mentioned it years ago—but she never gave me any details." She paused, giving him space to decline. "You don't have to talk about it if you don't want to... I'm just genuinely curious."

Chase was silent long enough that she thought he might change the subject. Then he reached for the remote and paused the movie.

"Her name was Janice. Janice Hartman." He set the remote down, his hands resting on his knees. "We were both Marines. Met after my first deployment, and she just—she got it, you know? Understood the life, the work, the constant moving around."

Hallie stayed quiet, letting him find his words.

"We got married four years after I left Mistletoe Falls. Thought we had it all figured out." A rueful smile crossed his face. "Turns out shared military service isn't the same as a shared life. We'd go months without seeing each other. Different deployments, different schedules. We'd try to connect over video calls, but it's not the same as actually building a life with someone."

He picked up his water, took a drink, and set it back down.

"I was deployed for fifteen months, and when I came back, she told me she'd met someone else. Someone who was actually there." He glanced at Hallie. "She wasn't cruel about it. Just honest. Said she couldn't build a life with someone who was never present."

"I'm sorry."

"Don't be. She was right. We both realized we'd mistaken compatibility for love. We were good friends who thought that was enough. But marriage needs more than friendship. It needs presence, communication, and actual time spent building something together."

"Are you still in touch?"

"Some. The occasional message checking in. We're friendly, but not friends, if that makes sense." He looked at her directly now. "The whole thing taught me a lot about myself and about love."

"What about you?" he continued. "My mom mentioned you'd been engaged?"

"Daniel." She sighed, picking at the edge of a napkin. "We broke up about six months ago. He was an attorney from the next town over. Very respectable, very ambitious, very... practical."

"But?"

"But he told me one day that he wasn't in love with me anymore." The words still stung, though less than they had initially. "Said he'd tried, but the feelings just weren't there. He was kind about it, which somehow made it worse."

"I'm sorry. That's rough."

"It was. For a while." She smoothed the napkin flat. "But looking back, I think part of me knew. I kept waiting to feel that big, overwhelming thing everyone talks about. That certainty. And it never came."

"Do you think that exists? That certainty?"

"I want to believe it does. I've seen it. My parents had it before my dad died. Your parents have it. That kind of partnership where you know exactly who you're supposed to be with."

"My mom said something to me the other day." Chase shifted, angling toward her slightly. "About how she knew she'd marry my dad the night they met. Not because it was dramatic or fate or anything like that. Just because talking to him felt easy in a way nothing else ever had."

"That's beautiful."

"She also said the easy part was recognizing it. The hard part was choosing it every day after."

The conversation had taken them into deeper waters than she'd expected. The movie sat paused on a scene they'd both forgotten about, and the pizza box sat mostly empty on the coffee table.

"Can I ask you something?" His voice had gone quieter. "About your mom."

Hallie's stomach tightened, but she nodded.

"Dad mentioned that after your father died, she just—left. Pretty quickly. Sold the house, gave you the business, moved to Florida. What happened?"

She'd known this question would come eventually. Chase deserved the truth, especially after he'd been so open with her.

"I came back to Mistletoe Falls about two months before Dad died." She pulled a throw pillow onto her lap, needing something to hold. "I'd been in Charleston, working in retail management for this big corporate chain. Good money, decent benefits, but I felt so disconnected from everything. I missed home. Missed my parents."

"So I came back. Dad was thrilled. He'd been wanting to slow down a bit, and having me there to help manage the shop took some pressure off. Mom was deep into her writing by then—she'd published a few romance novels and was getting some recognition." Hallie's throat felt tight. "We had two months. Two perfect months where everything felt right. Like I'd finally made the choice I was supposed to make."

"And then?"

"Heart attack. Completely unexpected. Dad was gone before the ambulance even arrived." She blinked against the burn behind her eyes. "Mom just—she fell apart. Wouldn't eat, wouldn't sleep, wouldn't talk to anyone. I tried everything. Grief counseling, support groups, just being there. Nothing worked."

She pulled the pillow tighter.

"Then about six weeks after the funeral, she just—changed. Like she'd made some decision I wasn't part of. She handed me the deed to the shop, listed the house with a realtor, and told me she was moving to Florida. When I asked why, she said she couldn't stay in a place where everything reminded her of him. That she needed a fresh start."

"Hallie—"

"I begged her to stay. Or at least to wait longer before making such huge decisions. But she'd already made up her mind." The old hurt bubbled up, familiar and sharp. "She was gone within weeks. Left me alone with a business I was barely qualified to run, a mountain of grief I didn't know how to process, and the constant question of what I'd done wrong. Why I wasn't enough reason for her to stay."

The last words came out broken, and she was mortified to feel tears slipping down her cheeks.

Chase reached over and took her hand, his palm warm and solid against hers. She didn't let go.

"You did nothing wrong," he said, his voice firm. "Grief does strange things to people. Your mom leaving was about her pain, not your worth."

"I know that. Logically." She wiped at her cheeks with her free hand. "But there's this part of me that still feels like I wasn't enough. Like if I'd been a better daughter, or more supportive, or just—more—she wouldn't have needed to run away."

"That's not how it works." His thumb brushed across her knuckles, a gesture probably meant to comfort but that sent awareness skittering up her arm. "Sometimes people are so buried in their own pain they can't see who they're hurting. It doesn't make it okay, but it's not your fault."

She looked down at their joined hands, his larger one engulfing hers.

"She calls sometimes," Hallie said. "Birthday, Christmas, a random Tuesday afternoons. Always cheerful, always talking about her book tours and her new friends in Florida. Never asks how I'm doing. Never acknowledges what she did."

"Do you want her to?"

"I don't know. Part of me wants her to apologize, to admit she messed up. But another part thinks maybe it's better this way. We have this surface relationship now where we pretend everything's fine, and I don't have to deal with the anger underneath."

"Anger's allowed, you know."

"I know. I just—" She looked at him finally, at the genuine concern in his eyes. "I've built this whole life around making sure other people don't feel abandoned and feel loved and wanted. Operation Christmas Cheer, the shop, showing up for everyone who needs anything. Because I know what it feels like to be left behind."

"You know you matter too, right? That you're allowed to need things, to ask for help, to not be the one holding everything up all the time?"

"In theory."

"Hallie." He squeezed her hand gently. "I'm serious. You don't have to earn love by being useful. You're allowed to just—be."

The words lodged somewhere near her heart. She wanted to believe him. Wanted to think she could stop proving her worth through constant service.

"Thank you," she said.

"For what?"

"For listening. For not making it weird. For—" She gestured at their joined hands. "For this."

He smiled, and it transformed his entire face. "Anytime."

They sat like that for a moment, hands linked, the movie forgotten. Then, Chase released her hand and reached for the remote.

"Want to finish this ridiculous plot, or should we find something else?"

"Let's see how it ends." She said as she settled back on the couch.

The movie resumed, building toward its inevitable happy ending. But Hallie's attention kept drifting to Chase—the way his profile looked in the lamplight, the steady rise and fall of his breathing, and the fact that he seemed as aware of her as she was of him.

They finished the film in near-silence, making occasional comments but mostly just existing in the same space. When the credits rolled, Hallie realized she had no desire to leave.

"I should probably go," she said as she forced herself to stand, and he followed suit. They navigated the short distance to his door, and he grabbed his coat from the hook.

"You don't have to walk me down," she protested.

"It's dark." He opened the door. "I'm walking you home."

They descended in silence, their footsteps echoing off the metal treads. At the bottom, they walked the distance between his building and hers and climbed her stairs.

At her door, they stopped. Hallie dug her keys from her pocket, suddenly reluctant to end an evening that had felt important in ways she couldn't quite name.

"Thanks for tonight," she said. "The pizza, the terrible movie, the conversation—all of it."

"I'm glad you agreed to it." His hands were in his pockets, but he didn't move to leave. "I had a really good time."

"Me too."

They stood there, neither quite ready to say goodnight. The alley was quiet, just the distant sound of traffic on Mistletoe Lane.

"Hallie—" Chase started, then stopped.

"Yeah?"

He looked at her for a long moment. "Nothing. Just—good night."

"Good night, Chase."

She unlocked her door and slipped inside, closing it softly behind her. Through the small window, she could see him still standing there, hands in his pockets, looking at her door.

Then he turned and headed back down the stairs.

Hallie leaned against the door, her heart doing complicated things in her chest. The evening played back through her mind—the easy conversation, the vulnerable confessions, and the moment their eyes had met with something that felt dangerously close to promise.

She'd spent the past two weeks telling herself that friendship was enough. That she didn't need more, couldn't risk more, shouldn't want more.

The question wasn't whether she wanted more with Chase.

The question was whether she was brave enough to stop protecting herself long enough to find out if he wanted it too.

Chapter 17

The bell above the entrance to Bells & Whistles jingled as Hallie stepped inside, immediately enveloped by the Saturday morning energy of the toy store. A family with three children clustered around the educational toy display, the youngest pointing excitedly at a wooden puzzle while her siblings debated the merits of various board games. Near the front counter, a grandmother studied a handcrafted rocking horse with the careful attention of someone selecting an heirloom rather than a simple gift.

Mark stood behind the register, ringing up a sale. Two employees Hallie recognized were working on the sales floor—one restocking the train display near the front window, another answering questions about age-appropriate science kits for a harried-looking father.

Mark glanced up as she approached, his smile immediate and genuine. "Hallie! Good morning."

"Morning." She waited while he finished the transaction, watching him wrap the items. "Is Liz available?"

"She's in the office with Chase. They've been back there for about an hour going over the inventory systems." He handed the bag to his customers with a warm farewell, then nodded toward the back. "Go on through. They're expecting you."

"Thanks."

Hallie made her way past the shelves of colorful merchandise, through the door marked "Employees Only," and into the storage area behind the retail space. Boxes lined metal shelving units, each labeled with Mark's precise handwriting. The scent of wood shavings drifted up from the basement workshop where he created his custom pieces.

The office door stood open, and she paused at the threshold, taking in the scene. Liz sat at her desk, and Chase occupied the chair beside her, both of them studying a spreadsheet displayed on the monitor.

"Knock knock," Hallie announced.

They both looked up and smiled.

"Perfect timing." Liz rolled her chair back slightly to create more space. "We were just finishing up the inventory review."

Chase stood and grabbed a folding chair from against the wall, setting it up near the desk before adjusting his own chair to face the small circle they'd formed. Liz maneuvered her wheelchair into position, completing the triangle.

"I've already explained to Chase how our donation system works," Liz said, gesturing to the papers spread across her desk. "I've shown him the records from previous years so he understands what we typically contribute and how it's been received."

"The numbers are impressive." Chase leaned back in his chair, one ankle crossed over his knee. "You've donated thousands of dollars worth of toys over the past five years."

"It's become one of our favorite parts of the business." Liz's expression reflected genuine pleasure. "Knowing that children wake up

Christmas morning with something special because we were able to help—that matters more than any profit margin."

Hallie pulled her notebook from her bag, flipping to the pages where she'd compiled this year's requests. "I have the list of specific items children have asked for, organized by age group. Some are general—'a doll,' 'building blocks'—but others are surprisingly specific."

"Let's see what we're working with." Liz said as she adjusted her reading glasses.

They spent the next thirty minutes reviewing the list. Hallie explained each request. Liz made notes, occasionally asking clarifying questions. Chase listened, sometimes offering suggestions about which toys might work best for particular age groups or interests.

"What about this one?" Chase pointed to an entry. "Ten-year-old boy interested in space and science. What do you think about one of those telescope starter kits? We've got several in stock."

"That's perfect." Hallie made a note. "I was thinking maybe a book about astronomy, but a telescope is so much better."

"We can do both." Liz was already writing. "Education and imagination."

They worked through the entire list, with Liz's generosity exceeding even Hallie's hopeful expectations. Educational toys, wooden puzzles that Mark had crafted in his workshop, board games that encouraged family time, art supplies, books, building sets—the donations added up to easily double what the store had contributed in previous years.

"Are you sure?" Hallie asked. "I have funds set aside from donations we've received, and I'd be happy to pay you for some of this."

"I'm sure." Liz's tone was firm. "The business is flourishing. We can afford to give more, and we want to. These children deserve the best we can offer."

"Thank you. This is going to make such a difference."

"It's our privilege." Liz set down her pen, her expression softening. "Now, let's talk about logistics. When do you need everything delivered?"

They discussed timing and coordination, settling on early next week, so she and her employees had time to sort and wrap the donations before next weekend's delivery to the Angel Tree at the Community Center. Chase offered to handle the physical delivery himself.

As their business conversation wound down, Liz shifted in her chair, her gaze turning thoughtful. "Goodness, I can't believe Thanksgiving is this week already. The year has flown by."

"It really has." Hallie closed her notebook.

"What are your Thanksgiving plans?" Chase asked.

Hallie kept her expression cheerful, practiced at deflecting concern about her solitary holidays.

"Actually, I'm planning a quiet day at home. I have reading to catch up on, maybe binge-watch something I've been meaning to see. It'll be peaceful, and I'm looking forward to a day of doing nothing but whatever I feel like."

Liz's expression shifted. "What about Nina? Or Sofia? Won't you be celebrating with them like usual?"

"Nina's driving to Knoxville to spend the day with her sister's family. Sofia's going to her in-laws in Nashville. Lucy's headed to Bristol to see her family." Hallie shrugged, maintaining her casual facade. "Everyone's traveling to be with extended family this year. It just worked out that way."

Chase was looking at her with an expression she couldn't quite read, and Liz had gone still.

"You're not spending Thanksgiving alone." Chase's statement held no room for argument.

"It's really fine—"

"Come to our house." He glanced at his mother for confirmation. "We're doing the whole traditional thing. Turkey, stuffing, way too many side dishes."

"Chase, I appreciate the offer, but I don't want to intrude on your family celebration—"

"Intrude?" Liz's voice carried genuine distress. "Hallie Rose Dawson, you listen to me right now. You are family. You've been like a daughter to us for years. You think I'm going to let you sit alone in your apartment eating a frozen dinner on Thanksgiving?"

"I wasn't planning on a frozen dinner. I make excellent grilled cheese."

"Not happening." Chase leaned forward, his elbows on his knees. "You're coming to dinner. That's final."

"I really don't want to impose—"

"You're not imposing." Liz's firm tone left no room for further protest. "You're accepting an invitation from people who love you and want you there. There's a difference."

"I don't know what to say."

"Say yes." Liz's expression had softened now, maternal warmth replacing the earlier firmness. "Please, sweetheart. It would mean so much to us to have you there."

Hallie looked between them—Liz's hopeful face and Chase's steady gaze. The invitation was genuine; she could see that. They truly wanted her there, not out of pity but out of affection.

"Can I at least contribute?" she asked, her resistance crumbling. "Bring something to help with the meal?"

"Absolutely not." Liz shook her head.

"Then I'm not coming."

"Hallie—"

"I mean it, Liz. Either I get to bring something and help cook, or I'll stay home with my grilled cheese."

Liz studied her for a moment, then a small smile curved her lips. "You're as stubborn as your father was."

"Learned from the best."

"Fine. Come early and help cook. And bring whatever groceries you want to contribute."

"Deal. What time should I be there?"

"Come around nine." Liz was already making mental calculations, Hallie could tell. "We'll get the turkey in the oven first thing, then work on everything else."

Chase had been watching their negotiation with barely contained amusement. "You two crack me up."

Liz smiled as she reached over and patted Hallie's hand. "I'm glad you're coming."

"Thank you." Her voice came out thicker than intended. "Both of you. This means more than you probably realize."

"We know exactly what it means." Liz squeezed her hand once before releasing it.

A knock on the doorframe interrupted the moment. One of the store employees poked his head in, looking apologetic. "Chase? Sorry to interrupt, but your dad needs help on the floor. We've got a rush, and he's swamped."

"On my way." Chase stood, then paused to look down at Hallie. "I'm glad you're coming Thursday. Really glad."

"Me too."

He squeezed her shoulder as he passed and then disappeared into the hallway.

Liz watched him go, then turned back to Hallie. "Now then. Let's make a list of what you can bring. I'm thinking maybe ingredients for that cranberry sauce your father used to make. The one with the orange zest."

"You remember that?" Hallie was surprised.

"Of course I remember. Your father brought it to our Christmas open house every year." Liz pulled a fresh sheet of paper toward her. "Tony was proud of that recipe. Said it came from his grandmother."

They spent the next twenty minutes crafting a grocery list. The conversation flowed easily between practical meal planning and shared memories—stories about Tony's cooking experiments, Corinne's tendency to burn something when she got in a hurry, and the year a Thanksgiving turkey had somehow ended up overcooked on the outside but frozen in the middle.

"Your mother called that turkey's confusion 'a metaphor for life,'" Liz recalled, laughing. "Said she was going to use it in a novel."

"Did she?" Hallie hadn't read very many of her mother's books. The romance novels Corinne wrote felt like they belonged to a different woman than the one who'd abandoned her.

"I don't know." Liz's expression sobered slightly. "Gosh... I miss those days when we used to spend the holidays together. Those were good times. Have you talked to your mom lately?"

"She called a few months ago. Usually, I only hear from her on my birthday, at Christmas, or random calls when she's between book events." Hallie studied the grocery list, not quite meeting Liz's eyes. "She tells me about her life in Florida. Her condo, her writing group, the beaches. Never asks much about me."

"I'm sorry, sweetheart."

"It is what it is."

"No, it's not." Liz's voice held quiet firmness. "It's a mother failing her daughter. And you're allowed to be angry about that."

Hallie looked up, meeting Liz's steady gaze. In it, she saw understanding born from watching the situation unfold, from picking up pieces Corinne had left scattered when she'd fled.

"I am angry. But I don't know what to do with it. So I just—keep going. Keep working, keep helping people, keep pretending I'm fine."

"You don't have to pretend with me," Liz said as she reached over, covering Hallie's hand with her own. "You're allowed not to be fine sometimes."

"I'll work on that," she managed.

"Good." Liz squeezed her hand once more, then returned to the grocery list with renewed focus. "Now, what about green beans? Do you want to bring those, or should I handle them?"

They finished planning the meal contribution, and Hallie tucked the list carefully into her notebook, gathered her things and stood to leave.

"Thursday morning, nine o'clock," Liz confirmed. "Don't you dare back out on me."

"I won't." Hallie leaned down to hug her, breathing in the familiar scent of Liz's floral perfume and feeling arms that had held her through worse grief than holiday loneliness wrap around her shoulders. "Thank you, Liz. For everything."

"That's what family does." Liz pulled back to look at her, eyes suspiciously bright. "We show up. We stay. We make sure nobody spends Thanksgiving alone eating grilled cheese in their apartment."

Hallie laughed despite the emotion clogging her throat. "The grilled cheese was going to be really good though."

"Save it for another day."

Chapter 18

The blade sliced through tender turkey meat with surgical precision, releasing a fresh wave of steam that carried the aroma of rosemary and thyme. Chase's hands moved slowly, following his father's steady guidance as Mark stood beside him at the kitchen counter.

"Keep the knife parallel to the cutting board, son," Mark said, his voice calm and instructional. "Let the blade do the work. You're just guiding it."

Chase adjusted his angle, and the next slice came away clean and even.

"You got it." Mark clapped his son on the shoulder.

Mark reached for another knife and began working on the second breast. "You know, the last time we carved a Thanksgiving turkey together, you were sixteen."

Chase paused mid-slice, memory flickering across his features. "I remember. You let me do the whole thing myself that year."

"You shredded half the meat." Mark's laugh was warm and teasing.

"I remember."

"You tried. That's what mattered. It's good to have you home, son. Really good."

Chase met his father's eyes. "It's good to be home."

From the dining room came the soft clink of silverware and Hallie's voice asking Liz where she kept the cloth napkins. The house hummed with life, warm and inviting.

"She's special, you know." Mark kept his voice low, meant only for his son.

Chase's hands stilled. "I know."

"Just making sure you do."

They finished carving the turkey, piling the last slices onto the platter. Chase lifted the heavy dish, feeling the warmth through the ceramic, and carried it toward the dining room where Hallie and his mother had transformed the table into something out of a magazine spread.

The dining room table stretched before them, laden with the rewards of their collective labor. The turkey took center stage, surrounded by dishes that represented hours of preparation—creamy mashed potatoes whipped to cloud-like perfection, green bean casserole with its crispy onion topping, sweet potato casserole dotted with toasted marshmallows, sage stuffing still steaming in its serving dish, a bowl of rich gravy that caught the light from the chandelier overhead, and Tony's cranberry sauce in its crystal dish, the recipe Hallie had made from memory.

Fresh rolls wrapped in cream-colored linen sat in a woven basket, their tops golden and brushed with butter. A second basket held cornbread muffins that Liz had insisted on making because Mark loved them. Serving spoons and ladles rested beside each dish, ready for the feast.

Hallie stood back from the table, hands clasped in front of her as she took in the display. The chandelier's warm glow reflected off polished silverware and crystal glasses, and the centerpiece—a low arrangement of autumn leaves, miniature pumpkins, and cream-colored candles—added the finishing touch.

"It's beautiful," she said.

Liz wheeled closer, adjusting one napkin that had been folded slightly crooked. "We make a good team."

They did. The last hour had flown by in a blur of synchronized movement—Hallie and Liz setting the table together and carrying dishes of food into the dining room. There had been laughter when Hallie couldn't remember where she had set the gravy boat after getting it from the cupboard and mild panic when they'd forgotten the rolls in the oven.

But now, looking at the finished table, Hallie felt a swell of emotion she wasn't quite prepared for. This wasn't just food arranged on dishes. This was what it looked like when people showed up for each other and when effort translated into love and found family.

"Everyone ready to dig in?" Mark asked.

"More than ready." Liz gestured to the empty chairs. "Let's eat before everything gets cold."

They settled around the table—Mark at the head, Liz to his right, Chase across from his mother, and Hallie beside Chase. For a moment, no one moved, each of them simply absorbing the sight before them.

"All right, let's not let this magnificent spread go to waste." Mark reached for the turkey platter. "Who wants white meat?"

Dishes began to circulate, each person serving themselves and passing dishes in a choreographed dance. The turkey was perfectly moist, its herb-roasted skin crackling with flavor. The mashed potatoes were creamy and buttery, the green bean casserole offered satisfying crunch, and Tony's cranberry sauce provided the tart-sweet contrast that completed each bite.

"This turkey is incredible," Hallie said after her first taste. "Chase, you and your dad outdid yourselves."

"Mom's seasoning recipe." Chase gestured with his fork toward Liz. "We just followed orders."

"Following orders well is a skill." Liz smiled at her son, pride evident in every line of her face. "And you both did beautifully."

"These rolls are perfect too." Mark buttered a second one, ignoring his wife's amused glance. "What? It's Thanksgiving. Calories don't count."

"That's not how it works." But Liz was laughing, reaching for a roll herself.

The conversation flowed as easily as the food, moving from compliments on the meal to stories that spanned years.

"Hallie, how are the preparations for Operation Christmas Cheer going?" Liz asked, redirecting the conversation as she served herself more stuffing. "It must be getting intense now."

"It is." Hallie set down her fork. "We've collected about eighty percent of our target donations for the toy drive. The food basket program is going well—we're serving forty-seven families this year. And the veterans' home baskets are ready to go."

"That's incredible." Mark shook his head in admiration. "The coordination alone must be massive."

"It helps having good volunteers." Hallie glanced at Chase, smiling. "Chase has been great about coming and helping us get things assembled."

"I'm just helping where I can."

"You're doing more than that." Hallie meant every word. "The wreath assembly went much faster with your help. And you reorganized my entire basement storage system this past week so we can actually find things easier."

"It needed organizing," Chase said, deflecting.

"You saw what needed doing and did it." Hallie turned to Mark and Liz. "He color-coded the donation boxes, created a tracking system for completed projects, and built additional shelving so we're not tripping over supplies."

"That's my boy." Mark raised his glass of sweet tea in salute. "Always solving problems."

The meal continued, plates gradually emptying as conversation wove through topics both weighty and light. They discussed the upcoming Christmas season in Mistletoe Falls, debated whether the town should add more light displays to the square, and laughed over memories of past holiday mishaps.

Through it all, Hallie was acutely aware of Chase beside her—the way his shoulder occasionally brushed hers when he reached for the bread basket, how his laugh rumbled warm and genuine, the attentiveness with which he listened when others spoke. Every small interaction added to the undeniable truth she'd been trying to ignore: her feelings for Chase weren't fading. They were growing, deepening, becoming impossible to categorize as anything other than what they actually were.

She wanted more than friendship. Had wanted it since the moment he'd walked into her shop three weeks ago. But wanting and allowing herself to have were different things entirely.

"Hallie?" Liz's voice broke through her thoughts. "I asked if you wanted more turkey."

"Oh." Hallie blinked, realizing everyone was looking at her. "No, thank you. I'm completely full. Everything was delicious."

"There's always room for more... a little later maybe," Mark joked, but he too pushed his plate away with a contented sigh.

"We'll wait a bit and have dessert later," Liz said as she surveyed the table, satisfaction clear in her expression.

As if on cue, they began the natural progression toward cleanup. Plates stacked on plates, serving dishes passed hand to hand, the organized chaos of clearing a table that had supported a feast. Hallie stood and began gathering silverware while Chase collected the empty bread basket and butter dish.

In the kitchen, they fell into an efficient rhythm—Hallie at the sink with hot water and soap, Chase stationed beside her with a clean towel. Mark and Liz worked at the counter, transferring leftovers into containers and debating how much turkey to freeze for later and how much to keep in the fridge and use over the next few days.

"We could make turkey soup," Liz suggested.

"Turkey sandwiches, turkey soup, turkey casserole, turkey salad..." Mark ticked off options on his fingers. "We'll be eating turkey until Christmas."

"You're the one who insisted on the twenty-pound bird."

"It was a good price!"

Hallie smiled at their banter as she scrubbed the serving platter. Beside her, Chase dried dishes with careful attention, his movements methodical and thorough.

"You're good at this," Chase said quietly, his voice just for her.

"Dishes?"

"Everything. It's been a great day... you know my parents love you, right?"

"I love them too."

"And me?" Chase's question was soft, almost lost beneath the running water.

Hallie's hands stilled in the soapy water. She looked up at him, meeting blue eyes that held something vulnerable and hopeful. Her heart hammered against her ribs.

"Of course I do," she said, keeping her voice light, friendly. Safe. "You're my oldest friend."

He nodded and returned to drying, the moment passing as Mark announced he'd successfully crammed six days' worth of turkey into five storage containers.

The kitchen gradually restored itself to order. Counters wiped clean, floors swept free of crumbs, dish towels hung to dry. The four of them stood back to admire their work, with the tired satisfaction that came from a day well spent.

"I vote for the living room," Mark said, pressing a hand to his stomach. "And possibly a nap."

"You and your Thanksgiving naps." Liz said as she headed toward the living room.

They migrated together, settling into comfortable spots—Mark in his recliner, which he pushed back with a groan of contentment, Liz near him with the remote control for the television, Chase and Hallie on the sofa.

"There's always a movie marathon on during Thanksgiving," Liz said, scrolling through channels. "Let's see what we've got. Oh, look—holiday movies already. They start earlier every year."

"Put on whatever you'd like," Mark mumbled, his eyes already drifting closed. "Just let me rest my eyes for a minute..."

"Uh-huh. A minute," Liz said as she smiled.

The opening credits of a cheerful Christmas movie filled the screen, all twinkling lights and snow-covered small towns. Hallie leaned back against the sofa, the fullness in her stomach mixing with emotional contentment into something almost drowsy.

This was nice. More than nice. This was the ordinary extraordinary that she'd been missing. The simple pleasure of being with people who cared, of belonging somewhere without having to earn it through service or usefulness.

Beside her, Chase shifted, stretching his arms over his head. The movement drew her attention despite her attempt to keep her eyes on the television. He looked relaxed, at ease in a way she'd rarely seen during his time back in Mistletoe Falls. Like he'd finally stopped waiting for the next mission, the next deployment, or the next requirement to pick up and move.

"I could use some fresh air," Chase said, lowering his arms. "If I sit here much longer, I'm going to end up joining Dad in a nap."

Mark snored softly from his recliner, validating the concern.

Chase turned to Hallie, his expression casual but his eyes warm. "Want to take a walk?"

"Sure, movement and fresh air sound perfect."

They stood, reaching for jackets that hung on hooks near the front door. Liz's voice followed them, warm with knowing amusement. "Don't be gone too long! We still have pie to eat."

"We won't," Chase promised, holding the door open for Hallie.

She stepped past him into the November evening, the cold air hitting her face like a wake-up call.

Chapter 19

Hallie walked beside Chase down his parents' driveway with her hands tucked deep in her jacket pockets, her breath forming small clouds that dissipated quickly in the cold.

"Your parents really know how to throw a Thanksgiving," she said. "I can't remember the last time I ate that much."

"Dad's convinced we need enough food to feed a small army." Chase smiled, remembering his father's expression of pure satisfaction when surveying the loaded table. "It's always been like that. Every holiday, every family meal—way more than we could possibly eat."

"It was perfect." Hallie's voice softened. "Thank you for including me. Really. I know I said it earlier, but I mean it. If I'd stayed home today, I probably would've been bored out of my mind by evening, reorganizing my closet for the third time this month just to have something to do."

"You're always welcome," he said. "My parents love having you around."

"They're good people. I'm lucky to have them in my life."

And I'm lucky to have you here, Chase thought.

They passed a house on the left already decorated for Christmas, with strands of lights outlining the roof and wrapping around the porch columns. Simple white lights in the windows and evergreen wreaths on the door. The yard featured an elaborate inflatable display—Santa in a sleigh pulled by reindeer that bobbed gently in the breeze.

"I love when people get into the Christmas spirit," Hallie said, gesturing toward the house. "In some places, putting up Christmas decorations before December is practically criminal. But here, it's just part of who we are."

"Living in a town called Mistletoe Falls kind of demands commitment to the theme."

They walked in silence for a few moments, their footsteps synchronized without conscious effort. The residential street stretched ahead of them, quiet and peaceful, lined with mature trees. Their childhood neighborhood—the place where he'd learned to ride a bike, where he'd played countless games of hide-and-seek, and where he'd spent summer evenings catching fireflies and winter afternoons building snow forts with Hallie and several of his other friends on the street.

The first house on the right loomed ahead, set back from the road with a long driveway and a front yard that sloped gently toward the street. Chase noticed Hallie's pace slow beside him, then stop entirely, staring at the house. Her hands remained in her pockets, but her shoulders had gone rigid, her breathing shallow.

Chase followed her gaze to the two-story home with its white siding and dark blue shutters. Christmas lights outlined the windows and wrapped around the porch railing in neat rows. A wreath hung on the front door. The yard looked well-maintained; the shrubs trimmed and the flower beds mulched for winter.

"They take good care of it," Hallie said. "The new owners. It looks nice."

Chase's throat tightened. This was Hallie's childhood home. The place where she'd grown up, where her father had taught her to love Christmas, where her mother had been present and loving before grief had driven her away. He'd been in this house countless times as a kid, running through the front door without knocking because he and Hallie had that kind of friendship.

"Do you ever think about what it would look like if you still lived here?" he asked.

Hallie didn't answer immediately. She stared at the house, and Chase watched emotions flicker across her face—nostalgia, grief, and something that might have been longing.

"Sometimes," she finally said. "I think about Dad still being alive. Mom still being here." She paused, releasing a breath that clouded white in the cold air. "I wonder what Christmas mornings would be like. If we would still do all the traditions we used to do."

"Mom used to decorate every single window," Hallie continued. "Not just put up a wreath or some lights, but actually decorate. She'd create these little scenes—miniature Christmas villages in some windows, candles and greenery arrangements in others. From the street, the entire house looked like something out of a storybook."

"I remember."

"And Dad—" Hallie's voice caught slightly, but she pushed through. "Dad would let me help him with projects in the garage. There was this one time he was determined to build a bookcase for me. He showed me how to sand the wood smooth, how to measure twice and cut once, and how to stain the wood with a steady hand." She smiled, the expression bittersweet. "I wasn't very good at it, but he never told me that. He just praised my efforts and helped me fix whatever I'd messed up."

"He was a wonderful dad."

"He was the best." Hallie's gaze remained fixed on the house. "I played in that yard for years. Climbed those trees, picked dandelions to make wishes, built snowmen that Dad would help me decorate with actual coal for the eyes and carrot noses. We'd have snowball fights out here—me and you and your family sometimes."

The memories surfaced—Hallie's delighted laughter as she'd pelted him with a perfectly aimed snowball, her father joining the fray and showing surprisingly good aim, the way her mother had eventually called them all inside for hot chocolate with marshmallows that were half-melted by the time they'd peeled off their wet gloves.

"I wonder what life would be like if things had been different," Hallie said. "If Dad were still alive. If Mom hadn't left. If I still had that—" She gestured toward the house. "—instead of what I have now."

Chase moved closer, drawn by the vulnerability in her voice. Without overthinking it, he reached for her hand. She pulled it from her pocket and let him take it, her fingers cold against his palm. He wrapped his hand around hers, sharing warmth.

"What you have now isn't nothing," he said. "You've built something pretty incredible, Hallie."

"I know." She squeezed his hand. "But sometimes I still wonder."

They stood together on the sidewalk, hand in hand, looking at the house that represented a life that could have been. The Christmas lights twinkled in the windows, cheerful and bright, a reminder that life continued even when people left.

Eventually, Hallie took a breath and started walking again, tugging gently on Chase's hand. He fell into step beside her, and neither of them let go as they moved down the sidewalk, past other houses with their own stories and histories.

Chase was acutely conscious of her hand in his—the delicate bones, the slightly rough patches on her fingers from constant work.

He was falling for her. Not just attracted. Not just drawn to her warmth and kindness and the way she laughed at his terrible jokes. He was genuinely, terrifyingly falling for Hallie Dawson. For the woman she'd become, for the strength she carried so gracefully, and for the way she made him want to be better just by existing in his orbit.

The realization should have scared him. Maybe it did, a little. But mostly it felt right—like finding something he'd been missing without knowing he'd lost it.

"I think about it sometimes too," Chase said as they turned onto another street. "What my life would have been like if I'd done things differently."

Hallie glanced at him. "What do you mean?"

"If I'd only served four years instead of twelve. If I'd come home after my first enlistment ended instead of re-upping." He kept his voice even, trying to articulate thoughts he'd never quite voiced before. "Would I have figured out civilian life a bit easier? Would I have stayed in Mistletoe Falls? What kind of man would I be now if I'd made different choices?"

"Do you regret it? The Marines?"

"No." The answer came immediately, certain. "The Marines made me who I am. Taught me discipline, leadership, and how to function under pressure. It gave me purpose when I didn't have any. I needed that." He paused, considering. "But I do wonder about the roads not taken. The life I might have had here if I'd come home sooner."

"You're home now," Hallie said simply.

"Yeah. I am."

They walked in silence for several paces. The sun was starting to set, and the cold intensified, making Chase grateful for his jacket and the warmth of Hallie's hand in his.

She stopped abruptly on the sidewalk, holding his hand firm to stop him as well. She looked at him with an expression he struggled to interpret—part confusion, part hope, part something that might have been fear.

She raised their clasped hands. "What are we doing here, Chase?"

His heart rate kicked up. "What do you mean?"

"This." She gestured with their joined hands. "We're friends. We've been friends since we were kids. So what's going on between us? I need to hear you tell me."

Chase's mind raced, searching for words that would be honest, that would convey truth without pushing too hard. "I'm drawn to you," he said finally. "I don't know exactly when it started—maybe the moment you walked out from behind that counter in your shop, maybe when we had lunch at the diner, maybe it's been building this whole time. But I look at you and I feel something I can't quite explain."

"Drawn to me," Hallie repeated, testing the words.

"Yeah. You're—" He struggled for the right description. "You're magnetic, Hallie. I want to know more about you. The woman you are now, not just the girl I remember from childhood. I want to spend time with you, talk to you, understand what makes you tick."

Hallie's expression remained guarded. "You've only been back home for three weeks, Chase. Maybe we should slow down. Take our time figuring this out."

"I don't think three weeks is too fast." Chase took a breath. "Hallie, I'm falling for you. That's what's happening here. I'm naturally drawn to you in a way I've never experienced with anyone else, and it doesn't feel rushed or premature. It feels right."

She stared at him, processing. "Why now? Why not back when we were teenagers?"

Chase had asked himself the same thing—why hadn't he seen Hallie this way when they were eighteen? Why had he been so oblivious to what was right in front of him?

"Back then, I always just thought of you as a friend," he admitted. "I was too wrapped up in myself to see anything else. At that age, I was completely confused about who I was or who I was supposed to be. I spent all my time hanging out with the guys when I wasn't around you, worrying about graduating, terrified of having to become an adult." He shook his head at the memory of his younger self. "Becoming an adult scared the daylights out of me, Hallie. I had no direction, no plan, no idea what I was doing with my life. That's why I enlisted—I needed someone to tell me what to do, other than my parents. I needed structure to figure out who I was."

"And now?"

"Now I know who I am." Chase met her eyes directly. "I'm not that confused kid anymore. I've got twelve years of experience, of growing up, of learning what matters. And what matters is this—" He squeezed her hand. "—you."

Hallie looked down at their joined hands, her expression shifting through emotions too quickly for Chase to track. "I had a crush on you our senior year. Did you know that?"

The revelation hit him like cold water. "What?"

"Senior year. I had the biggest crush on you." A rueful smile touched her lips. "I thought maybe you'd notice. But you never did."

Chase felt like the ground had shifted beneath his feet. "I had no idea."

"I know you didn't. You were too busy being eighteen and oblivious." She pulled her hand from his, and Chase immediately missed the contact. "But here's what you need to understand, Chase. I can't have you breaking my heart. I've had my heart broken so many times over the years since you left—by guys who seemed interested but weren't really, by relationships that went nowhere, by people who left when things got complicated. If you break my heart, if you decide this isn't what you want or isn't what you thought it would be—" Her voice cracked slightly. "I couldn't take it. Not from you. You're one of my best friends. This isn't some passing thing for me. I've had feelings for you since senior year in high school. I thought they'd gone away, but they never really did."

Chase stood motionless, absorbing the magnitude of what she'd just revealed. She'd carried feelings for him for twelve years.

"Say something."

Chase reached for her hand again, and she let him take it. He raised their joined hands to his lips and pressed a kiss against her knuckles, feeling her sharp intake of breath at the contact.

"I would never intentionally hurt you, Hallie." He lowered their hands but kept holding on. "We're both adults now. I'm not the same young and dumb kid I was in high school. I think that whatever this is between us is real. I feel it. I'm sure you feel it too." He paused to make sure she was listening. "I'd like to get to know you better. I think what we have is special."

Hallie's eyes searched his face, looking for something—certainty, maybe, or proof that he meant what he said.

"I'm scared," she admitted.

"I know." Chase started walking again, still holding her hand, guiding them back toward his parents' house. "But I'm here. I'm not going anywhere."

They walked in silence, hands clasped, navigating the familiar streets that led back to his parents' home. Christmas lights glowed in the distance, marking houses where families gathered and life continued on its ordinary-extraordinary path. The cold deepened, making Chase grateful for the warmth of movement and Hallie's presence beside him.

As they approached his parents' driveway, Chase saw the living room lights still blazing and could imagine his father snoring softly in his recliner while his mother watched whatever movie marathon she'd found. Normal, comfortable, home.

They climbed the porch steps together, and Chase paused with his hand on the doorknob. Hallie stood beside him, her face tilted up toward his, waiting.

"Let's just go inside," Chase said. "Have some dessert, watch movies with my parents, and enjoy the rest of the evening. No pressure. No expectations. Just you and me spending time together."

Hallie's smile was small but genuine.

Chase opened the door, releasing her hand to let her enter first. But as he followed her into the warmth, watching her greet his mother and settle onto the couch, he recognized with startling clarity what he felt.

This wasn't just falling. This was love—real, complicated, terrifying love. And he had absolutely no idea what to do about it except keep showing up and hope that would be enough.

Chapter 20

Chase knocked on Hallie's apartment door. Cold air stung his cheeks, and he tucked his hands into his jacket pockets while he waited.

The door swung open, and Hallie appeared, her smile immediate and genuine. "Hey. Give me just one second."

She stepped back, leaving the door ajar while she grabbed her heavy coat from the hook near the entrance. Chase caught a glimpse of her apartment—warm light spilling from lamps, a throw blanket draped over the arm of her couch, a mug sitting on the coffee table. The space looked lived-in and comfortable, entirely Hallie.

She pulled her coat on, shrugging it up over her shoulders before zipping it closed. Chase stepped back to give her room to lock the door behind them.

They descended the metal staircase together and walked through the alley that ran between their stores until they emerged onto the sidewalk.

Hollyberry Lane stretched before them, the shops on either side already closed for the evening but their windows glowing with Christmas displays. Holly & Hearth Furniture had arranged a cozy living room scene complete with a leather sofa positioned before a faux fireplace, while Mountain Memories Crafts showcased handmade ornaments hanging at varying heights like a forest of crystallized wishes. The Reindeer Rack's window featured a mannequin dressed in winter hiking gear, posed as if mid-stride on a mountain trail.

They walked north, side by side, following the sidewalk toward the intersection where Hollyberry Lane connected with Mistletoe Lane. Chase matched his pace to Hallie's, their shoulders occasionally brushing as they navigated around other pedestrians heading in the same direction.

"I can't believe it's already time for the tree lighting," Hallie said, her breath clouding white in the cold air. "This year has flown by."

"It really has. I can't believe we may have snow by morning."

As they drew closer, Chase could make out the massive Fraser fir rising from the center of the square, standing at least twenty feet tall. Even unlit, it commanded attention—perfectly symmetrical, dense with branches, positioned directly in front of the Victorian gazebo like a queen before her throne. The square itself teemed with people, thousands of them bundled in winter coats and scarves.

Mistletoe Lane had been closed off to vehicle traffic, transforming the road that circled the square into an extension of the celebration space. People spilled across the pavement, clustering in groups or weaving through the crowd in search of friends and family. The businesses surrounding the square glowed from within—the Sugarplum Bakery, Mistletoe Mercantile, Once Upon a Time Bookshop, and all the others forming a ring of light and warmth around the central gathering place.

Chase spotted three large white tents set up near the gazebo, their peaks illuminated by strings of lights. The scent of coffee and chocolate drifted on the air, mixing with the sharp bite of winter and the evergreen perfume of the massive tree.

"I'm not sure if you remember or not, but the Sugarplum Bakery always provides snacks and hot beverages for this event," Hallie explained, noticing his gaze toward the tents. "Claire Whitfield, the new owner of the bakery, and her staff are carrying on the tradition her grandmother started. I ran into Clair the other day, and she said they'll serve free coffee, hot chocolate, and decorated cookies during the tree lighting."

"That's generous."

"That's Mistletoe Falls." Hallie's smile held affection for the town and its people. "Everyone contributes what they can. Gabe Mills from the Christmas tree farm donated the tree again this year, and volunteers decorated the entire square. It takes the whole community to create this."

They worked their way through the crowd, excusing themselves as they squeezed between groups of chattering teenagers and families with small children perched on parents' shoulders. The energy was infectious—anticipation mixed with joy, the collective excitement of a community gathering to mark something meaningful.

"Do you see your parents?" Hallie asked, standing on her toes to scan the crowd.

"Not yet. Mom said they'd be near the tree where the accessibility area is set up." Chase used his height advantage to survey the mass of people. "There—I think I see them."

He placed a hand on Hallie's lower back, gently guiding her through the crowd in the direction he'd spotted his parents.

They found Mark and Liz near the front of the crowd in a roped-off section that provided space for wheelchairs and those with mobility challenges. Mark stood beside his wife's chair, one hand resting on her shoulder, both of them smiling as Chase and Hallie approached.

"There you are!" Liz's face lit up. "We were worried you'd gotten lost in this madness."

"Just took a while to navigate through everyone." Chase took up a position beside his mother while Hallie moved to stand next to him. The four of them formed a compact unit at the edge of the accessibility area, close enough to see the tree clearly.

"This turnout is incredible," Mark said, surveying the crowd. "Has to be the biggest one yet."

"Mayor Hayes will be thrilled." Liz said as she adjusted her scarf against the cold. "He's been promoting this event for months."

Music began to play through speakers mounted around the square—instrumental Christmas carols that created a soundtrack for the gathering. Near the gazebo steps, a group of elementary school children assembled in neat rows, their teacher directing them into position. They wore matching red scarves and looked both excited and nervous in the way children do when performing for a crowd.

The first notes of "Jingle Bells" filled the air as the children began to sing, their youthful voices carrying across the square with enthusiastic volume. The crowd quieted to listen, parents and grandparents straining to spot their own children among the rows of small singers.

Chase felt Hallie lean slightly closer beside him, and he glanced down to find her watching the children with an expression of pure delight. She caught his gaze and grinned, mouthing "adorable" while gesturing toward the performers.

He nodded in agreement, but his attention was on Hallie herself, watching as happiness transformed her features and how the cold had brought color to her cheeks. She was beautiful, yes, but it went deeper than physical appearance. She was beautiful in the way she engaged with the world, in her capacity for finding wonder in simple moments.

The children finished their first song and immediately launched into "Deck the Halls," complete with enthusiastic fa-la-la-las that made several adults in the crowd laugh with affection. They performed three songs in total before their teacher dismissed them with applause and proud smiles, the children scattering into the crowd to find their families.

Mayor Roger Hayes stepped forward then, climbing the gazebo steps to take a position at the microphone. He was a portly man in his late fifties with a gray beard and a booming voice that needed no amplification, though he used the microphone, anyway.

"Welcome, welcome everyone!" His greeting echoed across the square. "What a beautiful evening to celebrate the official start of our Christmas season here in Mistletoe Falls!"

The crowd cheered, the sound rising like a wave before settling back into attentive silence.

"I want to take a moment to thank all the volunteers who came together this past week to decorate this magnificent tree and transform our town square into the winter wonderland you see before you." Mayor Hayes gestured broadly. "Their hard work and dedication make events like this possible."

More applause rippled through the crowd.

"I also want to extend my gratitude to Gabe Mills, owner of Mistletoe Christmas Tree Farm, for once again donating this stunning Fraser fir. Gabe, wherever you are out there, thank you for your generosity!"

Chase spotted a tall man in a plaid jacket raising his hand in acknowledgment, grinning as people around him offered congratulations.

"Tonight represents more than just turning on some lights," the mayor continued, his tone shifting to something more reflective. "It represents our community coming together, year after year, to celebrate what makes Mistletoe Falls special. We're not just a town—we're a family. And like any good family, we show up for each other, we support one another, and we find reasons to celebrate together."

"So as we light this tree tonight, let's remember what this season is truly about—connection, generosity, and the joy that comes from being part of something bigger than ourselves." Mayor Hayes raised his hand, his voice lifting with renewed energy. "Now, who's ready to see this tree light up?"

The crowd roared in approval, children bouncing with excitement and adults calling out affirmations.

"And now," Mayor Hayes announced with a theatrical flourish, "the moment we've all been waiting for. In ten seconds, our magnificent community Christmas tree will officially welcome the holiday season to Mistletoe Falls!"

The crowd erupted into a unified countdown, children's voices tumbling over one another with giddy excitement while the deeper tones of the adults kept the rhythm steady. Anticipation shimmered in the snowy air like static before a storm.

"Ten! Nine! Eight!"

"Seven! Six! Five!"

"Four! Three! Two!"

"One!"

The massive tree exploded into light. Thousands of bulbs illuminated simultaneously, transforming the Fraser fir into a beacon of warmth and celebration. White lights wound through every branch, creating layers of brilliance that made the tree look like it was carved from stars. A large golden star topped the tree, casting its own glow across the uppermost branches.

The crowd gasped and then erupted into cheers, a collective sound of wonder and delight. Children pointed and exclaimed, adults hugged each other, and cameras appeared throughout the crowd to capture the moment.

Chase watched Hallie's reaction—the small intake of breath, the way she swayed slightly with emotion. Without thinking, he slipped his arm around her waist and pulled her closer to his side. She came willingly, naturally, leaning into him as they both gazed up at the illuminated tree.

Her body fit perfectly against his, the top of her head just reaching his shoulder. She was warm and solid and real, and having her this close felt like the most natural thing in the world. Chase rested his chin lightly against her hair, breathing in the faint scent of her shampoo.

"It's beautiful," Hallie said softly, her words meant just for him.

"Yeah," Chase agreed, though he was thinking about her. "Really beautiful."

They stayed like that while the crowd slowly began to disperse, people drifting away from the concentrated mass near the tree to explore the square or visit the coffee tents or simply continue celebrating in smaller groups. The moment felt suspended, perfect in its simplicity—just the two of them surrounded by light and joy and community.

Eventually, Liz's voice broke through. "That was lovely. I also enjoy the tree-lighting ceremony."

"Every year, it's just as magical as the last," Mark said as he looked at his wife with obvious affection. "Would you like to walk around the square a bit? See the window displays up close?"

"I'd love that." Liz's eyes brightened at the prospect. "Hallie, Chase, want to join us?"

Chase reluctantly released Hallie, stepping back to give her space. She glanced up at him, her cheeks flushed and her eyes bright, before turning to answer Liz.

"Of course. I love seeing what the other businesses do with their displays this time of year."

They set off as a group, Mark pushing Liz's wheelchair through the thinning crowd while Chase and Hallie followed a few paces behind. They crossed Mistletoe Lane to the sidewalk that circled the square in front of the businesses, and they moved slowly, pausing at each window to admire the creativity on display.

The Sugarplum Bakery had created an elaborate gingerbread village, complete with miniature houses, shops, and even a tiny replica of the town square's gazebo. Sugar-work trees and candy cane street-lamps completed the scene, all arranged on artificial snow that glittered under strategic lighting. This year they even had a gorgeous Christmas tree in their dining area, all decorated heavily with lights and vintage ornaments.

"Claire did a beautiful job. I'm so glad she moved back to town," Liz said, her nose nearly pressed to the glass. "Look at the detail on those little buildings."

"Is that supposed to be the bakery itself?" Hallie pointed to one structure that did indeed bear a resemblance to the actual building, complete with a miniature hunter green door.

"I think it is." Liz laughed with delight. "How charming."

They moved to the next window—Mistletoe Mercantile's display of vintage Christmas toys arranged as if Santa's workshop had been transported to the mountains. Old-fashioned dolls, wooden trains, tin soldiers, and hand-carved animals created a nostalgic scene that made several passersby stop and point out toys they remembered from their own childhoods.

At the Once Upon a Time Bookshop, Emma Sullivan had created a literary winter wonderland. Classic Christmas stories stood open on display stands, their pages fanned to reveal illustrations, while artificial snow drifted across stacks of books arranged to look like an alpine village. A small Christmas tree decorated entirely with paper ornaments—each one cut from old book pages and featuring literary quotes—provided the centerpiece.

"Oh, I love this," Hallie breathed, clearly enchanted. "Look at those ornaments."

"Emma always puts so much thought into her displays." Liz leaned forward in her chair, reading one of the visible quotes. "That's from 'A Christmas Carol'—'I will honor Christmas in my heart, and try to keep it all the year.'"

As they moved from window to window, Hallie naturally gravitated toward Liz, eventually taking over pushing the wheelchair so the two women could discuss each display in detail. They moved at their own pace, pausing longer at windows that particularly caught their interest, exclaiming over details and comparing this year's displays to previous years.

Chase and his father followed at a more leisurely pace, content to let the women set the tempo. Mark walked with his hands in his pockets, his attention divided between watching his wife and observing the passing scene.

"Hallie seems happy," Mark said quietly.

"She does," Chase agreed.

"And you?" His father glanced at him. "Are you happy, son?"

Chase considered how to answer, what his father was really asking beneath the surface inquiry.

"I am," he said finally. "Working at the toy store, being home, being close to you and Mom again—it all feels right."

"Planning to stay then?" Mark kept his tone casual, but Chase heard the hope underneath. "Or are you still looking at other options?"

"Before I came back to Mistletoe Falls, I'd put in some applications." Chase said as he watched Hallie and his mother pause at the Holly Belle Boutique window, their animated conversation carrying back to him in fragments. "I sent out feelers to some Marine buddies who'd transitioned into civilian jobs."

"But?"

Chase shrugged. "Since I've been home, I haven't thought much about those applications. Haven't checked job boards or reached out to contacts. I'm just living in the moment, building a life here."

Mark nodded slowly, processing. "And is Hallie part of that life?"

There it was—the real question his father had been circling. Chase appreciated the directness even as it made him consider carefully before responding.

"I want her to be. We're spending more time together. Getting to know each other as adults rather than just childhood friends."

"I've noticed." Mark's voice held warmth, not judgment. "Your mother and I both have. Hallie seems different around you—lighter, maybe. Happy in a way we haven't seen in a while."

"I have feelings for her dad," Chase admitted. Saying it out loud to his father made it more real, more concrete. "I'm not entirely sure when it happened or how, but it's there."

"Feelings," Mark repeated, testing the word. "That's a good start."

They walked a few more paces in silence, watching Liz and Hallie move to the next window. The Heritage House Antiques display featured vintage Christmas decorations arranged by decade, creating a visual timeline of holiday celebrations from the 1920s through the present.

"Can I give you some advice?" Mark asked. "Father to son?"

"Always."

Mark stopped walking, turning to face Chase directly. His expression was serious but kind, the look of a man who'd lived long enough to learn hard lessons and wanted to spare his son the same pain.

"Hallie is a good woman with a kind and generous heart," he said. "I've watched her grow up, seen how she handles loss and loneliness with grace. Your mother and I have always thought you and Hallie made a good match—even back when you were teenagers, though you were too young and foolish to see it then."

Chase smiled ruefully. "I was definitely foolish."

"We all are at that age." Mark placed a hand on his son's shoulder. "But here's what you need to understand. Hallie is a lot like your mother in many ways. They both love with their whole hearts. They're giving, kind women who think deeply and work hard. When they commit to something or someone, they commit fully."

Chase listened, absorbing every word.

"You and I, son, we're alike too. Both of us have military backgrounds—yours much more extensive than mine, but the same foundation. We're trained to be strong, to think independently, to make quick decisions and stick with them. That's not a bad thing, but it can create challenges in relationships."

"What kind of challenges?"

"Women like your mother and Hallie need room to grow and be independent, even while they're part of a partnership." Mark's voice held conviction born from experience. "They need to know their thoughts and feelings matter, that decisions are made together, that they're valued."

"Your mother taught me this early in our marriage," Mark continued. "I'd come home and make decisions about our life—where we'd live, how we'd spend money, what commitments we'd make—without consulting her. I thought I was being decisive, taking care of things. But what I was actually doing was making her feel like her voice didn't matter."

"What changed?"

"She called me on it. Told me she wasn't interested in being married to someone who saw her as a supporting character in his story rather than a partner with equal say." Mark smiled at the memory. "Best conversation we ever had, even though it was uncomfortable at the time. Changed everything between us."

"So what's the advice?" Chase asked, though he suspected he already knew.

"Be gentle with Hallie. Put her needs and desires before your own, not because you're weak but because that's what love requires. Listen more than you talk. Ask questions rather than make assumptions. Give her space to figure out what she wants without pressuring her to move at your pace." Mark squeezed Chase's shoulder once before releasing it. "And most importantly, be patient. Hallie's been hurt multiple times in the past... more than her fair share, really. She may need time to trust that you'll actually stay, that you won't disappear when things get difficult."

The words settled heavily in Chase's chest, a weight that felt like responsibility and promise combined. His father was right—Hallie needed patience, needed gentleness, and needed to know beyond doubt he was committed for the long haul.

"Thanks, Dad."

"Anytime, son." Mark resumed walking, and Chase fell into step beside him. "That's what fathers are for—sharing wisdom gained through their own mistakes."

They caught up to Liz and Hallie at the Sugar & Spice Candy Shop, where the window featured an elaborate candy landscape complete with a chocolate river, gummy bear mountains, and candy cane forests.

"This is dangerous," Hallie said as they approached. "Looking at all this candy is making me crave something sweet."

They completed their circuit of the square, pausing at a few more windows before Liz declared herself tired and ready to head home. The evening had grown colder; the temperature dropping as night deepened, and even the warmth from the crowd and surrounding businesses couldn't fully combat the chill.

"We parked on Cranberry Court," Mark said, orienting himself toward the street where Town Hall and the municipal building stood. "You two heading back to Hollyberry Lane?"

"Yeah." Chase glanced at Hallie, who nodded confirmation.

They said their goodnights, Mark reminding Chase they had a large shipment coming in around nine on Monday morning. Then the older couple headed off through the dispersing crowd.

Chase and Hallie turned south, retracing their earlier path toward Hollyberry Lane. The crowd had thinned considerably. A few dedicated souls remained in the square, standing near the illuminated tree to take photos or simply soak in the atmosphere.

"Did you enjoy tonight?" Hallie asked as they walked.

"I did. The tree lighting was beautiful, and spending time with you and my parents—" He paused, searching for adequate words. "It felt good."

"I'm glad." Hallie smiled up at him. "Are you still planning to help me tomorrow? With the toy delivery to the Community Center?"

"Absolutely. What time do you need me?"

"Around noon? That gives me the morning to finish organizing everything, and we should be able to load up and make the delivery by mid-afternoon."

"I'll be there."

They turned onto Hollyberry Lane, leaving the glow of the town square behind. The street was quieter here, the shops dark for the evening, the sidewalk nearly empty of pedestrians.

Chase reached for Hallie's hand, and she gave it willingly. Their gloved fingers intertwined, creating a connection even through layers of winter protection.

His father's words circled through Chase's mind as they walked—*be gentle, be patient, put her needs first, give her time to trust.* Sound advice, wisdom earned through years of marriage to a woman who shared many of Hallie's qualities. Chase wanted to follow that advice and wanted to do this right.

But he also wanted to tell Hallie everything—that he was in love with her, that he couldn't imagine his life without her in it, and that coming home to Mistletoe Falls had led him to the one thing he'd been searching for without knowing he'd lost it.

"You're quiet," Hallie observed. "Everything okay?"

Chase squeezed her hand gently. "I'm fine. Just thinking."

"About?"

"About how right this feels." He raised their joined hands and pressed a kiss to her glove-covered knuckles. "Walking with you, being with you. All of it."

Hallie's expression softened in the streetlight's glow, her eyes reflecting something tender and vulnerable. She didn't respond with words, just squeezed his hand back and kept walking.

They reached the alley that led to their apartments, and Chase guided her between the buildings. At the base of her stairs, they paused.

"Tomorrow at one," Hallie confirmed.

"I'll be there."

She stood on her toes and pressed a kiss to his cheek, lingering just long enough to make Chase's heart rate spike. Then she released his hand and climbed her stairs, calling goodnight over her shoulder.

Chase watched until she safely entered her apartment before climbing his own stairs. Inside, he shed his coat and gloves; the apartment's warmth was a welcome relief from the cold. But even as he moved through the familiar space, his mind remained occupied with the evening's moments—Hallie leaning into him during the tree lighting, his father's advice delivered with the weight of experience, and the simple perfection of walking hand-in-hand through the quiet streets.

He thought about how she'd looked tonight—her face illuminated by thousands of Christmas lights, her genuine joy at simple pleasures, the way she'd naturally gravitated toward his mother and taken over pushing her wheelchair so they could enjoy the window displays together. She was extraordinary, this woman who gave so freely while guarding her own heart so carefully.

And he was absolutely, completely in love with her.

Chapter 21

Chase hefted another bulging bag from the bed of his truck, the plastic crinkling as he adjusted his grip. The bag was lighter than it looked, filled with wrapped toys, but awkward to carry. He navigated carefully across the recently plowed parking lot. Five inches of powder had fallen overnight and transformed Mistletoe Falls into a winter postcard.

The community center's double doors stood propped open, warm air spilling out. Inside, a massive Fraser fir dominated the main hall, reaching nearly to the vaulted ceiling. Angel ornaments of every size and material covered its branches—porcelain angels with delicate wings, wooden angels carved by local artisans, fabric angels sewn by the quilting circle, glass angels that caught and reflected light like prisms. The Angel Tree, Hallie had called it, and Chase understood why.

Beneath the tree, a growing mountain of wrapped presents created a colorful display. Red and green paper, silver and gold bows, packages of every size and shape already formed the foundation of what would become a much larger collection.

Hallie followed behind him carrying a bag of her own, her cheeks flushed from exertion and cold. She'd worn jeans and a thick cable-knit sweater in deep burgundy, with a heavy-duty winter puffer vest on, practical clothes for hauling toy donations—her hair was pulled back in a ponytail that swung as she walked.

"That's the last load from my car," she announced, setting the bag down near the tree. "How many more do you have?"

"Six or seven," Chase said as he deposited his bag and turned back toward the doors. "Your car was packed to the ceiling, yet you got it emptied fast."

She grinned, following him back outside to help with the last few bags from his truck.

They worked in companionable silence, making trips back and forth between their vehicles and the tree. The snow muffled sound, creating a hushed quality to the afternoon broken only by their footsteps and the distant laughter of children in the building.

Chase grabbed the final two bags from his truck bed, one in each hand, and carried them inside as Hallie arranged the gifts under the tree with care, ensuring each one was visible and accessible. She picked up a medium-sized box wrapped in blue paper with silver snowflakes and adjusted its position so the gift tag faced outward.

"These tags are important," she explained, noticing his attention. "Each one has a family code and child's name on it. During the week before Christmas, my volunteers will come here and separate everything by family, then deliver them so parents can put them under their own trees on Christmas morning."

Chase examined one tag—a simple white label with "F-12, Billy" written in Hallie's neat handwriting. "F-12?"

"Family twelve. I assign each family a number to maintain their privacy." She continued arranging gifts as she talked. "The system works well because we can track what each family receives without broadcasting their identities to the entire community. Dignity matters as much as generosity."

"How many families are you serving this year?"

"Forty-seven, with a hundred and thirty-two children total." Hallie stepped back to survey the gift arrangement, changed one package, then nodded with satisfaction. "This year's been incredible. Between the donations we've received plus your parents' generous donation from Bells & Whistles, every child will have multiple gifts."

Chase watched her work, noting the methodical care she put into positioning each present. This wasn't just about dumping gifts under a tree—this was about creating something beautiful, about honoring both the givers and the receivers by treating their contributions with respect.

"Why here instead of the storage room at your store?" he asked. "Seems like it would be easier to keep everything in one place."

"It used to be that way." Hallie bent to pick up another bag, pulling out wrapped packages and adding them to the display. "But Operation Christmas Cheer has grown so much over the past few years that I ran out of storage space. The storage room and basement can only hold so much, and I needed room for the food baskets and gift baskets we assemble. So I approached Mayor Hayes about using the Community Center as a collection point for the toy drive."

"Interesting,"

"Mayor Hayes loved the idea, said it would give the community a visual reminder of everyone's generosity and might inspire additional donations." She gestured to the growing pile beneath the tree. "Other people bring gifts here too—families who've bought toys for random children in need but aren't part of the formal program. Those gifts that are brought in just have tags that read 'Boy age 9 or girl age 2' and everything ends up under this tree, all combined into one enormous collection."

"You've really thought this through."

"I've had years of practice. Trial and error teaches you a lot."

The sound of children's voices rose from the far end of the hall, drawing Chase's attention. He straightened, looking past the Angel Tree to where a group of kids were clustered. Several adults moved among them, holding scripts and gesturing as they directed small groups through what appeared to be a rehearsal.

"What's going on over there?" Chase asked.

Hallie followed his gaze. "Oh, that's the Christmas program rehearsal for the Operation Christmas Gala. Every year we host our biggest holiday event here with a children's play, performances by the high school choir and band, a silent auction, dinner, and dancing afterward. The entire community's invited—it's our major fundraiser for the veterans' home."

Chase's interest sharpened. "Fundraiser for the veterans' home?"

"The proceeds from ticket sales and the silent auction go directly to supporting the facility. They use it for improvements, activities for those that live there, medical equipment—whatever the veteran's need most." Hallie's expression softened. "It's always a fun night. You should come."

"I will."

They finished arranging the last of the gifts, creating a display that looked both abundant and organized. The Angel Tree rose majestically above the presents, its angel ornaments seeming to stand guard over the generosity gathered below.

"Hallie!" A child's voice rang out, high and excited. "Hallie, you're here!"

Chase turned to see two kids racing toward them across the polished floor—a boy and a girl who looked to be about ten, both with dark hair and matching grins. They wore jeans and coordinating red sweaters, and they moved with the synchronized energy of twins used to doing everything together.

The girl reached Hallie first, throwing her arms around her waist in an enthusiastic hug. The boy followed a split second later, wrapping his arms around both his sister and Hallie in a group embrace that made Hallie laugh with delight.

"Mitchell! Maya!" She hugged them back, her joy genuine and unrestrained. "I didn't know you'd be here today."

"We're practicing for the play," Maya said, bouncing slightly. "We're elves! We have lines and everything!"

"Very important lines," Mitchell added with the gravity of someone entrusted with a crucial mission.

Hallie disentangled herself from the hug and gestured toward Chase. "Guys, I want you to meet my friend Chase. Chase, these are Sofia's twins—Mitchell and Maya."

"Hi, Chase!" Maya's greeting was immediate and friendly. "Are you Hallie's boyfriend?"

"Uh—"

"Are you helping Miss Hallie with Operation Christmas Cheer?" Mitchell interrupted before Chase could formulate a response. "Mom says it's really important."

"Your mom's right," Chase said. "It is important, and yes, I'm helping."

Both children held papers covered in handwriting—their scripts, Chase realized. Maya waved hers in the air with enthusiasm.

"Will you help us practice our lines?" she asked, looking between Hallie and Chase with hopeful eyes. "We're supposed to practice with grown-ups so we get used to performing for them, and you're grown-ups!"

"Please?" Mitchell added. "We only have a few lines, but they're really important ones."

Hallie glanced at Chase, a question in her expression. "What do you think? Want to help?"

Chase opened his mouth to say he was no actor, that he'd spent twelve years in the Marines not drama class, that there were probably better qualified people to help with play rehearsal. But looking at the twins' eager faces and Hallie's encouraging smile, he nodded instead.

"Sure. Why not?"

Maya squealed with excitement, grabbing Hallie's hand and tugging her toward a quieter corner of the hall. Mitchell took Chase's hand with similar enthusiasm, pulling him along.

They settled in a spot near the windows where afternoon light streamed through, creating a natural stage. Maya handed her script to Hallie while Mitchell gave his to Chase.

"Okay, so you can be Mrs. Claus," Maya informed Hallie with the confidence of a director. "And Chase, you're Santa Claus."

"Of course I am," Chase said as he scanned the lines on the script.

"And we're elves," Mitchell added unnecessarily. "The important ones who help save Christmas."

The scene was simple—Mrs. Claus and Santa discovered that two elves had accidentally mixed up all the toy orders, requiring quick thinking and teamwork to fix the problem before Christmas morning. Maya and Mitchell had three lines each, plus some physical comedy involving pretend toys falling off a conveyor belt.

They ran through it once with everyone reading stiffly from the scripts. Then Hallie suggested they try it again with more expression, and suddenly the quiet corner erupted into animated performance.

Hallie adopted an exaggerated motherly tone for Mrs. Claus, complete with gestures and concerned expressions. Chase attempted his best Santa impression, which mostly consisted of deepening his voice and trying not to laugh at how ridiculous he felt.

Maya delivered her lines with theatrical flair, throwing her hands up in dismay when announcing the mixed-up orders. Mitchell practiced his comedic timing, pretending to trip over imaginary toys with exaggerated stumbles that made everyone laugh.

"No, no, no!" Maya called during their third run-through. "Santa has to sound more jolly. Like ho-ho-ho!"

"Come on," Hallie teased, her eyes dancing with amusement. "Give us your best Santa."

Chase sighed, knowing he was defeated. "Ho-ho-ho," he said flatly.

"That was terrible!" Mitchell declared, but he was grinning. "You sound like a bad Santa."

"I'm a Marine," Chase defended. "We don't do jolly."

"Try again," Maya encouraged. "Think about cookies and Christmas morning and presents!"

Chase tried again, putting more energy into it, and this time both children applauded. They ran through the scene twice more, with everyone committing fully to their roles. Hallie proved surprisingly good at physical comedy, miming catching falling toys with increasingly elaborate gestures. Chase discovered that being ridiculous in front of ten-year-olds was actually kind of fun, especially when it made Hallie laugh so hard she had to pause to catch her breath.

When they finished their final run-through, Mitchell tilted his head to one side, studying Chase and Hallie with the unfiltered curiosity of childhood.

"So are you boyfriend and girlfriend?" he asked.

Hallie looked at Chase, clearly waiting for him to field this question.

"We're—" He struggled to find phrasing for a ten-year-old audience. "We're dating. Sort of. We've been spending time together."

"So yes," Maya concluded with satisfaction. "You are boyfriend and girlfriend." She paused, then asked with the innocence of someone who didn't yet understand the implications of such questions, "Are you getting married? Like our mommy and daddy are married?"

Chase's face went from warm to absolutely burning. He opened his mouth, closed it, tried again, and produced no coherent sounds. Beside him, Hallie pressed her lips together, clearly fighting back laughter at his complete inability to respond.

"Chase and I have only started seeing each other," Hallie said, coming to his rescue with remarkable composure. "It's still very new."

"Well, that means you're gonna get married, right?" Mitchell said this as if it were obvious logic. "That's what people do when they see each other."

"No, Mitchell," Maya corrected with the authority of someone who clearly knew better. "They have to date for three more weeks. Then they get married."

"Three weeks?" Mitchell looked skeptical. "Wow. I'm sure glad I'm not a grown-up."

"It's the rule," Maya insisted.

Chase stood frozen, completely out of his depth. He could plan military operations, manage complex logistics under pressure, lead men through hostile territory—but nothing in his training had prepared him for this particular conversation with two precocious ten-year-olds.

Hallie had abandoned all pretense of composure and was now actively trying not to laugh, one hand pressed to her mouth and her shoulders shaking slightly.

"Cookies and punch!" A woman's voice called. "Everyone, come get your snack!"

"Cookies!" Maya's attention shifted immediately to this more pressing concern. She hugged Hallie quickly, then surprised Chase by hugging him too. "Thanks for helping us practice! Bye!"

"Yeah, thanks!" Mitchell added his own hug to both of them before racing after his sister toward the promised treats.

Chase watched them go, then turned to Hallie with an expression of complete bewilderment. "What just happened?"

Hallie's careful control finally broke, and she laughed—a full, genuine laugh that made her eyes crinkle and her entire face light up. She reached out and placed her hand on his arm.

"Don't worry," she said, her voice still bubbling with amusement. "I won't hold you to the three-week timeline."

Chase looked down at her hand on his arm, then up to her face where laughter still danced in her eyes. He was struck again by how beautiful she was—not just physically, though she was that too, but in the way she moved through the world with such open-hearted delight and generosity.

She'd dropped everything to help two kids practice their lines. Had created a system to deliver Christmas gifts to over a hundred children while protecting their families' dignity. Had turned her own grief into a force for good that touched countless lives.

And she was standing here laughing about marriage timelines with him.

The realization hit him with crystalline clarity: he didn't want just three weeks or any arbitrary timeline. He wanted all the time she'd give him. Wanted mornings and evenings and ordinary moments and extraordinary ones. Wanted to be the person she called when she needed help and the one she laughed with over ridiculous conversations with children.

"Chase?" Hallie's voice broke through his thoughts. "You okay? You've got this weird look on your face."

He realized he'd been staring at her for several seconds without speaking. "I'm good," he said, his voice rougher than intended. "Just thinking."

"About?"

About how he was absolutely going to marry her someday, if she'd have him. About how three weeks or any timeline felt both too short and exactly right. About how terrifying and wonderful it was to recognize love when it was standing right in front of you with her hand on his arm and laughter in her eyes.

"About how glad I am that I came home," he said instead, because that was true and safe and wouldn't send her running for the hills.

Hallie's expression softened, her amusement giving way to something warmer and more vulnerable. "I'm glad you came home too."

Chapter 22

Hallie's phone buzzed against the coffee table, pulling her attention from the spreadsheet that had been blurring before her eyes for the past twenty minutes. She reached for it, grateful for the interruption from budgeting projections that made her head ache.

Chase: *What are your plans today?*

She smiled at the screen, setting down her pen.

Hallie: *Nothing exciting. Just catching up on paperwork.*

Chase: *It's Sunday. Time for you to take a day off.*

Hallie: *Day off? What's that*

Chase: *Wanna go on an adventure?*

Hallie's heart did a small flip at the word. Adventure. When had she last done something spontaneous, something just for fun?

Hallie: *Adventure?*

Chase: *My parents need a Christmas tree. Want to come help me pick one out at the tree farm?*

Hallie: *Yes! I'd love to.*

Chase: *Perfect. Meet me at my truck in thirty minutes. Dress warm—more snow fell last night.*

Hallie looked down at her pajama pants and oversized sweatshirt, then at the clock. Thirty minutes. She could do thirty minutes.

She launched herself off the couch and headed for her bedroom, already mentally cataloging what she'd need. Warm layers, definitely. Her good winter boots. That burgundy scarf Nina had given her last Christmas. Maybe the knit hat with the pompom that made her look ridiculous but kept her ears from freezing.

Twenty-five minutes later, she'd transformed from lazy Sunday Hallie into winter-adventure Hallie—jeans tucked into insulated boots, a thick cream-colored sweater under her heavy coat, the burgundy scarf wrapped snugly around her neck, and yes, the pompom hat because function trumped fashion when temperatures hovered in the low thirties.

She grabbed her gloves and headed downstairs, her boots clanging on the metal steps. Chase's truck sat in the alley behind the buildings, engine already running, exhaust puffing white clouds into the cold air. Through the windshield, she could see him fiddling with the radio.

He looked up as she approached, and his grin was immediate and genuine. He leaned across to push open the passenger door from inside.

"Right on time," he said as she climbed in, bringing cold air with her. "I was expecting at least ten more minutes."

"I'm very efficient when properly motivated." Hallie settled into the seat, pulling the door closed and immediately appreciating the warmth blasting from the vents. "What's the proper motivation, you ask? The promise of Christmas trees and adventure."

"Good to know for future reference." Chase shifted into gear and guided the truck out of the alley. "Fair warning—I've never actually cut down a tree before. My family always bought pre-cut ones. So if this goes badly, I'm blaming you."

"How can cutting down a Christmas tree possibly go badly?"

"I don't know, but I'm sure we'll find out."

They headed north through downtown Mistletoe Falls, passing the town square where the massive Fraser fir from Friday's lighting ceremony still stood in all its illuminated glory. Even in daylight, the tree commanded attention.

Fresh snow blanketed everything—rooftops, sidewalks, tree branches, and parked cars transformed into soft white sculptures. The town looked like it had been dipped in powdered sugar, pristine and perfect in the late morning light.

"I can't believe how much snow fell last night," Hallie said, watching snow-covered buildings slide past her window. "It has to be at least five inches."

"More like seven according to the weatherman. I had to dig my truck out this morning." Chase turned onto the road leading out of town, following signs toward Pinecone Pass. "Worth it though. Everything looks incredible."

They drove through residential neighborhoods where families were outside building snowmen and engaged in snowball battles. Children pulled sleds up small hills, their laughter carrying across the cold air. A group of teenagers worked together on what appeared to be an ambitious snow fort.

"I love this about Mistletoe Falls," Hallie said. "The first good snow and everyone just goes outside to play. No one stays inside wishing they could go somewhere warmer."

"That's because everyone here is slightly crazy." But Chase was smiling as he said it. "In the best possible way."

As they left the town proper, the landscape opened up into rolling hills and forestland. Pinecone Pass wound through the mountains like a ribbon. The road was well-maintained but bordered by pristine snowbanks that sparkled in the sunlight. Ancient evergreens stood sentinel on either side, their branches heavy with snow that occasionally released in small avalanches when wind disturbed the delicate balance.

"So I have to ask," Chase said, glancing at her with barely suppressed amusement. "Did Mitchell and Maya traumatize you yesterday with all that marriage talk?"

Hallie laughed, the sound bright in the truck's warm interior. "Are you kidding? That was the best part of my day. The look on your face—I thought you were going to pass out."

"I wasn't prepared for that level of direct questioning from ten-year-olds." His ears had gone slightly pink. "They're very... thorough."

"They're honest. Kids that age don't have filters yet." Hallie adjusted her scarf, still grinning at the memory. "Plus, they clearly adore you. Maya hugged you goodbye like you were a long-lost uncle."

"They seemed like good kids." Chase slowed as they approached a curve, the truck handling the snowy road with ease. "But I'm never saying 'ho-ho-ho' like that ever again. That was humiliating."

"It was adorable. You were a very grumpy Santa at first."

"Marines aren't supposed to be adorable."

"Too late. You've been classified as adorable. There's no appealing the decision."

They bantered easily as the miles passed; the conversation flowing as naturally as breathing. Chase told her about helping his dad reorganize the toy store's inventory system, creating a digital tracking method that would make reordering more efficient. Hallie shared Nina's latest romantic disaster—a first date that had ended with the guy asking if he could borrow money for the check.

"He didn't," Chase said, horrified.

"He absolutely did. Nina paid for her own meal and left."

"Good for her."

"She's sworn off men until February. She makes this declaration every few months."

A wooden sign appeared on the right: "Mistletoe Christmas Tree Farm - 2 Miles." Then another: "Christmas Magic Ahead - 1 Mile." The anticipation built with each marker, the promise of something special waiting just ahead.

When they rounded the last curve, Hallie gasped. She'd been to the farm countless times over the years, but seeing it transformed by fresh snow took her breath away. The entrance looked like something from a fairy tale—twin stone pillars topped with enormous evergreen arrangements, the hand-carved wooden sign announcing "Mistletoe Christmas Tree Farm - Est. 1924 - Mills Family" in elegant script.

The paved drive curved between towering Fraser firs, their branches so laden with snow they created a tunnel of white beauty. At the traffic circle, the vintage 1952 Ford pickup sat in its permanent spot, decorated for Christmas with wreaths, garland, and lights that looked even more charming against the snowy backdrop.

"This place is incredible," Chase said, taking in the view as they followed the drive toward the main parking area.

"Wait until you see the rest of it." Hallie was already unbuckling her seatbelt, ready to explore. "It just gets better."

The parking lot held a surprising number of vehicles for a Sunday morning—families clearly had the same idea about taking advantage of the perfect snow and selecting Christmas trees. Chase found a spot near the edge, and they climbed out into air that bit with cold but smelled of pine and wood smoke.

The main complex spread before them—the historic red barn with white trim that served as the operations center, and next to it, the North Pole Trading Post with its large windows and welcoming entrance. Smoke curled from the Trading Post's chimney, and through the windows, Hallie could see people gathered inside, probably warming up with hot chocolate.

"Should we check in?" Chase asked, gesturing toward the barn.

"Trading Post first," Hallie said decisively. "I need hot chocolate before we go tree hunting."

They crunched across the snowy parking lot and up the cleared walkway to the Trading Post entrance. The moment they stepped inside, warmth enveloped them along with the mingled scents of pine, cinnamon, and fresh-baked cookies.

The interior was everything the farm's reputation promised—rustic wooden displays showcasing local artisan crafts and Christmas decorations, vintage holiday items creating nostalgic vignettes, and twinkling lights strung throughout the space. A central stone fireplace crackled with an actual fire, surrounded by comfortable seating where several families had claimed spots to warm up and plan their tree selection strategies.

But the real draw was the coffee and hot chocolate station along the back wall, where Claire Whitfield from the Sugarplum Bakery had set up an impressive display of baked goods. Gingerbread cookies decorated to look like Christmas trees, sugar cookies frosted in festive designs, and what appeared to be fresh cinnamon rolls still warm from the oven.

"Oh, this is dangerous," Hallie said, eyeing the cookies. "I'm getting hot chocolate and at least two cookies."

"Make it three," Chase said. "We're going to need energy for tree hunting."

They ordered from a cheerful teenager wearing a red vest that identified her as farm staff, then carried their steaming cups and cookies to a small table near the windows. From here, they had a perfect view of the tree fields stretching across the landscape—neat rows of Fraser firs and Noble firs creating patterns against the snow.

"So here's the thing," Chase said, wrapping his hands around his cup. "I have no idea how to pick a good Christmas tree. What am I looking for?"

"Well, what kind of tree do your parents usually get?"

"Tall. Very tall. And full. My mom likes them to look like they came straight from a Christmas card."

"Then we're looking for a Fraser fir, with good needle retention and a nice symmetrical shape." Hallie bit into her gingerbread cookie, closing her eyes briefly at the perfect blend of spice and molasses. "These are incredible."

"How do you know all this?"

"I've been coming here since I was a kid. My parents brought me every year to pick out our tree. Dad would let me choose, even when I was little and had terrible taste. One year I picked this scraggly thing that was missing branches on one entire side because I felt sorry for it."

Chase smiled. "What did your dad do?"

"Bought it. Took it home and spent an hour arranging it so the bare side faced the wall, then helped me decorate it until you couldn't tell it had ever been anything but perfect." Her throat tightened slightly, but in a good way—the kind of emotion that came from cherishing memories rather than drowning in loss. "He was like that. Never made me feel silly for caring about things."

"He was such a good man; I miss him."

"He was." Hallie took a sip of hot chocolate, letting the warmth chase away the bittersweet ache. "Anyway, I'm somewhat of a Christmas tree expert. You're in good hands."

They finished their treats and headed back outside, stopping at the barn to check in with staff and get directions to the Fraser fir section. A friendly older man in a red vest and warm flannel jacket gave them a map and told them to take their time, have fun, and flag down any staff member if they needed help with cutting or loading.

The walk to the tree fields was like stepping into a winter wonderland. Pathways had been cleared of snow but were still magical, bordered by split-rail fencing decorated with evergreen garland and red bows. Other families moved through the fields in various directions, their voices carrying across the crisp air as children pointed excitedly at potential trees and parents debated heights and fullness.

The Fraser fir section sprawled across forty acres of gently rolling land. Wooden stakes marked the most exceptional specimens, and small signs showed height ranges and pricing.

"Okay," Chase said, surveying the acres of options before them. "Where do we start?"

"We start by looking for the eight-to ten-foot section, then we narrow it down from there." Hallie started walking down a row, her practiced eye scanning trees. "Your parents' house has high ceilings."

"Probably ten feet in the living room."

"Then we want something in the nine-foot range to leave room for the tree topper and to keep it from scraping the ceiling." She stopped at a full specimen, walking around it to check for bare spots or irregular growth. "This one's nice, but the top is a little crooked."

They moved methodically through the section, Hallie pointing out qualities to look for—good needle density, even branch distribution, a strong central trunk, fresh green color with no browning. Chase proved to be a quick study, soon spotting potential candidates on his own and calling her over for evaluation.

"What about this one?" He stood beside a nine-foot Fraser that did indeed look like it belonged on a Christmas card—perfectly symmetrical, lush branches at ideal intervals, and that classic triangular silhouette that screamed "ideal Christmas tree."

Hallie circled it slowly, examining from every angle. The tree was gorgeous. Not a bare spot to be found, no weird gaps or scraggly growth. The needles were deep green and healthy; the trunk straight and strong.

"It's perfect," she announced. "Your mom is going to love it."

"Really? We found it that fast?"

"When you know what you're looking for, it doesn't take long." Hallie grinned at his surprised expression.

Chase pulled out his phone and took several photos from different angles. "Mom's going to want to see what we picked before I cut it down. She's very particular about her Christmas trees."

While he texted the photos to his mother, Hallie studied the surrounding landscape. Fresh snow covered everything in soft contours, untouched except for the pathways and the footprints of other tree hunters. The sun had climbed higher, making the snow sparkle as if someone had scattered diamonds across the fields. In the distance, she could see the horse-drawn wagon making its rounds and hear the faint sound of children's laughter carrying on the cold air.

This place held so many memories—good ones that she'd tucked away. Coming here with Chase, creating new memories, felt like reclaiming part of herself she'd thought was gone forever.

"Mom says it's perfect," Chase announced, pocketing his phone. "She also said, and I quote, 'That Hallie has excellent taste, and you should listen to everything she says.'"

"Your mother is a wise woman."

"She also said we should get trees for our apartments while we're here." He looked at her with a question in his eyes. "What do you think?"

"Sounds good."

A staff member appeared with a bow saw and brief instructions about cutting technique—low and straight, watching for the tree to tip, having someone ready to catch it. Chase accepted the saw with the same confidence he applied to any new task, and Hallie stepped back to give him room to work.

He knelt in the snow beside the tree, positioning the saw against the trunk about six inches from the ground. The first strokes were tentative as he found his rhythm, then settled into steady back-and-forth motions that sent sawdust scattering onto pristine snow.

Hallie watched him work, admiring the focused competence he brought to even simple tasks. His flannel coat stretched across his shoulders with each motion, his breath creating small clouds in the cold air, and there was something attractive about watching him do manual labor.

The tree began to creak, signaling its imminent fall. Chase stopped sawing and stood, positioning himself to guide the tree's descent. It tipped slowly, gracefully, landing with a soft whoosh in the snow.

"Success!" Chase announced, grinning with satisfaction. "I didn't kill us or destroy the tree."

"Very impressive for your first time. Your mom and dad are going to be thrilled."

"One down, two to go." Chase brushed snow off his jacket. "Ready to find yours?"

They flagged down another staff member, who promised to tag Chase's parents' tree for pickup, then headed back toward the fields.

But as they walked, Hallie noticed untouched snow between some rows—perfect pristine powder that practically begged for mischief.

An idea formed. A terrible, wonderful, absolutely necessary idea.

She slowed her pace, letting Chase move a few steps ahead while she casually bent down and scooped up a handful of snow. The powder packed beautifully, forming a solid projectile that fit perfectly in her gloved hand.

Chase was completely oblivious, studying the map the staff member had given them and muttering something about where the smaller Fraser firs were located.

Hallie took aim, pulled her arm back, and let the snowball fly.

It hit him square in the back of the head with a satisfying splat, exploding in a shower of white powder that dusted his dark hair and shoulders.

Chase slowly turned around, with snow sliding down his neck and an expression of complete shock on his face.

"Did you really just do that?"

"I have no idea what you're talking about." Hallie tried to keep a straight face and failed spectacularly. "Snow must have fallen from a tree branch."

"There are no trees directly above me."

"Wind is mysterious."

Chase wiped snow from his neck, his eyes narrowing with an expression that made Hallie's heart skip. Not anger—something far more dangerous. Playful intent.

"You know," he said slowly, bending down to scoop his own handful of snow, "I seem to remember you starting these fights when we were teenagers too."

"I have no memory of that." Hallie was already backing up, grinning. "I was a perfect angel as a teenager."

"You were trouble then and you're trouble now."

He formed his snowball with quick efficiency, and Hallie knew she was in for it. She turned and ran, her boots crunching through the snow as she darted between rows of trees, laughter bubbling up from her chest.

Chase's snowball whizzed past her left ear, missing by inches.

"Your aim is terrible!" she called over her shoulder.

"I'm just warming up!"

Hallie ducked behind a Fraser fir quickly, packing another snowball. She waited until she heard his footsteps crunching closer, then popped out from behind the tree and fired. This one caught him in the shoulder, another perfect hit.

"Two for two!" she crowed. "I'm the reigning champion!"

"The battle's not over yet, Dawson!"

What followed was pure mischief—the best kind of adult mischief. They chased each other through rows of Christmas trees, snow flying in both directions. Chase had better arm strength, but Hallie was faster and more nimble, darting around trees and changing directions with the agility of an athlete.

She nailed him in the back. He got her in the leg. She managed a spectacular shot that hit him in the chest. He retaliated with one that exploded against the tree trunk right next to her head, showering her with powder.

Other families working their way through the farm stopped to watch, kids pointing and giggling at the two adults engaged in full-scale snowball warfare. A little girl tugged on her father's jacket and asked if they could have a snowball fight too, and soon multiple battles erupted.

Hallie packed another snowball while running, not looking where she was going, completely focused on Chase's location several feet behind her. Which meant she didn't see the slight depression in the snow, the place where the ground dipped just enough to catch her boot at the wrong angle.

She stumbled, her momentum carrying her forward into a full fall that would have been embarrassing if Chase hadn't lunged to catch her. His arms wrapped around her waist from behind, steadying her, but their combined momentum was too much. They both went down in a tumble of limbs and laughter, landing in a snowbank with Hallie sprawled on top of Chase.

For a moment, they just lay there, breathing hard and laughing. Snow covered both of them from head to toe, cold seeping through jackets and jeans, but neither moved. Hallie was acutely aware of Chase beneath her—solid and warm and very much not moving to dislodge her.

"I think that's a draw," Chase said, his voice slightly breathless. "We both fell."

"No way." Hallie said as she turned over and propped herself up on her elbows, looking down at him. His hair was a mess, sticking up at odd angles from the combination of snow and their fall. His cheeks were flushed from the cold and exertion. "I got you at least twice as many times as you got me."

"That's not how snowball fights work. It's not about quantity; it's about quality."

"Says the guy who's currently on the bottom of this pile."

"That's a tactical position. I can push you off anytime I want."

"So why haven't you?"

Chase's expression changed, the laughter fading into something more serious, more intense. "Maybe I don't want to."

Hallie's heart hammered against her ribs. She could see snow crystals caught in his eyelashes and the faint scar on his chin from a childhood mishap.

She thought about being careful. About protecting her heart. And about all the reasons she'd been holding back from this exact moment since Chase had returned to Mistletoe Falls.

And then she stopped thinking entirely.

Hallie leaned down and kissed him. It was brief—a gentle press of cold lips against cold lips that sent warmth cascading through her entire body despite the snow and the temperature. His mouth was soft and surprised beneath hers, and for one perfect heartbeat, the entire world narrowed to just this—just them, just now.

She pulled back, grinning even as her heart threatened to pound right out of her chest. "I won."

Before he could respond, Hallie pushed herself up and off him, climbing to her feet and brushing snow from her jeans.

Chase remained on the ground, staring up at the sky with an expression of complete bewilderment. Snow covered him from shoulders to boots, and the look on his face was somewhere between stunned and delighted—like someone had just told him he'd won the lottery but he needed a minute to process the information.

Hallie glanced back at him as she started to walk away, still lying there like a snow angel who'd forgotten how to move. His grin widened.

"Well, come on, soldier," she called, turning to walk back toward the main pathways. "We still have work to do. Those trees aren't going to pick themselves."

Chase sat up slowly, like someone waking from a dream, and looked at her with an expression that made her stomach flip.

But he was smiling—that slow, genuine smile that transformed his entire face and made her knees weak. He pushed himself to his feet, brushing snow off his jacket but not taking his eyes off her.

"Hallie—"

"Trees," she interrupted, her voice too bright, too cheerful, covering the terror and exhilaration fighting for dominance in her chest. "We need trees. Your apartment, my apartment, remember?"

He studied her for a long moment, and she knew he wasn't fooled by her deflection. But he nodded, falling into step beside her as they headed back toward the tree fields.

"For the record," he said, "I'm pretty sure that kiss means I won the snowball fight."

"That's not how it works."

"I'm making new rules."

"You can't just make new rules."

"Sure, I can. I just did."

They bickered all the way back to the tree sections, holding hands.

Hallie knew one thing with absolute certainty: she'd meant what she'd said.

She'd won.

Chapter 23

Hallie tugged at the hem of Liz's oversized sweatshirt, which hung nearly to her knees over Mark's borrowed sweatpants that she'd had to roll up three times at the ankles. The outfit was absolutely ridiculous—a fashion disaster of epic proportions—but at least she was warm and dry. Her own clothes tumbled in the dryer down the hall, the rhythmic thumping a reminder of just how thoroughly soaked she and Chase had gotten during their snowball battle.

The Christmas tree stood in its place of honor before the Montgomery living room's front window, its branches still settling into their natural positions after being freed from netting. The Fraser fir was even more impressive inside than it had been in the snowy fields—a solid nine feet of perfectly symmetrical evergreen beauty that would look spectacular once decorated.

Chase emerged from the hallway wearing his father's navy sweatpants and a gray Mistletoe Falls High School sweatshirt. His hair was still damp from toweling off, sticking up at odd angles that made him look younger.

"Well," Liz said from her position near the tree, her eyes dancing with barely suppressed amusement as she surveyed their borrowed attire. "You two look absolutely adorable. Very coordinated."

"We look like we raided a thrift store," Chase said, but he was grinning.

"I think the word you're looking for is 'comfortable,'" Mark added from his spot on the couch, where he'd been organizing boxes of ornaments. "Though I have to say, those sweatpants look better on you than they ever did on me, Hallie."

Liz wheeled closer to examine the tree, running her hand along a branch to test its sturdiness. "It really is perfect. You two did an excellent job. Now I just need to know—" She turned to look at them with exaggerated innocence. "—how exactly did you end up soaking wet at a Christmas tree farm?"

Hallie felt heat creep into her cheeks. She glanced at Chase, who was suddenly very interested in straightening ornament boxes.

"There was a minor incident," Hallie said carefully.

"A minor incident," Liz repeated, clearly not buying it for a second.

"With snowballs," Chase added.

"Multiple snowballs, actually," Hallie clarified. "It's possible there was a minor snowball fight."

"Minor?" Chase turned to her with mock indignation. "You started a full-scale war in the middle of the tree fields."

"I did not start anything. I merely threw one innocent snowball."

"At the back of my head!"

"I was testing your reflexes. You failed, by the way."

Mark laughed, a deep rumbling sound that filled the room. "Let me guess—Hallie initiated combat, and you retaliated?"

"Extensively," Chase confirmed. "Though she maintains she won."

"Because I did win," Hallie said. "Definitively."

"We fell into a snowbank together. That's a draw at best."

"You were at the bottom. I was on top. That's a victory."

Liz was laughing now too, her shoulders shaking with delight. "This sounds like the snowball fights you two used to have when you were kids. Except back then, you'd come home covered in snow and mud, tracking it all through my kitchen."

"I never tracked mud," Chase protested.

"You absolutely tracked mud. Multiple times." Liz smiled at the memory.

"I remember those fights," Mark said. "You two were relentless. One time you were out there for two hours, just absolutely pelting each other with snowballs until you were both so cold you couldn't feel your fingers."

"And you came inside and sat in front of the fireplace drinking hot chocolate until you thawed," Liz added, looking between them with obvious affection. "Some things never change."

"So after this epic snowball battle," Mark said, getting them back on track, "you ended up choosing two more trees, soak and wet. Or were those selected before the warfare commenced?"

"After," Chase said. "Hallie's very particular about tree selection."

"I am not particular. I'm discerning. There's a difference."

"You rejected seven trees before finding one that met your exacting standards."

"They had flaws! One was lopsided, two had bare patches, and the others were too tall for your apartment ceiling."

"See? Particular."

"Discerning!"

"I love listening to you two bicker," Liz said, wheeling toward the ornament boxes. "It's like watching a married couple who've perfected the art of affectionate arguing."

Hallie's breath caught at the word "married," and she saw Chase go still beside her. Neither of them looked at each other, suddenly fascinated by the Christmas tree's lower branches.

If Liz noticed the awkward moment, she graciously ignored it. "All right, let's get this tree decorated before dinner. Mark, can you string the lights while Chase and Hallie start unpacking ornaments?"

They fell into an easy rhythm, Mark carefully wrapping strands of white lights around the tree from top to bottom while Chase and Liz worked on untangling ornament hooks. Hallie opened the first box and gasped with delight.

"Oh, these are beautiful!" She lifted out a delicate glass ball in deep burgundy, hand-painted with gold filigree. "This looks vintage."

"It is," Liz said, her voice warm with memory. "That one belonged to Mark's grandmother. She brought it from Scotland when she immigrated. It's very old."

Hallie turned it carefully to admire the craftsmanship. "It's stunning."

"There are stories behind most of these ornaments," Liz explained. "That one you just picked up, Mark made for me our first Christmas together. We were so broke we couldn't afford decorations, so he spent evenings in his workshop carving ornaments from scrap lumber."

"I made twelve of them that year," Mark said from his position by the tree. "Thought I was being practical. Turned out she cried when I gave them to her."

"They were beautiful," Liz protested. "And meaningful. Much better than store-bought."

Chase lifted out a felt stocking ornament with his name embroidered across the top in childish stitching. "Did I make this?"

"You did. First grade, if I remember correctly. You were so proud of it."

They continued unpacking, each ornament revealing another piece of the Montgomery family history. The glass pickle ornament that had been a gift from a neighbor who'd since passed away. The photo ornaments from various Christmases, showing Chase's progression from baby to teenager. The collection of sports-themed decorations marked milestones—his first soccer goal, making the high school football team, graduating basic training.

Hallie absorbed it all, cataloging each story, feeling honored to be trusted with these memories. This was what family looked like—not perfection, but accumulated moments preserved in glass and wood and felt, each one treasured not for its monetary value but for what it represented.

"Oh my goodness," she breathed, reaching into a box and pulling out a slightly lopsided clay ornament painted in garish colors. "Is this—?"

"The ornament you and Chase made together," Liz finished, smiling. "You were both twelve. We had that craft day when you and your mom and dad came over to make ornaments."

"I remember this," Chase said, moving closer to examine the ornament. "We were supposed to make something Christmas-themed, and we couldn't agree on what to make."

"So we compromised and made something completely bizarre." Hallie traced the outline of what might have been a tree or possibly a deformed snowman—it was hard to tell after thirteen years. "I think this was supposed to be a snowman next to a Christmas tree."

"I maintain it looks exactly like what we intended."

"It looks like a blob attacked another blob."

"It's abstract art."

"It's a disaster."

"It's a masterpiece," Liz declared, taking it from Hallie and hanging it prominently on a front-facing branch. "Every year this goes on the tree, and every year I remember that afternoon. You two sat at the kitchen table for hours making ornaments and arguing about paint colors."

"Hallie wanted everything to be realistic colors," Chase recalled. "I wanted to make a purple Christmas tree."

"Because that makes no sense! Christmas trees are green!"

"Not in my artistic vision."

Mark had finished with the lights and stepped back to admire his work. The tree glowed with warm white bulbs, creating the perfect backdrop for ornaments. "All right, team. Let's get these decorations on this tree."

They worked together, Chase passing ornaments to Mark, who hung them on higher branches, and Liz, who had claimed the lower branches for herself. Hallie joined in picking ornaments at random and adding them to the tree. The process was neither quick nor efficient, but it was fun—full of laughter and storytelling and debates about whether certain ornaments should go on the front or the side.

Hallie relaxed completely, enjoying decorating a Christmas tree with people she loved, creating fresh memories.

"You're doing it wrong," Chase said, reaching past her to adjust an ornament she'd just hung.

"There is no wrong way to hang an ornament."

"This one is unbalanced. See? It's tilting."

Hallie swatted his hand away. "It's fine. You're being particular."

"I thought the word was 'discerning.'"

"That only applies to me."

"That seems like a double standard."

"It's called being right."

Liz and Mark exchanged glances, their expressions amused and knowing. Hallie caught the look and felt her cheeks warm, but she didn't stop bantering with Chase. This was who they were together—playful and easy, challenging each other while somehow moving in perfect synchronization.

The tree gradually transformed from bare branches into a tapestry of memories and colors. Glass balls in jewel tones caught the light, wooden ornaments added rustic charm, and the slightly ridiculous clay creation from their twelve-year-old selves held pride of place where everyone could see it.

When the last ornament was hung, they stood back to admire their work. The tree was magnificent—full and lush and glowing with lights.

"Perfect," Liz declared. "Absolutely perfect."

"We make a good team," Mark said, putting his arm around his wife's shoulders.

"We do," Liz agreed. Then she looked at Hallie and Chase. "All of us."

Hallie felt Chase shift beside her, and she looked up to find him grinning.

"I should make hot chocolate," Liz announced, breaking the spell. "We can't have a tree-decorating party without hot chocolate."

"I'll help," Hallie said immediately.

"Perfect." Liz maneuvered her wheelchair toward the kitchen.

Liz directed her to the cocoa and milk while she gathered mugs from the cabinet, four of them painted with various Christmas scenes.

"The trick to great hot chocolate," Liz said, measuring cocoa into a saucepan, "is to use whole milk and add a pinch of salt. Brings out the chocolate flavor."

Hallie measured milk and added it to the pan, stirring while Liz adjusted the heat.

"I'm glad you came today," Liz said. "Not just to help with the tree, but—" She paused, seeming to choose her words carefully. "I'm glad you're spending time with Chase. He's happy and more settled now. That first week home was rough on him."

Hallie kept stirring, not trusting herself to look at Liz. "He seems to be adjusting well to civilian life."

"He is. But I think you're a big part of that adjustment." Liz added sugar to the mixture, testing the temperature with her finger. "He cares about you, Hallie. I can see it in the way he looks at you."

Heat flooded Hallie's cheeks.

"I know this might be awkward. I'm his mother, and I'm sure the last thing you want is for me to meddle in whatever is or isn't happening between you two. But I need you to know something."

Hallie finally met her eyes, seeing nothing but warmth and affection in Liz's expression.

"You've been like a daughter to me for years now," Liz continued. "Even when Chase was gone, you were here. You showed up after my accident when you didn't have to. You brought meals and helped when I was too proud to ask for help. You made me laugh when I wanted to cry about losing my independence." Her voice thickened slightly. "What I'm trying to say is that I love you, Hallie. Not just because of Chase, but because of who you are."

Tears pricked at Hallie's eyes.

"So whatever happens between you and my son—whether it's friendship or something more—I want you to know you'll always have a place in this family. Always. You understand?"

Hallie nodded, not trusting her voice.

"And just between us girls," Liz added, her tone shifting to something lighter, more conspiratorial, "I've never seen Chase look at anyone the way he looks at you. Not even that girl he dated in high school—what was her name?"

"Vicky," Hallie supplied, surprised she remembered.

"Vicky. Right. He liked her well enough, but there was no spark. With you, there are sparks everywhere. You two light up around each other."

"It's complicated," Hallie said. "We're still figuring things out."

"Of course you are. That's what dating is—figuring things out together." Liz smiled. "Just don't overthink it so much that you miss out on something wonderful. You both deserve wonderful."

Hallie stirred the hot chocolate, watching chocolate and milk blend into rich brown perfection. "I'm scared," she admitted. "Of getting hurt. Of losing him again."

"That's what love is, honey. It's being scared and choosing to try, anyway." Liz reached over and squeezed her hand. "And for what it's worth, I don't think you'll lose him. That boy came home for a lot of reasons, but I think you might be the biggest reason he'll stay for good."

They finished preparing the hot chocolate in companionable silence, Liz adding a dash of vanilla and a sprinkle of cinnamon to each mug while Hallie arranged them on a tray. The scent was divine—rich and sweet and promising comfort.

Before they headed back to the living room, Hallie set down the tray and pulled Liz into a careful hug. Liz's arms came around her immediately, strong and warm and maternal in a way that made Hallie's throat tighten.

"I love you and thank you," Hallie whispered against Liz's shoulder. "For everything. For accepting me, for caring about me, for—" Her voice broke slightly. "For being here when my own mom isn't."

Liz hugged her tighter. "Oh, sweetheart. You don't have to thank me for loving you. That's just what family does."

When they pulled apart, both of them were crying. Liz laughed and wiped at her cheeks with the back of her hand.

"Look at us, getting all emotional over hot chocolate."

"It's very good hot chocolate," Hallie said, her voice still thick. "Worth getting emotional about."

"The best hot chocolate," Liz agreed. She squeezed Hallie's hand once more. "Now let's get these to the men before they come investigating. Mark has absolutely no patience when chocolate is involved."

Chapter 24

Chase balanced the takeout bag in one hand and knocked on Hallie's open office door with the other. Hallie glanced up, surprise washing across her features. Her hazel eyes widened, and a smile broke across her face.

"Chase! What are you doing here?"

He held up the takeout bag like evidence in his defense. "Thought you might not have taken a lunch break yet. Am I right?"

She glanced at her computer screen, then at the clock on the wall, and her expression shifted to sheepish acknowledgment. "It's almost two o'clock."

"That's a yes, then."

"That's definitely a yes. I'm starving. I was just going to run up to my apartment when I finished this project I'm working on and grab an apple or something."

Chase stepped into the small office, closing the door behind him. He set the bag on her desk and began unpacking containers. "Turkey and Swiss panini from the Fireside Diner for you. I got the roast beef and cheddar. And I brought soup—tomato basil, because I remembered you defending soup with concerning intensity during that debate at the wreath-making session."

Hallie laughed, the sound bright and easy. "Soup is the superior comfort food, and I stand by that position." She accepted the container he handed her, opening it to release a cloud of fragrant steam. "This is really thoughtful, Chase. Thank you."

"You're welcome." He settled into the chair across from her desk, unwrapping his own sandwich. The office wasn't large, but sitting here across from Hallie while she smiled at him like he'd just solved all her problems felt comfortable in a way that made him forget about the thoughts that had been circling his mind all morning.

Almost forgot, anyway.

They ate in companionable silence for a few minutes. Hallie made appreciative sounds over her soup, dipping her sandwich into the tomato basil soup. Chase watched her between bites of his own lunch, noting the way her shoulders gradually relaxed, how the tension lines around her eyes softened.

She looked tired but content. Busy but fulfilled. Like someone who knew exactly what she was doing and why it mattered.

The observation stirred something uncomfortable in his chest—not resentment or envy, but a restless wondering that had been growing louder since last night's phone call.

"So what really brings you by?" Hallie asked, setting down her soup spoon and studying him with those observant eyes that seemed to see straight through any pretense he might attempt. "And don't say it's just because you thought I needed lunch. You've got that look."

Chase paused mid-bite. "What look?"

"The one where you're thinking about something heavy and trying to decide whether to talk about it or keep it to yourself." She tilted her head slightly. "You're not quite yourself today. What's wrong?"

Chase set down his sandwich, suddenly less hungry than he'd been a moment ago. "I got a phone call last night. From Sam Webb—one of my Marine buddies."

"Okay. How's he doing?"

"Really well, actually." Chase leaned back in his chair, searching for the right words. "Sam got out about six months before I did. He's in Denver now, working for a private security firm that does international consulting. High-level stuff—protecting executives, coordinating security for major events, training corporate teams. He just bought a house. Three bedrooms, a backyard, the whole deal."

Hallie nodded slowly, listening without interrupting.

"And he's not the only one. I've been in touch with a few guys from my unit since getting out. Connor's doing structural engineering for a firm in Seattle—designing bridges, working on projects that'll last generations. Tyler started a construction company in North Carolina, building custom homes. They've all found careers that seem to fit them perfectly. They know what they're doing with their lives. They have direction and purpose, and they're making good money doing work that matters to them."

"And you're wondering if managing the toy store is enough," Hallie said.

Chase met her eyes. "Yeah. I am."

She didn't rush to reassure him or dismiss his concerns. Instead, she took another sip of soup, considering her response. When she finally spoke, her voice was gentle but direct.

"Why are you questioning whether it's enough? You seem to enjoy the work. Your parents say you're doing a wonderful job. The customers love you. You're good at it."

"I know. And I do enjoy it—more than I expected to, honestly." Chase rubbed the back of his neck, trying to articulate the distinction that had kept him awake until two in the morning. "But there's a difference between enjoying something and knowing it's what you're supposed to be doing. Between being good at something because you're competent, and being good at something because it's your purpose."

Hallie leaned forward slightly, her elbows resting on the desk. "Tell me more about that. What's the difference to you?"

"In the Marines, I had purpose. Every mission had an objective. Every skill I developed served a larger goal. I was building infrastructure that protected people, clearing routes that saved lives, and training others to do the same. I could see the impact of my work, measure it, know that what I did mattered beyond just me. Now I'm here because my parents needed help. Because my mom got hurt, and my dad couldn't manage everything alone. I came home out of duty and love, which are good reasons. But I'm starting to wonder if duty is enough to build a life on."

"So you're not questioning whether you're capable," Hallie said. "You're questioning whether this is your path or just the path circumstances put you on."

He nodded. "I love my parents. I want to help them. But is this my calling, or am I just filling a need because I was available when they needed someone?"

Hallie was quiet for a moment, her fingers tracing the rim of her soup container.

"Can I tell you something?"

"Of course."

"When my dad died and then my mom left, I took over this store out of necessity, not choice. I was twenty-five years old, barely out of college, and suddenly I was running a business I'd never planned to own. I did it because someone had to, because my mom couldn't and didn't want to, because walking away felt like abandoning everything my dad had built. For the first two years, maybe longer, I was just going through the motions. Keeping the doors open, maintaining inventory, and making sure the business survived. I told myself I was honoring my dad's legacy, but really I was just treading water."

"It took me a long time to make this store truly mine," she continued. "To transform it from duty into purpose. I started small—changing the window displays to reflect my aesthetic, expanding the Christmas focus because that's what brought me joy, creating Operation Christmas Cheer because I needed to do something that felt meaningful beyond just selling merchandise. Little by little, I stopped managing my dad's store and started building my vision. But that transformation didn't happen overnight. It took years of showing up, of trying things, of slowly figuring out what mattered to me."

"So you think I need to give it more time."

"I think you've been home less than two months," Hallie said. "You spent twelve years in an environment where every day had structure and clear expectations. You knew your role, your rank, your mission. Now you're expecting yourself to have everything figured out immediately, but that's not how civilian life works—especially when you're also processing everything else. Your mom's injury, your parents are aging, your rebuilding connections with people you left behind, and adjusting to a completely different pace and purpose. That's a lot to navigate."

Chase considered her words, recognizing the truth in them even as part of him resisted the idea of simply waiting for clarity.

"I look at you," he said, "and I see someone who's settled. You know what you're doing and why it matters. You've found your purpose—in this store, in Operation Christmas Cheer, and in serving this community. It's like you've figured out the equation I'm still trying to solve."

Hallie's laugh was soft and slightly self-deprecating. "Chase, I still question whether I'm doing enough, whether I'm making the right choices, whether I should aim for something bigger or different. Just because I look settled doesn't mean I have it all figured out. I've just learned to be okay with not having all the answers."

"But you're not in transition," Chase countered. "You know this is where you're supposed to be."

"Do I?" She tilted her head, considering. "Or have I just decided to be present where I am while I figure out what comes next? Maybe that's the real difference—not having answers versus being at peace with the questions."

He'd been thinking about purpose as a destination, a clear endpoint he needed to reach.

"It's almost like you're feeling like you have to prove yourself to someone," Hallie said, her voice taking on a more direct quality. "Like managing the toy store isn't prestigious enough or important enough compared to what your Marine buddies are doing. Like you need to justify your choices to some invisible measuring stick."

"Maybe. I don't know. It's not that I think the toy store is unimportant. But when Sam talks about his work, there's this excitement in his voice. This sense that he's found exactly what he's supposed to be doing. And I wonder if I'm supposed to have that too, or if I'm settling for something that's just okay instead of great."

"Or maybe," Hallie said, "you're in a season of transition, and that's exactly where you're supposed to be right now. Not settled, uncertain, just present and learning and open to what might come next."

Chase wanted to argue, to push back against the idea that uncertainty could be purposeful. But looking at Hallie across the desk—her eyes warm with understanding, her expression free of judgment—he felt some of the tension in his chest begin to ease.

"I worry I'll disappoint my parents. They needed help, so I came home. But what if this isn't my forever answer? What if I realize in six months or a year that I need to do something different? They'll have restructured their lives around having me here, and then I'll be the person who let them down. Again."

"Again?" Hallie's eyebrows lifted.

"I left twelve years ago and barely looked back," Chase said. "I was so focused on my life and my career as a Marine that I didn't stay connected the way I should have. I missed years in their lives. Missed seeing my mom before her accident. And now I'm here, but what if I'm not here for the right reasons? What if I'm just trying to make up for lost time instead of actually choosing this life?"

Hallie stood from her chair and moved around the desk, settling on the edge so she was closer to him.

"Chase, listen to me. You didn't abandon your parents. You served your country honorably for twelve years, and they are proud of you. You didn't lose touch with them. Your mom told me they got letters every once in a while, phone calls when you could manage them, and a few sporadic visits when you had leave. You weren't perfect, but you weren't absent either."

"I should have been here when she got hurt."

"You came home as soon as you could. You were serving your country and couldn't just walk away to be here after her accident,"

Hallie countered. "You decided not to re-enlist so you could be present for what comes next. That's not failure, Chase. That's love and commitment and showing up. The fact that you're questioning whether this is your long-term path doesn't diminish any of that."

Chase looked up at her, seeing the conviction in her expression. "But what if I decide I need something different?"

"Then you'll have that conversation with your parents when the time comes, and you'll figure it out together. But you don't have to have that conversation today. You don't have to solve your entire future this afternoon. Maybe the question isn't whether the toy store is enough. Maybe the question is whether you're giving yourself permission to be in transition. You're allowed to not have all the answers yet. You're allowed to be figuring it out."

"How did you get so wise?" he asked, managing a small smile.

"Trial and error, mostly. And a lot of mistakes along the way." Hallie smiled back. "Plus, I've had good people in my life who've given me permission to be imperfect. Your parents especially."

Chase nodded, absorbing everything she'd said. The restless anxiety that had been churning in his gut since Sam's call hadn't disappeared, but it had quieted to something more manageable.

"Thanks for listening and not telling me I'm being ridiculous."

"You're not being ridiculous. You're being thoughtful and self-aware, which are actually really attractive qualities."

Chase smiled as her cell phone rang.

Hallie glanced at the screen and grimaced. "It's Bernard Mitchell. I should take this—he's playing Santa for the Letters to Santa Booth tomorrow at the Holiday Bazaar and probably has a few last-minute questions."

She swiped to accept the call, putting it on speaker. "Hi, Bernard. How are you?"

"I'm so sorry, Hallie." Bernard's voice came through rough and congested. "I woke up this morning with the flu. Full-on fever, chills, the whole miserable package. There's no way I can be Santa tomorrow. I can barely get out of bed."

Hallie's expression shifted from hopeful to distressed in the span of a heartbeat. "Oh no. Bernard, I'm so sorry you're sick. Don't even worry about tomorrow—just focus on getting better."

"I feel terrible leaving you in the lurch like this."

"It's not your fault. You can't help being sick. You just rest and take care of yourself, okay?"

"I will. Again, I'm really sorry."

"Don't be. Feel better soon." Hallie ended the call and immediately slumped against the desk, closing her eyes. "This is a disaster."

"What happens if you don't have a Santa?" Chase asked.

"The Letters to Santa Booth is one of our fundraisers for Operation Christmas Cheer. Parents pay five dollars so their children can deliver letters or their wishlists to Santa. Parents pay extra for photos. Last year we raised almost two thousand dollars in one afternoon." She opened her eyes, staring at the ceiling as if divine intervention might appear in the acoustic tiles.

"What about asking someone else in town?" he suggested.

"Everyone who usually helps is already committed to running other booths or volunteering for other events. The Holiday Bazaar is all-hands-on-deck." She drummed her fingers on the desk. "I suppose I could try calling around to neighboring towns, see if anyone knows someone who could fill in, but that's a long shot on such short notice."

"I'll do it."

Hallie's head snapped toward him. "What?"

"I'll be Santa."

She blinked at him as if he'd just offered to sprout wings and fly.

"You need a Santa, and I'm available. How hard can it be? Sit in a chair, listen to kids, say 'ho ho ho' a few times... with enthusiasm. I think I can manage that."

"It's more involved than that," Hallie warned, but he could see hope beginning to replace the panic in her expression. "You have to stay in character. Some of the kids are really young, and they completely believe. You can't break the magic."

"I won't break the magic." Chase grinned.

"And you have to be patient. Sometimes the kids get nervous and need time to warm up. And some of them have very long, very detailed lists."

"I excel in patience. Twelve years in the military, remember? I once spent six hours in the same position waiting for clearance to move forward. I think I can handle long Christmas lists."

Hallie's smile broke through her worry like sun through clouds. "You're seriously willing to do this?"

"I'm seriously willing to do this. On one condition."

Her smile faltered slightly.

"You have to stay in the booth with me... just in case I need a little help."

Hallie laughed. "I think I can manage that since I play Mrs. Claus every year anyhow."

"Perfect. Then it's settled." Chase stood, gathering the empty food containers, stuffing them back in the takeout bag. "I'm your Santa. Just tell me what time to show up and what about the Santa suit."

"The suit's in the basement. We'll need to make sure it fits you, though. Bernard is quite a bit rounder around the middle."

"Are you saying I'm not round enough to be Santa?" Chase put a hand to his chest in mock offense. "I'm wounded."

"I'm saying you might need some strategic padding. But I can work with what we've got. I have pillows. Lots of pillows."

"This is going to be interesting." Chase moved toward the door, then paused, turning back to look at her.

"Hey, Hallie?"

"Yeah?"

"For what it's worth, I meant what I said earlier. About looking at you and seeing someone who's figured things out. You make it look easy, but I'm starting to understand that it's not about having answers. It's about showing up anyway, even when you're uncertain. You do that every single day, and it's one of the things I admire most about you."

Color rose in Hallie's cheeks, and her smile softened into something that made Chase's heart beat faster. "Thanks Chase. That means a lot."

"I'll see you tomorrow, Mrs. Claus." He grinned, letting the moment lighten again. "Think you can handle being married to Santa for an afternoon?"

"I think I can manage," Hallie said, her eyes sparkling with amusement. "Though I reserve the right to correct your 'ho ho ho' technique if it needs work."

"My 'ho ho ho' technique is flawless. I've been practicing."

"You have not."

"How do you know? Maybe I practice in the shower. Maybe I've been preparing for this moment my entire life."

Hallie laughed, the sound bright and unguarded. "Get out of here, Chase. I have work to do, and you're being ridiculous."

"Ridiculous is my specialty." But he was smiling as he opened the door and then paused, looking back at her one more time. At the woman who'd listened without judgment, who'd offered wisdom without pretense, who'd seen his uncertainty and met it with grace.

He walked back to where she stood by the desk and cupped her face gently with one hand and kissed her. Tender and sweet, unhurried and genuine—the kind of kiss that said everything he was still learning how to put into words. Hallie's hand came up to rest against his chest, and she kissed him back with the same warmth that had been growing between them since that snowy afternoon at the tree farm.

When they pulled apart, Chase smiled down at her, his thumb brushing softly along her cheekbone.

"That will never get old," he said.

He traced his thumb along her cheekbone once, then stepped back. "I should let you get back to work."

"Probably," she agreed, but she was still smiling, her cheeks flushed and her eyes bright. "Though I'm not sure how much work I'm going to get done now."

"Sorry about that."

"No, you're not."

"You're right. I'm not. I'll see you tomorrow, Mrs. Claus."

"See you tomorrow, Santa."

Chapter 25

Hallie crouched beside a little girl who couldn't have been more than four years old, her tiny hand clutching a crumpled piece of paper covered in crayon scribbles and what might have been an attempt at spelling "Barbie." Tears streaked down the child's cheeks, and her bottom lip trembled as she stared at the red-suited figure sitting in the ornate chair ten feet away.

"Sweetie, what's your name?" Hallie kept her voice soft and gentle, adjusting the wire-rimmed glasses perched on her nose—part of her Mrs. Claus costume that included a long red velvet dress with white fur trim, a matching cape, and a white wig styled in a neat bun.

"Emma," the little girl whispered, not taking her eyes off Santa.

"That's a beautiful name. I'm Mrs. Claus, and that's my husband, Santa." Hallie gestured toward Chase, who was currently listening with exaggerated interest to a boy explaining something involving dinosaurs and spaceships. "He's very nice. See how he's smiling?"

Emma nodded but didn't move.

The Mistletoe Falls High School gymnasium had been transformed into a bustling holiday marketplace. Vendor booths lined the walls and created aisles throughout the space, each one draped in festive decorations and filled with handmade crafts, baked goods, candles, wooden toys, knitted scarves, and every other conceivable Christmas item. The air smelled of cinnamon rolls from the bakery booth, fresh pine from the wreath station, and the particular warmth that came from hundreds of bodies packed into a space meant for basketball games. Christmas music played through the sound system—currently "Silver Bells"—competing with the general cheerful noise of vendors calling out to shoppers and children exclaiming over treasures they'd discovered.

The Letters to Santa Booth occupied prime real estate near the main entrance, impossible to miss with its elaborate setup. A large wooden throne-style chair sat on a raised platform, draped in red velvet and flanked by two decorated Christmas trees. Garland wrapped around the booth's frame, interwoven with twinkling white lights that cast a warm glow over everything. A professional photographer had set up equipment to one side, ready to capture each child's moment with Santa.

Nina stood at the booth's entrance in a green and red elf costume complete with pointed shoes and a hat with bells, collecting five-dollar donations and directing families toward the line. Sofia, dressed in a matching elf outfit, managed the queue that currently stretched fifteen families deep, keeping children entertained with candy canes and Christmas trivia while they waited.

And there, in the center of it all, sat Chase in full Santa regalia—red suit stuffed with strategic pillow padding, white beard and wig, black boots, and an expression of patient joy that Hallie had been watching transform throughout the day. He'd started the day with a hint of self-consciousness, his "ho ho ho" a little too practiced, his movements slightly stiff. But three hours into the event, he was much more at ease. Now he inhabited the role completely, leaning into the magic with the same commitment he'd probably brought to military missions, and the result was pure enchantment.

"What if Santa doesn't like my letter?" Emma's small voice pulled Hallie's attention back.

"Oh, sweetheart, Santa loves every letter he gets. Each one is special because it comes from a special child like you." Hallie held out her hand. "How about this—I'll walk up there with you? We can give Santa your letter together. Would that help?"

Emma considered this, then nodded and placed her tiny hand in Hallie's much larger one.

They approached the throne together, Emma's grip tightening with each step. The dinosaur-and-spaceship boy had just climbed down from Santa's lap, his face glowing with satisfaction, and his parents were collecting him from the photographer's station where they'd captured the moment.

Chase's eyes met Hallie's over his fake beard, and he winked at her. Then his attention shifted to Emma, and his entire demeanor gentled even further.

"Well, well, well," he said in the deep, jolly voice he'd perfected over the past few hours. "Who do we have here?"

"This is Emma," Hallie said, still holding the little girl's hand. "She has a very important letter for you."

"A letter! Those are my favorite." Chase leaned forward slightly, making himself less imposing. "Emma, would you like to come sit on Santa's lap and tell me what's in your letter?"

Emma looked up at Hallie, seeking reassurance.

"I'll be right here," Hallie promised. "I won't go anywhere."

That seemed to be enough. Emma took three brave steps forward, and Chase carefully lifted her onto his lap while she clutched her letter like a lifeline.

"Now then," Chase said, his voice kind and unhurried. "What would you like for Christmas this year?"

Emma whispered something Hallie couldn't hear.

Chase nodded seriously. "A Barbie with long hair and a purple dress. That's a wonderful choice." He paused, then added, "You know what makes you extra special, Emma?"

The little girl shook her head.

"You were brave enough to come talk to me even though you were scared. That takes real courage, and I admire that courage very much."

Emma's face broke into a smile—tentative at first, then blooming into full radiance. She leaned against Chase's padded chest, suddenly comfortable, and launched into a detailed description of the exact Barbie she wanted, including accessories and the name she planned to give the doll.

Hallie stepped back to let the photographer capture the moment, her chest tight with an emotion she couldn't quite name. Watching Chase with this frightened child, seeing his patience and gentleness, observing how naturally he'd found the exact right words to ease her fear—it did something to her heart that had nothing to do with the Santa costume and everything to do with the man wearing it.

The afternoon continued with a steady stream of children approaching the throne, each one bringing their own personality and wishes. Hallie moved through the booth like a dancer who'd memorized every step, offering candy canes to waiting children, chatting with parents about Operation Christmas Cheer, and stepping in whenever Chase needed support.

She was refilling the candy cane basket from the supply box when she heard a boy's voice ring out with a confidence that suggested he was used to being listened to.

"Santa, I need to ask you some questions."

Hallie turned to see a child of about ten climbing onto Chase's lap with the air of someone conducting an important interview. The boy wore glasses that kept sliding down his nose, and he pushed them back up with one finger before fixing Chase with a serious look.

"Questions are good," Chase said, settling the boy on his lap. "I love questions. What would you like to know?"

"How do you deliver presents to every house in one night? You'd have to travel faster than the speed of light. But nothing can go faster than the speed of light except maybe quantum particles, and you're definitely not a quantum particle."

Hallie bit back a laugh, watching Chase's eyes widen. But he recovered quickly, leaning back in his throne as if settling in for a proper discussion.

"Well now, that's an excellent question, and it shows you've been thinking carefully about the logistics." Chase's voice took on a professorial quality that somehow stayed perfectly in character. "You're absolutely right that regular time wouldn't work. That's why I operate on Christmas magic time, which differs from regular time. It's like when you're having so much fun that hours feel like minutes, except reversed. On Christmas Eve, one minute of regular time becomes hours of Christmas magic time, but only for me."

The boy considered this, his forehead wrinkling. "But what about the reindeer? How do they fly?"

"Christmas magic," Chase said simply. "Same magic that lets me know whether children have been naughty or nice. Magic doesn't have to follow the same rules as science, and that's what makes it special. It fills in all the places where regular rules can't reach."

"Can you teach me Christmas magic?"

"You already have Christmas magic. Every time you're kind to someone, every time you help your family, every time you believe in something good even when you can't see it—that's Christmas magic at work. You don't need flying reindeer to have magic in your life."

The boy thought about this for a long moment, then nodded slowly. "Okay. That makes sense. Can I still have the Lego set I asked for?"

"Absolutely. I think a smart boy like you deserves a good Lego set."

After the photographer snapped several photos, the boy climbed down and walked back to his parents, who'd been watching the exchange with barely concealed amusement. The father caught Hallie's eye and mouthed, "That was perfect," and Hallie felt a surge of pride that had everything to do with Chase and nothing to do with herself.

She moved closer to the throne during a brief gap in the line, handing Chase a bottle of water.

"You're really good at this," she said.

"I have an excellent Mrs. Claus supporting me," Chase replied, his voice pitched low enough that only she could hear. "Makes all the difference."

Before Hallie could respond, Sofia gestured that the next child was ready, and the moment passed.

The next several children were straightforward—a girl who wanted art supplies, twin boys who'd coordinated their wish lists to request matching superhero costumes, and a toddler who mostly wanted to pull Santa's beard.

Then, an older girl approached, maybe nine or ten, moving with the cautious dignity of someone trying very hard to look grown up.

She wore a dress that was slightly too formal for the casual bazaar, and her expression carried a seriousness that made Hallie's heart ache.

The girl climbed onto Santa's lap with care, as if afraid she might break something.

"Hello there," Chase said. "What's your name?"

"Olivia." She sat very straight, her hands folded in her lap. "I'm probably too old to be sitting on Santa's lap."

"Nobody's too old for a visit with Santa," Chase assured her. "I've had grandmothers sit on this lap. You're just fine."

That earned a small smile. "Okay."

"So, Olivia, what would you like for Christmas this year?"

The girl was quiet for a moment, and Hallie watched her struggle with something internal. When she finally spoke, her voice was soft but clear.

"I don't really want toys. I mean, toys are nice, but that's not what I really want."

"What do you really want?"

"I want my mom to get better. She's been sick for a long time, and the doctors say she's going to be okay, but she's tired all the time and sometimes she hurts. I want her to feel good again." Olivia looked up at Chase with eyes that held too much understanding for someone so young. "Can you do that?"

The bazaar noise seemed to fade as Chase looked at this child. Hallie's throat tightened, and she watched Chase gather his thoughts.

"Olivia," he said finally. "I wish with all my heart that I could make your mother completely better right away. But some things are bigger than Christmas magic. What I can tell you is this: the love you have for your mother, and the love she has for you—that's the strongest magic in the entire world. Stronger than flying reindeer or fitting down chimneys or delivering presents. That kind of love helps people get through tough times. It gives them strength when they're tired and hope when things are difficult."

Olivia listened with the intensity of someone memorizing every word.

"Your mother is lucky to have a daughter who loves her so much. And I bet that just knowing you're there, just having you be her daughter, helps her more than you think. Sometimes the best gift we can give isn't something wrapped in paper—it's just being there, being loving, and being patient when things are hard."

"So you can't make her better?" Olivia's voice wavered slightly.

"I can't promise that. But I can promise that you're doing exactly what you should do—loving your mother and being brave even when you're worried. That matters more than any toy I could bring."

Olivia nodded slowly, processing this. Then she leaned forward and hugged Chase. She held on for several seconds, and Chase's arms came around her, returning the embrace with the same genuineness.

When she pulled back, Olivia's eyes were damp, but she was smiling. "Thank you, Santa."

"You're very welcome, Olivia. And you know what? I'm going to put something special under your tree. Because even when we're worried about the big things, we still deserve a little Christmas joy."

After Olivia left with her parents—her mother, Hallie noticed, did indeed look tired but smiled warmly at her daughter—Hallie blinked back tears she couldn't afford to shed while wearing Mrs. Claus make-up. She busied herself reorganizing candy canes that were already perfectly organized, trying to regain her composure.

Mark and Liz arrived just as Hallie was getting herself under control. They'd clearly come specifically to see Chase in action, and Hallie watched Liz's face light up as she took in the sight of her son in full Santa mode.

"Look at him," Liz said to Hallie, her voice full of maternal pride. "He's wonderful."

"He really is," Hallie agreed, meaning it with every fiber of her being.

Mark snapped several photos with his phone, grinning like someone who'd just won the lottery. "Never thought I'd see the day when my Marine son would play Santa Claus in his hometown, but I have to say, it suits him."

They stayed for three children's visits, watching Chase interact with each one with the same patience and attention he'd shown all afternoon. A little boy who wanted a puppy, a girl who couldn't decide between dolls and wanted to list every option she could think of, and a toddler who mostly just stared at Santa in awe without saying a word.

"This is amazing, Hallie," Liz said, gesturing to the whole booth setup.

"It takes a lot of help to pull this off every year," Hallie said, nodding toward Nina and Sofia, who were currently entertaining the line with an impromptu Christmas carol. "And Chase has been incredible. I don't know what I would have done if he hadn't stepped up and offered to play Santa."

"You would have figured something out," Mark said. "You always do. But I'm glad Chase stepped in. Gives him purpose, you know? Something meaningful to focus on while he's finding his footing."

The comment resonated with what Hallie knew about Chase's internal struggle from yesterday's conversation. Looking at him now, watching him bring joy to child after child, she wondered if he could see what she saw—that purpose didn't always look like an impressive career title or a hefty salary. Sometimes it looked exactly like this: showing up, serving others, and making people smile.

The afternoon stretched on. More children, more wishes, more photos. Hallie's feet ached in the Mrs. Claus boots, and she'd lost count of how many candy canes she'd distributed. The gym remained packed with shoppers moving between vendor booths, and the Letters to Santa station maintained its steady stream of families.

Around four o'clock, an elderly couple approached the booth—Mr. and Mrs. Jameson, who'd been fixtures of the Mistletoe Falls community for as long as Hallie could remember. They weren't there with children or grandchildren, just themselves.

"We wanted to stop by and say thank you," Mrs. Jameson said to Hallie. "Our grandson was blessed by Operation Christmas Cheer last year when he was going through a rough patch. The food basket you put together and all the toys you provided for his family—it wasn't just toys and food. It was hope. It was someone showing him he wasn't alone in the struggle he was having."

Hallie felt her eyes well up for the second time that afternoon. "That's what we're here for. I'm so glad we could help."

"And your Santa is wonderful," Mr. Jameson added, nodding toward Chase. "Best we've seen in years."

After they left, Hallie stood for a moment just watching Chase. He was listening to a little girl explain her wish list with the same complete attention he'd given the first child hours ago. No signs of impatience, no checking his watch, just genuine presence with each person who sat on his lap.

She loved him.

She loved this man, who'd come home after twelve years and stepped back into her life like he'd never left. Who volunteered for her charity work because it mattered. Who'd wrestled with questions about purpose and calling but showed up anyway. Who kissed her in quiet moments and made her believe in possibilities she'd stopped letting herself imagine.

She loved him, and watching him be Santa for a gymnasium full of children only made her love him more.

Sofia appeared at her elbow, making Hallie jump. "You okay? You've got a look on your face."

"I'm fine," Hallie said. "Just tired. It's been a long afternoon."

"Mmm hmm. We're almost at the end. Just a few more families in line."

The final children came through—a set of triplets who wanted to sit on Santa's lap together and nearly knocked him over, a boy with a list so long he'd typed it on the computer and printed it out, and a tiny little girl who was mesmerized by Santa and barely spoke three words.

Finally, no more families waited. Chase sagged slightly on the throne, his shoulders dropping with relief.

Nina approached the throne with a mischievous grin. "You know what we haven't gotten yet? A photo of Santa and Mrs. Claus together."

Chase's eyes met Hallie's, and he spread his hands in invitation. "What do you say, Mrs. Claus?"

"I suppose Santa's lap looks comfortable," Hallie said, playing along.

Chase helped her settle onto his lap, one arm coming around her waist to steady her while she arranged her Mrs. Claus dress.

"Okay, look at the camera," the photographer called out. "Big smiles, you two. This is going to be adorable."

Hallie draped one arm around Chase's neck and turned toward the camera. She could feel Chase shift slightly beneath her, adjusting his position. They both smiled, and the photographer raised the camera.

Just as the shutter clicked, Chase leaned in and kissed her cheek.

"Oh, that's perfect!" the photographer called out, reviewing the image on the camera screen. "This is my favorite photo of the day."

Nina and Sofia were laughing, clapping their hands in delight.

Chase's arm was still around her waist, and Hallie was still sitting on his lap, and they were both grinning at each other like children who'd gotten away with something wonderful.

"Surprise," Chase said softly, just for her.

"You're terrible," Hallie whispered back, but she was laughing.

"You love it."

And heaven help her, she did. She loved it, and she loved him, and she loved this absurd, perfect moment at the end of a long day spent bringing joy to their community.

The photographer showed them the photo on the camera screen, and Hallie smiled. They looked happy. They looked right together. They looked exactly like what they were pretending to be—a couple who belonged together, who'd found something worth holding onto.

"Can you send me that photo?" Hallie asked the photographer.

"Already planning to. This one's too good not to share."

Hallie carefully climbed off Chase's lap, suddenly shy under the attention of Nina, Sofia, and the handful of shoppers who'd witnessed their photo moment. But Chase caught her hand briefly as she stepped away, giving it a quick squeeze that sent warmth all the way to her toes.

Chapter 26

Chase knocked on the door marked 118, balancing a gift basket wrapped in red cellophane against his hip while Hallie checked her clipboard for the veteran's name.

"Rick Kuiper," she said. "Navy veteran, served in the Pacific Theater during the Korean War. He loves crossword puzzles and big band music."

The door opened to reveal a man in his nineties, his face creased with deep lines that somehow made his smile even more brilliant. "Well, well. What do we have here?"

"Mr. Kuiper, I'm Hallie from Operation Christmas Cheer, and this is Chase. We brought you something special for the holidays." Hallie's voice carried the same warmth it had held for every veteran they'd visited in the past hour, genuine and unhurried.

"Come in, come in." Mr. Kuiper waved them inside a small room that held a lifetime compressed into careful organization. A narrow bed with military-precise corners, a recliner positioned near the window, and shelves displaying photographs in frames polished to gleaming. The scent of Old Spice aftershave mixed with the institutional smell that permeated the Mistletoe Falls Veterans Home—industrial cleaner, cafeteria food from down the hall, and something indefinable that Chase recognized from his visits to military hospitals overseas.

Hallie presented the basket. "We put together some things we thought you might enjoy."

Mr. Kuiper accepted it carefully, setting it on the small table beside his recliner. His hands trembled slightly as he unwrapped the cellophane, revealing the contents—three crossword puzzle books, a CD collection of Glenn Miller and Benny Goodman, a warm fleece blanket in Navy blue, packages of his favorite butterscotch candies, and a handwritten card in Hallie's elegant script.

The old veteran's eyes glistened as he picked up the CD. "How did you know? Glenn Miller was what we listened to on the ship when we had downtime. Takes me right back."

"We do our research," Hallie said.

Mr. Kuiper looked up at Chase, his gaze sharp despite his age. "You serve, son?"

"Marines, sir. Combat engineer. Twelve years, just discharged in October."

"Good man." Mr. Kuiper extended his hand, and Chase shook it. "Thank you for your service. And I thank both of you for bringing me this Christmas gift. Means a lot to me."

After they left Mr. Kuiper's room, continuing down the hallway, Chase glanced at Hallie. She was consulting her clipboard again, her winter boots squeaking against the polished linoleum floor. She'd dressed for efficiency today—jeans, a deep green sweater, her blonde hair pulled back in a ponytail, minimal makeup. She looked beautiful.

They delivered baskets to three more rooms in quick succession. Margaret Foster, an Army nurse from Vietnam, cried when she saw the vintage nursing pin Hallie had tracked down through an online collector. Thomas Banks, Air Force mechanic, who laughed with delight at the model airplane kit and promised to display it on his shelf when completed. James Rodriguez, Marine Corps rifleman, who stood at attention when Chase introduced himself and insisted on showing them his Purple Heart while recounting the story behind it with pride that hadn't dimmed in fifty years.

Each visit followed a similar pattern—Hallie presenting the basket with personal touches, Chase connecting through shared military experience, the veterans responding with gratitude that seemed disproportionate to the simple gifts they received. But Chase was understanding it wasn't about the items themselves. It was about being seen. Being remembered. Being treated like individuals with histories and preferences.

The hallway stretched ahead of them, with doors on both sides marked with numbers and Christmas wreaths. Christmas music played softly through speakers mounted in the ceiling, currently an instrumental version of "I'll Be Home for Christmas" that felt almost painfully appropriate. Large windows at intervals showed the December afternoon fading toward evening, the sky that shade of gray that promised snow.

"How many more?" Chase asked, adjusting his grip on the basket he carried.

"Four, then we're done." Hallie paused outside room 142, checking her notes. "Aaron Carmichael. Army, did two tours in Iraq. Served as a combat engineer, actually—like you."

Something in Chase's chest shifted. A fellow engineer, and recently discharged as well. He knocked, hearing the call to enter from inside.

The man who answered the door was younger than Chase expected—late thirties, maybe forty at most. Tall and lean with close-cropped dark hair going gray at the temples, wearing jeans and a flannel shirt that had seen better days. His room was spartan even by the standards of the veterans' home. A bed, a desk, a small television, and a bookshelf holding what looked like woodworking manuals and a few paperback thrillers. No photographs, no personal decorations except for a shadow box on the wall displaying military medals and unit patches.

"Aaron Carmichael?" Hallie asked.

"That's me." Aaron's gaze moved between them, settling on Chase with the particular recognition that existed between veterans. "You serve?"

"Marines. Combat engineer. Chase Montgomery." Chase extended his hand, and Aaron shook it, his grip firm.

"Army. Same field—route clearance, bridge construction, demolition. Small world." Aaron gestured for them to come inside. "What brings you by?"

Hallie stepped forward with the basket. "I'm Hallie, from Operation Christmas Cheer. We're delivering holiday gifts to the veterans here. We put together something special for you."

Aaron accepted the basket with visible surprise, carrying it to his desk and carefully removing the cellophane. Inside were woodworking magazines, a set of high-quality carving tools, a thick fleece jacket in Army green, a coffee mug with the combat engineer insignia, packages of beef jerky and dark chocolate, and Hallie's handwritten card.

He picked up the carving tools, examining them with the careful attention of someone who understood quality. "These are really nice. How did you know I'm into woodworking?"

"The staff mentioned you've been making small carvings to pass the time," Hallie said. "I thought you might appreciate some new tools."

"I appreciate them very much." Aaron set the tools down carefully, running his hand over the magazine covers. "This is thoughtful. Really thoughtful. Thank you."

"You're welcome." Hallie said.

"How long have you been here?" Chase asked.

"About eight months." Aaron moved to sit on the edge of his bed. "Got out of the Army a year ago. Thought I'd transition fine—had skills, experience, figured employers would value military training. Turns out civilian companies care little about combat engineering when you don't have the right pieces of paper."

"Certifications?" Chase asked.

"Trade licenses, union memberships, civilian education credentials. I can build a bridge and clear IEDs from supply routes, but I can't get hired to do basic carpentry without formal apprenticeship paperwork I never had time to get. Been working minimum wage jobs—retail, warehouse stuff, whatever I can find. I can't afford rent for housing on that, so I ended up here. The veterans' home takes in people who need temporary housing help. Supposed to be short term, but eight months later, here I am."

Chase absorbed this, seeing his own situation reflected in uncomfortable ways. "You're looking for work in construction? Carpentry?"

"Anything that uses my hands and pays more than nine dollars an hour." Aaron picked up one of the carving tools from the basket, testing its weight. "I'm good at what I do. I built furniture in my spare time on base, fixed everything that broke in our unit. I've got skills worth more than stocking shelves, but nobody wants to give me a shot without those magic certification papers."

Hallie leaned forward slightly in her chair. "What kind of furniture did you build?"

"Tables, chairs, shelving units. Whatever people needed. I had access to scrap wood on base and tools from the motor pool. I made a rocking chair once for a lieutenant's wife when their baby was born. She cried when she saw it."

"Really? That's impressive," Hallie said. "Mistletoe Falls has several businesses that might value those skills. Would you be open to my asking around?"

Aaron looked at her with cautious hope. "You'd do that?"

"Of course. Sometimes finding work is about connections, and I happen to know a lot of people in town." She pulled out her phone, making a note. "Let me get your contact information so I can reach you if something comes up."

While Hallie and Aaron exchanged information, Chase watched the interaction. This was who Hallie was—someone who saw a need and immediately moved to address it.

"That's rough," Chase said. "I've been struggling with transition too. Different circumstances, but still trying to figure out where I fit in civilian life."

"What are you doing now?" Aaron asked.

"Helping my parents run their toy store. Bells and Whistles Toy Shop, downtown. My mom was in a car accident last year, leaving her paralyzed from the waist down. My dad needed help to manage everything, so I came home after my discharge."

"That's good of you. Family needs you, you show up. That's what we're trained to do." Aaron set the tool back in the basket carefully. "But I'm guessing there's a 'but' coming?"

Chase exhaled slowly. "I don't know if it's what I'm supposed to be doing long-term. Managing a toy store. My Marine buddies are moving into careers—security consulting, engineering firms, construction companies. Buying houses and building lives. And I'm selling toys to families in my hometown."

"You think that's not purposeful?" Aaron asked.

"I don't know what I think." Chase ran his hand through his hair. "I love my parents. I want to help them. But I keep wondering if I'm just filling a need out of obligation, or if this is actually my path. If I'm settling for good enough instead of finding what I'm really meant to do."

Aaron was quiet for a moment, his gaze steady. "Can I tell you what I see? From my position?"

"Please."

"You've got family who need you and value what you bring, I imagine. You've got meaningful work that serves your community. You've got a place where you belong and people who want you there. That's more than most of us get when we come home. A lot of us would give anything to have someone need us the way your parents need you. To have work that matters, even if it's not combat engineering or whatever we thought we'd do. You're questioning whether it's enough, but from where I'm sitting, you've already got what I'm searching for."

The words landed with unexpected force.

"I appreciate your perspective and your honesty," Chase admitted.

"Transition messes with your head. Makes you think you need something bigger, something that matches what you did in uniform. But maybe the point isn't finding something as important as military service. Maybe it's finding something that matters in different ways." Aaron stood, moving to the window and looking out at the fading afternoon light. "I'm not saying don't question. Question away. Just don't dismiss what you've got while you're doing it."

Hallie rose from the desk chair. "Aaron, I meant what I said. I'm going to keep my ears open for opportunities. You deserve better than minimum wage work when you've got skills like yours."

"I appreciate that more than you know." Aaron's gratitude was genuine. "Most people just say 'thank you for your service' and move on. You actually seem to mean it."

"I mean it," Hallie said firmly. She glanced at Chase. "We should probably finish the last few deliveries. It's getting late."

They said goodbye to Aaron, leaving him with the basket and Hallie's genuine promise to keep him in mind. Chase carried the remaining baskets as they continued down the hallway, but his mind stayed in that sparse room, turning over Aaron's words.

The last three deliveries passed in a blur. By the time they finished, the winter evening had fully settled over Mistletoe Falls. The parking lot lights cast yellow circles on the snow-covered pavement as Chase and Hallie made their way back to his truck.

"You were quiet during those last visits," Hallie said. "Everything okay?"

"Just thinking about what Aaron said. About having what he's searching for." Chase leaned against the truck, looking back at the veterans' home building. Christmas lights outlined the windows, warm against the gray stone. "Made me realize I've been focused on what the toy store isn't instead of what it is. But talking about it also reminded me I'm still not sure if it's where I'm supposed to be long term."

"Right. Of course."

Something in her tone made Chase look at her more carefully. She'd gone still, her gaze fixed on the pavement rather than meeting his eyes. The easy warmth that had existed between them all afternoon had cooled, replaced by something more guarded.

"Hallie?"

"We should probably head back." She moved toward the passenger door, her voice carefully neutral. "I'm sure you're tired, and I have paperwork to finish at the store."

"Are you okay?"

"I'm fine." But she wasn't looking at him, and her smile when she finally did was practiced rather than genuine.

Chase watched her climb into the truck, her movements efficient and purposeful. She settled into the passenger seat and immediately pulled out her phone, scrolling through something with focused attention that felt deliberate.

He walked around to the driver's side, understanding dawning with uncomfortable clarity. His talk about questioning his path, about not being sure if the toy store was his long-term answer—she'd heard that as a warning. A preview of leaving. She was protecting herself by pulling back, creating distance before he could hurt her the way he had twelve years ago when he'd left Mistletoe Falls without looking back.

Chase started the truck, the engine's rumble filling the silence between them. He wanted to say something, to reassure her that questioning didn't mean leaving, that figuring out his future didn't mean abandoning what they were building together. But the words stuck in his throat because he couldn't make promises about his future when he genuinely didn't know what that future looked like.

Aaron's perspective had reframed things, made Chase see his situation through a different lens. But it hadn't answered the fundamental question of whether managing the toy store was his calling or just his current circumstance.

And Hallie, perceptive as always, had heard the uncertainty in his voice and understood what it might mean for them.

The drive back toward downtown passed in careful quiet. Not hostile, not tense, just measured. Hallie mentioned tomorrow's tasks at her store. Chase responded with acknowledgments, telling her what he needed to accomplish tomorrow in his parents' store as well.

They sounded like colleagues. Not like two people who were dating and getting to know each other again.

When Chase pulled into the alley behind their stores, Hallie was already reaching for the door handle before he'd fully stopped.

"Thanks for the help today," she said, climbing out.

"Hallie." Chase killed the engine, wanting to address what was happening between them. "About what I said—"

"You don't have to explain anything." She stood by the open door, backlit by the alley's security light. "You're figuring things out. That's completely understandable. I'll see you tomorrow. Goodnight, Chase."

"Goodnight."

He watched her as she climbed the stairs to her apartment and disappeared through the door.

She was scared he was going to leave. His questioning had triggered every abandonment fear she carried. She was pulling back now, creating distance, protecting her heart before he could break it.

And Chase couldn't blame her, because he'd given her every reason to believe history might repeat itself. He'd come home uncertain about his path. He'd questioned whether Mistletoe Falls could offer what he needed. He'd admitted he didn't know if the toy store was his answer.

All truths. All honest reflections of where he was in his life.

And all things that must sound to Hallie like a man preparing his exit strategy.

Chase climbed out of the truck, locked it, and headed up to his own apartment. The stairs creaked under his weight, and his key scraped in the lock louder than usual in the quiet evening. Inside, he flipped on the lights and stood in his living room surrounded by furniture they'd picked out together.

Chase pulled out his phone and almost texted her. Almost wrote something about how much today meant, how much she meant, how questioning his career path didn't mean questioning them.

But his thumbs hovered over the keyboard without typing because what could he say that would be true and reassuring simultaneously? He was questioning his path. He didn't know if the toy store was his future. He couldn't promise he wouldn't need something different eventually.

He set the phone down without sending anything.

Chapter 27

Chase set the day's closing reports on his father's desk in the office at Bells & Whistles. His father was reviewing a vendor invoice, reading glasses perched on his nose, while his mother sat nearby.

"The register's balanced," Chase said. "I did the deposit bag. It's in the safe."

His mother looked up from the computer screen. "Thank you, sweetheart."

Mark removed his reading glasses, setting them on the desk with deliberate care. "Chase, sit down for a minute."

"I should probably—"

"Sit." His father's tone wasn't harsh, just firm enough to make it clear this wasn't optional.

Chase lowered himself into the chair positioned against the wall, the same chair he'd sat in as a kid when his parents had needed to discuss his report card or his plans for after high school or any of the hundred other conversations that had happened in this office over the years.

Liz swiveled to face him fully, her expression gentle but concerned. "You've been quiet all day. Not yourself. What's going on?"

"Nothing. Just tired."

"Chase," his mother said.

He wanted to brush it off, to insist he was fine and escape to his apartment where he could process everything alone. But sitting here in this office with both his parents watching him with expressions of patient concern, the words came tumbling out.

"I went with Hallie yesterday to deliver Christmas baskets to the veterans' home."

"How did that go?" she asked.

"Fine. Great, actually. The veterans appreciated the baskets." Chase rubbed his hand over his face, feeling the day's stubble rough against his palm. "We met this guy. Aaron Carmichael. Army combat engineer. He's living at the veterans' home because he can't afford his own place on minimum-wage jobs. Has all these skills from military service but can't get hired for decent work because he doesn't have the right civilian certifications."

"That's rough," Mark said. "Happens to a lot of veterans. Civilian employers don't always value military experience the way they should."

"He told me he built furniture. From what it sounds like, he has a skill. But nobody will hire him for carpentry work without apprenticeship paperwork he never had time to get while he was serving." Chase leaned forward, elbows on his knees. "We got to talking, and I told him a few things about what I've been struggling with since coming home. And the thing is, he looked at my situation—helping you guys run the store, having a place to live, having family who needs me—and he said I already have what he's searching for. That I'm questioning whether it's enough when most veterans would give anything to have someone need them the way you need me."

Liz's expression softened with understanding. "That must have been hard to hear."

"It made me realize I've been so focused on what this store isn't that I've lost sight of what it is. Stable. Meaningful. Connected to the people I love. But it also made me keep thinking about whether I'm here because this is my path, or because circumstances put me here and I don't know how to leave."

The office was quiet except for the hum of the fluorescent lights and the distant sound of traffic on the street outside.

"And Hallie?" Liz asked. "How does she fit into all this?"

Chase exhaled slowly. "She heard the conversation with Aaron. Heard me questioning again whether this is what I'm supposed to be doing long-term. And she pulled back. Got careful and distant. I could see her protecting herself, and I understood why. She's scared I'm going to leave, like I did twelve years ago, and like her mother did. My questioning makes me sound like someone planning an exit strategy."

"Are you?" Mark's question was direct but not accusing. "Planning to leave?"

"I don't know. I don't want to disappoint you. Either of you. You needed help, and I came home, and I've been trying to be what you need. But I keep wondering if duty is enough to build a life on, or if I should look for something that feels more like a calling."

His mother wheeled closer, reaching out to take his hand. Her grip was warm and firm. "Chase, look at me."

He met her eyes—the same blue as his own, filled with a mother's unconditional love and also a surprising amount of steel.

"You don't owe us your life," Liz said, her voice carrying absolute conviction. "We love you. We're grateful you came home when we needed help. But if staying here and running this store isn't what you want, you have permission to choose something different. We'll figure it out. Your happiness matters more to us than keeping the store in the family."

"But Mom, you can't manage everything alone. Not with—" He gestured awkwardly toward her wheelchair.

"I manage fine," she said firmly. "I've adapted. Learned new systems. Your father and I have always worked well together. If you decided tomorrow that you needed to pursue something else, we'd adjust. We always do."

Mark leaned back in his desk chair, the springs creaking softly. "Your mother's right. We didn't ask you to come home so that we could trap you here. We asked because we wanted you here. We wanted you to have a job to come home to. We wanted to give you a purpose. You've been present, committed, and you've done excellent work while you've been home. But that doesn't obligate you to stay here forever."

Chase looked between his parents, seeing the sincerity in their expressions. They meant it. They'd let him go without resentment or guilt if that's what he needed.

Which somehow made the decision harder rather than easier.

"What if I don't know what I'm being pulling me toward?" Chase asked. "What if I'm just confused and restless and comparing myself to other guys who seem to have it all figured out?"

"Then you sit with the confusion until clarity comes," his father said.

Liz squeezed Chase's hand once before releasing it. "I want to tell you something. Something your father and I have been discussing for a while now... even way before we were certain you would not reenlist."

Mark nodded, picking up the thread. "We're ready to retire, Chase. Fully retire. We've run this store for years. It's been good to us, given us a livelihood and purpose and a way to serve this community. But we're tired. We want to travel while we still can. See places we've always talked about seeing. Spend time with each other without the constant demands of inventory and schedules and customer needs. Your mother's accident gave us both a jarring realization. Life is short, Chase, and your mother and I want to live it to the fullest and not be constrained to running this store forever."

"We've been waiting for the right time," Liz continued. "Waiting to see if you'd want to take over completely, or if we'd need to look for a buyer. Your coming home gave us breathing room to figure things out. But we're ready for that next chapter in our lives now, whatever it looks like."

Chase absorbed this information, recognizing it as significant even as his mind struggled to process all the implications.

"We've been trying to figure out the right moment to tell you," Mark admitted. "We didn't want to pressure you or make you feel obligated. But seeing you struggle... well, it seems like maybe now is the right time to be honest about where we are."

"So you need me to take over the store?"

"We want you to make whatever choice serves your life best," Liz said. "If that's taking over Bells & Whistles, wonderful. We'd love to keep it in the family, and we think you'd do excellent work with it. But you want to pursue something else entirely, we'll support that too. We can sell the business or find someone else to manage it full time, with us remaining in the background. The store's future isn't your responsibility to solve."

Mark leaned forward, his expression thoughtful. "But I will say this, son. If you wanted to take it over, it doesn't have to stay exactly as it is. Your mother and I built Bells & Whistles to reflect our vision, our values, our way of serving the community. If it became yours, you'd have the freedom to reshape it into something that reflects who you are and what matters to you."

"What do you mean?" Chase asked.

"I mean the foundation is solid—the building, the customer relationships, the community reputation. But what happens inside these walls could grow." Mark said. "Maybe you keep selling toys but add a different dimension. Maybe you shift focus to a particular type of product. Maybe you create programs or initiatives that align with your skills and interests. Shoot... turn it into a restaurant for all we care. We own the building, and if you take over this business, you can do with it as you please. The possibilities are limited only by your imagination and what makes sense for you."

His parents weren't offering him a simple solution or trying to solve his internal conflict. They were offering him freedom. Permission to choose without guilt. The space to figure out what he actually wanted instead of what he thought he should want.

"I don't know what to do with all this," Chase admitted. "You're giving me options, and somehow that makes it harder rather than easier."

"Good decisions are usually hard," Mark said. "If it were easy, it probably wouldn't matter as much."

Liz wheeled closer to the desk, her hands folding in her lap. "Can I ask you something, Chase? About Hallie?"

He nodded.

"Do you love her?"

The question was direct, simple, and impossible to deflect. Chase looked at his mother, seeing her watching him with the particular intensity of someone who already knew the answer but needed to hear him say it.

"Yes. I love her."

"Does she know that?"

"I think so. Maybe. I don't know." Chase ran his hand through his hair in frustration. "We're great together, getting closer every day. But then I voiced my uncertainty again last night, she heard that as me preparing to leave. She's protecting herself by pulling back, and I don't blame her for that. Why would she trust that I'll stay when I can't even tell her definitively that staying is what I want?"

"Love isn't about having everything figured out," Liz said. "It's about choosing to figure things out together. Hallie's scared—of course she is, given her history. But that fear is about the past, not about you specifically. If you love her, you need to give her something concrete to hold on to. Not empty promises about the future, but the truth about the present. Tell her how you feel. Let her see that you're committed to her."

"What if I decide I need to leave Mistletoe Falls? What if I figure out that my calling is somewhere else?"

Mark and Liz exchanged another one of those married-couple glances, and Mark spoke first. "Then you'll have a tough conversation with Hallie about what that means for your relationship. But Chase—and this is important—you don't get to decide about your future without considering how it affects the person you love. That's not how a partnership works. If you're serious about Hallie, then whatever you choose about your career has to be something you choose together, or at least something you're willing to include her in the decision-making process about."

"What if she doesn't want to leave Mistletoe Falls if I do?" Chase asked. "Her whole life is here."

"Then you'll have to decide what matters more," Liz said. "Your theoretical calling somewhere else, or building a life with her here. Neither answer is wrong, but you have to choose. And you have to be honest with her about the choice you're facing. Stringing her along while you're indecisive is not fair to her... it's cruel."

The office felt smaller than it had when Chase first entered; the walls pressing in with the weight of decisions that needed to be made and conversations that needed to be had.

"I appreciate this," Chase said finally, meeting his parents' eyes. "All of it."

"We just want you to be happy," Liz said. "Whatever that looks like."

Mark stood, stretching his back with an audible pop. "There's no pressure on any of this, Chase. Take your time. Figure out what you actually want instead of what you think you should want. The store will be here, and so will we. The only thing I'd encourage you not to wait on is talking to Hallie. The longer you let that distance grow between you, the harder it'll be to bridge it."

"I know." Chase stood as well, feeling the exhaustion of the day settling into his bones. "I need to think about everything. Process what you've told me."

"Of course." Liz began shutting down her computer; the screen went dark with a soft electronic chime. "Just remember, sweetheart—you don't have to have all the answers right away. You just have to keep asking the questions until you find your answer."

Chase helped his father gather the day's paperwork, filing things in their proper places with the automatic movements of someone who'd learned the system well over the past few weeks. His mother locked the desk drawers and organized the workspace—their evening routine as familiar now as it had been when he was a child watching them close the store at the end of a long day.

They left the office together, Mark turning off the lights and locking the door behind them.

At the back door leading to the alley, his parents stopped. Mark pulled on his coat while Liz wrapped a scarf around her neck and put on her own coat.

"Are you going to be okay?" Mark asked, his hand on Chase's shoulder.

"Eventually. Right now I'm just confused and tired."

"Get some rest. Things often look different in the morning." His father squeezed his shoulder once before releasing it.

Liz reached up to grasp Chase's hand. "We love you. We're proud of you. And we trust you to make the right decisions for your life, whatever those decisions are."

"I love you too. Both of you."

He followed them out the back door, his father pushing his mother's wheelchair to where their car waited. He watched them work together to get her transferred into the passenger seat, Mark folding the wheelchair and loading it into the back cargo area of his truck. He watched them drive away, their taillights disappearing around the corner toward home.

Chase stood alone in the alley behind Bells & Whistles, looking up at the dark windows of his apartment. Next door, lights glowed in Hallie's apartment windows—warm and inviting.

His parents had given him permission to choose. Freedom to pursue whatever path called to him. Honesty about their own readiness to move into retirement. Wisdom about relationships and decision-making.

But they hadn't given him answers, because answers weren't something anyone else could provide.

Chase climbed the metal stairs to his apartment, his boots ringing on the steps in the frigid evening air. Inside, he flipped on the lights and cranked the heat, shedding his coat and boots and collapsing onto the couch.

The conversation with Aaron yesterday. The distance in Hallie's eyes. His parents' revelation about retirement and their offer of the store. Liz's question about whether he loved Hallie—and his immediate, certain answer.

All of it swirled through his mind like snow in a winter storm, individual pieces that he couldn't quite see how to fit together into a coherent picture.

What did he want? Not what he should do, or what would disappoint the fewest people, or what made the most practical sense. What did Chase Montgomery actually want for his life?

The answer should have been simple. It felt like it should be obvious.

But sitting alone in his apartment with the evening stretching ahead of him, Chase realized he still didn't know. And not knowing felt like failing some fundamental test of adulthood.

His phone sat on the coffee table, Hallie's number just a few taps away. He could call her. Text her. Walk next door and knock on her door and try to bridge the distance that had opened between them.

But what would he say? That he loved her but didn't know if staying in Mistletoe Falls was his answer? That he wanted to build a life with her but couldn't promise what that life would look like? That he was confused and questioning and still trying to figure out who he was outside of a Marine uniform?

None of that was fair to her. None of it gave her the security she deserved.

Chase grabbed his phone anyway, opening his messages to Hallie's name. His thumbs hovered over the keyboard, and a dozen different texts composed themselves in his mind.

I love you.

I'm sorry for making you doubt my commitment.

Can we talk?

I don't have answers yet, but I don't want this distance between us.

He typed nothing. Sent nothing. Set the phone back down and leaned his head against the couch cushions, staring at the ceiling and wondering how you choose between competing goods when there is no clear right answer.

Chapter 28

Hallie stared at the spreadsheet on her computer screen, the numbers blurring into meaningless columns that refused to resolve into coherent information no matter how many times she blinked. She'd been working on it for the past forty minutes—or trying to work on it, anyway—and had accomplished exactly nothing.

The radiator ticked and hissed its familiar rhythm, and from the store beyond her closed door came the muted sounds of customers browsing and Lucy's cheerful voice offering help. Everything normal. Everything ordinary.

Except Hallie felt like she was watching her life happen from somewhere outside herself, disconnected and distant.

She clicked to a different tab on the spreadsheet, then back to the first one. Neither made more sense than they had a minute ago.

The office door opened without warning, and Nina stepped inside, closing it firmly behind her with a decisive click. She carried two takeout cups from the Fireside Diner.

"Break time," Nina announced, setting one cup in front of Hallie. "Hot chocolate. Extra whipped cream. And before you ask, Sofia's handling the floor, Lucy's restocking the ornament wall, and Taylor's managing the register. The store will survive without me."

Nina settled into the chair across from the desk, cradling her own hot chocolate. "What's going on? Every time one of us tries to talk to you, you suddenly have urgent inventory to check or paperwork to finish or phone calls to make."

"I've been working. It's a busy time of year."

"It's always busy this time of year, and you're never this checked out." Nina took a sip of her drink, her dark eyes watchful over the rim of the cup. "You've barely been on the sales floor the past two days. You're in this office constantly with the door closed. Lucy asked you a question about pricing yesterday, and you didn't even hear her. Taylor had to ask you a question twice before you registered she was talking to you."

Hallie set down the hot chocolate without tasting it. "I'm fine. Just distracted."

"Hallie. I've known you since high school. I know what 'fine' looks like on you, and this isn't it. What's going on?"

"Nothing. Really. I'm just—there's a lot happening with Operation Christmas Cheer right now, and the gala's this weekend, and—"

"Stop." Nina held up one hand. "You coordinate Operation Christmas Cheer every year. You've planned the same gala for the past couple of years. None of that explains why you look like someone stole Christmas and left you the empty box."

Hallie looked away, focusing on the bulletin board covered in coordination lists and volunteer schedules, anything to avoid Nina's too-perceptive gaze.

"I'm fine," she repeated.

Nina was quiet for a long moment. Then she stood, walked to the office door, and locked it. She returned to her chair and settled in with the air of someone prepared to wait as long as necessary.

"We're not leaving this office until you tell me what's going on," Nina said. "I'll sit here all afternoon if I have to."

"Nina—"

"Is it Chase?"

Hallie's throat closed. She wanted to deny it, to deflect again, to maintain the fiction that everything was manageable and under control. But sitting here under Nina's steady gaze, she couldn't summon the energy to keep pretending.

"Yes."

"Did he do something? Say something? Because if he hurt you, I'll—"

"No, he didn't do anything wrong." Hallie picked up her hot chocolate just to have something to do with her hands. "He's been nothing but good to me."

"Then what's the problem?"

Hallie took a sip of hot chocolate; the sweetness coating her tongue brought no real comfort. "On Sunday, we delivered Christmas baskets to the veterans' home together. It was good—really good. The veterans loved the personalized baskets, and Chase connected with them in this beautiful way because of his military background."

"So what went wrong?"

"We met this veteran. Aaron Carmichael. Younger guy, living there because he can't afford his own place. He and Chase talked about transitioning from military to civilian life, about struggling to find purpose, about questioning whether what you're doing is enough." Hallie set down her cup, her hands trembling slightly. "And Chase opened up about his own doubts. About whether managing his parents' toy store is what he's supposed to be doing long term. About feeling like he's settling for good enough instead of finding his real calling."

"And you interpreted that as his planning to leave."

"I heard that as him questioning whether Mistletoe Falls can give him what he needs. Whether this life here is enough for him. And I've heard that before, Nina. I heard it from my mother after my dad died. I heard it from Chase twelve years ago when he left for the Marines. Everyone I love eventually decides that what we have here isn't enough, and they leave."

"Hallie—"

"And the worst part is, I knew this was coming. I knew getting close to Chase again was dangerous. I knew that letting myself feel things for him was setting myself up to get hurt again. But I did it anyway because I'm apparently incapable of protecting myself when it comes to him. And on top of that, Chase brought up his confusion about not knowing what to do with his life, struggling with his purpose and questioning what he should do and what mattered... and I was supportive and listened and talked to him about it in this very office last week. But Sunday... when he talked about those same issues with Aaron... it hit me differently."

"I'm scared," Hallie finally admitted. "I'm terrified, Nina. What if I let myself believe this will work between Chase and me, and then he leaves anyway? What if I give him my whole heart and he decides that I'm not enough? I can't survive that again."

"You survived being left before," Nina said. "Your mother left, and you survived. Chase left to serve his country, and you survived. You built a life and a business and a community program that serves dozens of families. You're stronger than you give yourself credit for."

"I don't feel strong. I feel like I'm barely holding myself together."

"That's because you're in love with him." Nina's voice was matter-of-fact. "Love makes us vulnerable. That's terrifying. But it's also the only way to actually build something real with another person."

Hallie's hands shook as she set down her hot chocolate.

"I do love him."

"Does he know?"

"How can I tell him that when I don't even know if he's staying? When he's questioning his entire future here?"

Nina made an exasperated sound. "Hallie, listen to yourself. You're not telling him how you feel because you're scared he might leave. But by not telling him, by pulling away and creating distance, you're basically ensuring the relationship can't work. You're making the choice for both of you instead of deciding together."

"That's not fair."

"No, what's not fair is punishing Chase. What's not fair is deciding he's going to leave before he's even made that decision himself." Nina's voice softened. "I know you're scared. I know your mother's leaving broke something in you. But Chase isn't your mother. He's a grown man trying to figure out his life after twelve years of military service. Questioning his career path doesn't mean he's questioning you."

"But what if it does?" Hallie's voice cracked. "What if he realizes that staying here means giving up other opportunities, and he resents me for it? What if I become the reason he's stuck somewhere he doesn't want to be?"

"Then you'll deal with that if it happens. Hallie, you can't live your life trying to avoid potential hurt. If you continue to do this, you're guaranteed you'll be alone forever."

"I don't know how to do this. I don't know how to be open and vulnerable when every instinct I have is screaming at me to protect myself."

"You start by being honest. With yourself and with Chase. You tell him how you feel. You have an actual conversation about what's scaring you instead of just pulling away. You give him the chance to reassure you, or to tell you the truth about what he's thinking. Either way, you stop making assumptions and start communicating."

"What if he can't give me the reassurance I need? What if he's genuinely not sure about staying?"

"Then you deal with that reality instead of the imagined scenario in your head. But at least you'll know where you actually stand instead of torturing yourself with maybes." Nina picked up her hot chocolate again, taking a long drink. "Look, I'm not saying you shouldn't be scared. Fear is reasonable given your history. But you have to decide if you're going to let that fear control you for the rest of your life, or if you're going to be brave enough to risk getting hurt for the chance at something real."

Hallie absorbed this, feeling the truth of it settle uncomfortably in her chest. Nina was right. She'd been so focused on protecting herself that she'd forgotten to consider whether her protection was actually achieving anything except guaranteed loneliness.

"Self-protection is kind of my default setting, isn't it?"

"Yes, it is, and you need to learn a new default."

A knock on the office door interrupted them. Sofia's voice came through, slightly muffled. "Nina? Sorry to bother you, but we've got a situation with a customer return that needs manager approval."

Nina stood, draining the last of her hot chocolate. "Duty calls. You going to be okay?"

"I don't know," Hallie admitted. "But I'll figure it out."

"That's all any of us can do."

Nina paused at the door, looking back. "For what it's worth, I think Chase is in one of those strange in-between moments everyone hits eventually in their life. He's leaving one life behind and trying to figure out what comes next. It's a lot like when we graduated college. Back then, school felt safe—structured. We knew what was expected of us. But the moment we stepped into the real world, it was like someone opened the gate and said, go on, figure it out. Suddenly we were asking ourselves, Which way do I go? What am I supposed to do now? Hallie... I think Chase is one of the good ones. I think he's worth the risk. And I think you two could build something really beautiful together—if you let yourself try."

"Nina?"

"Yeah?"

"Thanks."

"That's what best friends are for." Nina unlocked the door, opening it to reveal Sofia waiting in the hallway with an apologetic expression. Then she was gone, leaving Hallie alone in her office with a cooling cup of hot chocolate and thoughts that wouldn't settle into any kind of comfortable arrangement.

Nina was right about so much. About fear creating distance. About punishing Chase for other people's choices. About needing to communicate instead of making assumptions.

But knowing something intellectually and having the courage to act on it were two entirely different things.

Chapter 29

Hallie positioned the gourmet coffee basket on the worktable, adjusting the angle of the French press so the handle faced outward. The donated items spread across the basement of Wrapped Up in Christmas created a landscape of generosity—spa products in jewel-toned bottles, outdoor gear still bearing price tags, books with pristine spines, wine bottles wrapped in tissue paper, and gift cards tucked into elegant holders.

"That coffee set is gorgeous," Nina said from across the table. "Someone's going to bid high for that one."

"Maybe." Hallie reached for the artisan chocolate bars that would complete the coffee lover's basket. Her movements felt mechanical, going through the motions her hands knew by heart while her mind remained somewhere distant and unreachable.

The basement air carried the mingled scents of vanilla candles, expensive soaps, and the faint mustiness that came with any below-ground space in an old building. Overhead lights cast everything in warm yellow tones, softening the exposed brick walls and concrete floor into something almost cozy. Christmas music played, an instrumental version of a carol that normally filled Hallie with joy but tonight felt like background noise she couldn't quite hear.

She'd been assembling silent auction baskets for this weekend's Operation Christmas Gala for forty minutes, and she honestly couldn't remember half of what she'd done. Her body moved, her hands worked, but some essential part of herself had disconnected from the present moment.

"You're awfully quiet tonight," Nina said as she cut a length of gold ribbon.

"Just focused."

"Mmhmm." Nina's tone suggested she wasn't fooled, but she didn't push. Instead, she held up the spa basket she had been working on for inspection. "What do you think? Should I add the bath bombs, or is it too much?"

Hallie glanced over, forcing her attention to the question. The basket overflowed with luxury—body butter, face masks, scented candles, a plush robe. "Add them. It's for the veterans' home fundraiser. More is better."

Nina tucked three bath bombs wrapped in shimmering paper among the other items, then secured everything with cellophane wrap that crinkled as she worked. The sound reminded Hallie of all the other years they'd done this together and all the other baskets they'd assembled. She and Nina had been doing this dance for years. Creating beauty from donated pieces. Transforming individual items into cohesive gifts that would raise money for people in need.

Tonight, it felt hollow, though.

Footsteps on the basement stairs made both women look up to find Chase. His expression shifted from neutral to something softer when his gaze found Hallie.

She looked away first, returning her attention to the coffee basket with more intensity than required.

"Well... look who's here," Nina said.

"Sorry, I'm a couple of minutes late. Traffic was terrible," Chase said, reaching the bottom of the stairs. "All twenty feet of it."

Nina laughed. "The commute from next door can be brutal."

Hallie didn't join the banter. She positioned the chocolate bars in a fan pattern, then second-guessed the arrangement and started over.

"Hallie," Chase said.

She made herself look at him. Made herself offer something resembling a normal greeting. "Hi. I wasn't sure you'd come."

"Why wouldn't I?"

Because I've been distant and cold for four days. Because I practically ran away from you Sunday night. Because I've been avoiding you, and you must have noticed, and you'd have every right to decide this isn't worth the effort. She thought.

"No reason," she said instead. "We have a lot to get through tonight."

Chase just nodded. "Put me to work then. What do you need me to do?"

Nina stepped forward with the efficiency of a woman seizing an opportunity. "I need to head upstairs and finish some inventory reconciliation. Year-end accounting waits for no one." She untied her apron, draping it over the back of a folding chair. "You two have this under control, right?"

Hallie shot her a look that clearly communicated You're abandoning me, but Nina pretended not to notice. She grabbed her water bottle from the table and headed for the stairs with purposeful strides.

Halfway up, she paused and turned back. Her gaze moved between Hallie and Chase with pointed intention. "You two need to talk."

Then she was gone, her footsteps fading into the sounds of the shop above, leaving Hallie and Chase alone in the basement with fifteen unfinished silent auction baskets and a chasm of unspoken words between them.

The silence stretched thin and uncomfortably. Hallie picked up a jar of gourmet jam, studying the label as if it contained the secrets of the universe. Strawberry rhubarb. Small batch. Locally sourced.

"So." Chase moved closer to the worktable. "Where should I start?"

"The outdoor adventure basket needs assembling." Hallie gestured toward a collection of camping gear, hiking accessories, and a nice fleece jacket still in its packaging. "Everything goes in that large wicker basket. Try to make it look balanced."

"Balanced. Got it." He picked up the fleece, examining it with the same careful attention she'd seen him give everything. "This is nice quality."

"Mountain Outpost donated it. They've been generous supporters for years."

They worked in careful silence. Hallie finished the coffee basket, tucking the last items into place before starting on the cellophane wrap. Chase arranged camping supplies in the wicker basket, his movements methodical and precise.

The old ease between them was absent. Every interaction felt measured and polite, like two acquaintances working together rather than two people who'd spent the past month and a half growing close again. No teasing. No laughter. No comfortable rhythm that turned work into something fun.

Hallie hated it. Hated that she'd created this distance. Hated that she couldn't seem to bridge it even though she wanted to. Hated the fear that kept her locked behind walls she'd built to protect a heart that had been broken too many times.

"How was your week?" Chase asked.

"Busy. The usual holiday rush."

"Yeah, same at the store." He said as he secured the camping lantern in the basket. "We had a run on board games yesterday. Apparently, everyone wants to give their families the gift of quality time."

"That's nice."

Another silence. This one heavier.

Chase set down the water bottle he'd been positioning and turned to face her fully. "Hallie."

She didn't look up from the cellophane she was wrapping around the coffee basket. "Hmm?"

"What are we doing here?"

The question hit her like cold water. She fumbled with the cellophane and had to catch it before the whole arrangement collapsed. "We're assembling silent auction baskets."

"That's not what I mean."

She knew that. Of course, she knew that. But acknowledging what he actually meant would require courage she wasn't sure she possessed. She secured the cellophane with tape, focusing on making the edges crisp and professional.

"Hallie, look at me. Please."

The please undid something in her chest. She set down the tape and lifted her gaze to his, finding blue eyes that held concern and frustration and something tender that made her throat tighten.

"This isn't us," Chase said. "This careful politeness. This distance. I've felt it since Sunday night, and I understand why it's there. But we need to talk about it."

"There's nothing to talk about." The lie tasted bitter. "We're fine."

"We're not fine." He moved around the table, closing the physical distance even though the emotional gulf remained. "You've been avoiding me. Brief texts. Excuses about being too busy to grab lunch. You practically ran away from me Sunday night after we came back from the Veteran's Home."

"I had work to finish."

"Hallie. I know you're pulling away. I recognize what you're doing because I understand why you're doing it."

She wanted to deny it. Wanted to maintain the fiction that everything was normal and manageable. But standing here under his steady gaze, she couldn't summon the energy for more lies.

"Okay," she said quietly. "Maybe I am pulling away."

"Because of what I said to Aaron. About questioning whether the toy store is my calling. About not being sure if what I'm doing is enough."

She nodded, not trusting her voice.

"You heard uncertainty and assumed I was planning to leave."

"Aren't you?" The question burst out before she could stop it. "You've said multiple times now that you don't know if managing your parents' store is what you're meant to do. That you're not sure if it's enough. That sounds a lot like someone who's going to leave."

"That's not what I meant."

"Then what did you mean, Chase?" She turned away, pressing her palms flat against the worktable, trying to regain composure that was slipping like sand through her fingers.

"I'm not your mother, Hallie," Chase said quietly behind her. "And I'm not the eighteen-year-old kid who left for the Marines. I'm trying to figure out my life after twelve years of following orders and executing missions. That doesn't mean I'm looking for an escape route."

"But you don't know what you want." She kept her back to him, unable to face him while speaking this truth. "You're questioning everything. And I can't—" Her breath hitched. "I can't watch someone else leave. I can't let myself care and then have you decide that life here isn't enough. That I'm not enough."

"Hallie, that's not—"

"Yes, it is." She spun to face him, and the words came pouring out like a dam breaking. "I'm scared, Chase. I'm terrified. Every person I've ever loved has left. My mother couldn't handle grief and ran to Florida. You left for the military. Daniel broke our engagement because he wasn't in love with me anymore. Everyone decides eventually that what I can offer isn't worth staying for. And I thought—" She pressed a hand to her chest, feeling her heart hammering beneath her palm. "I thought maybe your coming back meant something different. That maybe this time someone would stay."

Chase stood perfectly still, absorbing her words. His jaw worked, and she saw him processing everything she'd just thrown at him—her fear, her pain, her assumption that he would leave because everyone else had.

"I had a conversation with my parents yesterday," he said finally. "About the store. About my future here."

Hallie's stomach dropped. Here it came. The confirmation of her worst fears. The admission that he'd decided to pursue something else, somewhere else. She braced herself.

"They told me they're ready to retire. They've been waiting to see what I wanted to do before making any decisions about the business." Chase moved closer, stopping a few feet away from where she stood. "They offered me the store. Said if I wanted to take it over, they'd step back and let me run it however I thought best. But they also said if I wanted to do something else entirely, they'd support that too."

"Oh. So you have options."

"I do. And that's what's been on my mind the past few days. Not whether I'm leaving Mistletoe Falls, but what I'm going to build here."

The distinction took a moment to penetrate. "What are you going to build here?"

"I'm not leaving, Hallie." He said it clearly, firmly, leaving no room for misinterpretation. "That's not what my questioning was about. I'm trying to figure out how to create something meaningful. How to use what I learned in the Marines to serve a different kind of mission."

"I don't understand."

"Talking with Aaron on Sunday made me see something I'd been missing. There are veterans like him all over—men and women who served their country and came home to struggle with transition. They have skills but no civilian credentials. They need purpose and income while they figure out their next steps. They're trying to find their place in a world that doesn't always value what they bring, and not only that... some of us come home to a world we don't understand anymore."

Hallie watched emotions play across his face. This was important to him. She could see it in every line of his body.

"I've been doing research," Chase continued. "Looking into veteran unemployment rates, talking to people online who've gone through transition programs in other parts of the country. I've been thinking about what could actually help military men and women like me and Aaron. And I realized I could create something here. Something that honors what my parents built while serving veterans who need support."

"What kind of something?"

"A bridge program. Keep the toy store running on the main floor—employ veterans in transition, teach them retail and customer service skills while they earn income. Use my dad's woodworking shop in the basement to train them in carpentry. Aaron mentioned he builds furniture. He could manage the workshop, train other veterans, and create the handcrafted toys my dad's been making for years. I could expand the online business even more, possibly, and generate more revenue."

Hallie's mind raced to keep up, picturing what he was describing. The toy store she knew so well transformed into something bigger. A mission with layers.

"And my apartment upstairs," Chase continued, "I'd convert it into a headquarters for veteran services. Job counseling. Resume help. Skills translation—helping veterans understand how their military experience applies to civilian jobs. I'd partner with local businesses and create a network of employers willing to hire veterans. Connect transitioning service members with permanent positions that pay decent wages and value their skills."

The vision spilled out of him like water from a broken dam—detailed, thoughtful, clearly something he'd been turning over in his mind for days. He talked about three-to six-month positions that would give veterans time to heal and plan. About creating a model where successful veterans came back to help new ones. About maintaining dignity while providing support.

"Aaron would have purpose," Chase said. "Other veterans would have options. And I'd be using everything I learned in the Marines—leadership, logistics, program development—to serve people who understand what it means to come home and feel lost."

Hallie absorbed it all, watching him transform before her eyes. This wasn't the uncertain man questioning his place. This was someone who'd found direction. Purpose. A calling that combined his skills and values in a way that made his entire face light up.

"It would mean giving up my apartment," he added. "I'd need to find somewhere else to live. But that's fine. The space would serve veterans better than it serves me."

"Where would you go?"

"I'd figure something out. Maybe rent a place in town, or there are apartments over on Pinecone Ridge. Maybe even move back into Mom and Dad's place for a little while and save to buy a house. That's a minor detail, though, compared to what the program I'm trying to figure out could accomplish."

Minor detail. He was talking about displacing himself, reorganizing his entire life, and treating it like an afterthought because this mission mattered more.

"I want to run the business side of the toy store," he continued. "Management, operations, program development—the behind-the-scenes work that keeps everything functioning. I'm good at that. It's where my brain works best. I can hire people eventually who can handle the customer-facing retail, and I can focus on making sure the entire operation runs smoothly and grows sustainably."

He paused, and his expression shifted to something more vulnerable. More uncertain.

"But I need your opinion on this. I need your perspective. You know this community better than anyone. You've built Operation Christmas Cheer from nothing into something. You understand how to create programs that actually help people without making them feel like charity cases."

"Will this work?" Chase asked. "What am I missing? What problems do you see that I'm too close to notice? How do I approach the mayor about this? Which businesses would be excellent partners?" He ran a hand through his hair, a gesture of nervous energy she'd rarely seen from him. "I don't want to make this decision alone. I've spent years deciding alone, executing missions solo, and following orders without collaboration. This is different. This matters too much to get wrong, and I need—" He stopped, corrected himself. "I want your help to figure out if this is the right direction."

"You're staying," she said.

"Yes, I'm staying. I'm not questioning whether to be here. I'm figuring out how to build something meaningful here. There's a difference."

He hadn't been looking for an exit. He'd been searching for purpose. And he'd found it in a way that rooted him more deeply in Mistletoe Falls rather than pulling him away.

"I thought—" She swallowed against the tightness in her throat. "When you talked about not knowing if the toy store was your calling, I heard you planning to leave."

"I know." He took a step closer. "Hallie, you need to understand something. Questioning my career path isn't the same as questioning you. Or us."

Chase moved closer slowly, as if approaching something skittish that might bolt. "I'm not going anywhere, Hallie. I'm staying because this is where I want to be. Because there's work here that matters. Because everything I want is here. My family. My purpose. You."

The simple word—you—hit her with the force of a confession. Not I love you or declarations too big to process, just the acknowledgment that she factored into his decision to stay. That she mattered in the equation of his future.

"I'm scared to believe this," she whispered. "I'm scared to trust that you'll stay. That this program will work out. That I won't wake up six months from now to find out you've decided you need something different after all."

"I can't promise the future will be perfect. In fact, I know it won't be." Chase's honesty stung and soothed in equal measure. "I can't guarantee the program will succeed. But I can promise I'm committed to figuring it out here where I grew up. This is home."

Hallie studied his face, searching for any hint of doubt or reservation. She found only steady certainty and something that looked like hope.

"What do you think?" he asked. "About the program. Does it make sense? Can it work?"

The question pulled her into practical considerations, away from the emotional vertigo of the past few minutes. She thought about Operation Christmas Cheer, about what she'd learned by building it from nothing.

"You'd need buy-in from the veterans' home," she said, her mind engaging with the logistics. "They'd be your natural partner for connecting with veterans who need support. Mayor Hayes would probably support it too—he's always looking for programs that serve the community meaningfully."

Chase nodded, listening with the same focused intensity he'd given to Aaron's stories at the veterans' home.

"The job placement piece is critical," Hallie continued. "You'd need commitments from local businesses before you start. Promises of interviews, at minimum. Otherwise, you're training people for positions that don't exist."

"That makes sense. How do I approach businesses about that?"

"Personal connections first. You old friend Luke at the Reindeer Rack. Claire at the bakery. People who know you and would be willing to take a chance on veterans you vouch for. Then you use those successes to approach other businesses." She tucked a strand of hair behind her ear, warming to the topic despite her emotional exhaustion. "And you'd need to track outcomes. How many veterans go through the program, how many find permanent employment, average wages.

Data helps when you're asking for community support or applying for grants."

"Grants hadn't even occurred to me."

"There are veteran service grants. Small business development grants. Community improvement funds. You'd qualify for multiple categories." She moved to the worktable, pulled out a notepad, and started jotting down thoughts. "You'd need a website, social media presence and a way for veterans to find out about the program and apply. And clear criteria for who qualifies—recent discharge, local residency, that kind of thing."

Chase watched her write. "See, this is exactly why I need your help. I was thinking about the structure and mission but hadn't gotten to implementation details."

"Implementation is where good ideas succeed or fail." She added another note. "You should talk to the veterans' home director. Get their perspectives on what veterans struggle with most. That'll help you refine the program focus."

They talked for another twenty minutes, Hallie asking questions and Chase answering, both of them building on the vision until it felt less like a vague concept and more like something achievable. The conversation pulled her out of her fear and into familiar territory—problem-solving, planning, and figuring out how to serve people effectively.

And somewhere in the middle of discussing partnership agreements and program timelines, the tension that had gripped her chest for four days began to ease.

This was real. Chase had thought this through. He wasn't making empty promises or vague commitments. He was trying to build something concrete.

"I keep coming back to Aaron," Chase said, leaning against the worktable. "Thinking about his skills and how he can't get hired because civilian employers don't value military carpentry experience the same way. That's wrong. That needs to change."

"It does," Hallie agreed. "And your program could help change it. At least locally... at first. A program like this could actually grow into something much bigger... just a warning."

"Start local, prove the model works, maybe expand to help other communities develop similar programs." He rubbed the back of his neck. "I'm getting ahead of myself. Right now, I just need to figure out if this is viable."

"It is," Hallie said with more certainty than she'd felt about anything in days. "It'll take work, and there'll be challenges. But Chase, this is good. This is really good."

Relief crossed his features, so profound it made her realize how much her opinion had mattered to him. How vulnerable he'd been, sharing this vision and asking for her assessment.

"We should probably finish these baskets," Hallie said finally, gesturing at the work they'd abandoned. "The gala's Saturday."

"Right, baskets."

They worked together, and this time the silence felt different. Not comfortable yet, but not strained either. More like the quiet of two people who'd said difficult things and needed time to settle into new understanding.

Hallie assembled a gourmet food basket while Chase finished the outdoor adventure collection.

"Hallie," Chase said as she secured cellophane around the food basket.

"Yeah?"

"Thank you for listening and helping me think this through. For being honest about why you've been pulling away. I know that took courage."

She met his eyes across the table and nodded.

"I'm not going anywhere, and I mean it."

"Let's just finish these silent auction baskets up. It's getting late."

By the time they finished, the worktable held fifteen completed silent auction baskets in various themes—spa treatments, gourmet foods, outdoor adventures, book lovers' collections, wine and cheese, coffee connoisseur supplies. Each one wrapped in cellophane with elaborate bows, ready for Saturday's gala.

Chase helped her carry the baskets to the storage area where they'd be safe until the event. When the last basket was brought up, Hallie turned to find Chase watching her with an expression she couldn't quite read. Not quite a smile, but something warm and steady that made her pulse skip.

"Tomorrow evening then? I'll see you for the setup for the gala?" he asked.

"You sure you want to keep helping? You've got a lot to figure out with your new program."

"I'm sure. I committed to seeing Operation Christmas Cheer through Christmas Day, and I keep my commitments." He paused. "Plus, I enjoy working with you. Even when you're trying so hard to keep your distance from me to protect yourself."

The gentle teasing in his voice surprised a small laugh out of her. "Fair point."

"Come on, let's call it a night."

They exited the building together, and he watched her climb her stairs to her apartment.

"Hallie."

She turned to look down at him.

"I know we're not completely okay yet. I know you're scared. That's fine. Take whatever time you need. Do whatever you need to do. But please don't shut me out completely. Talk to me. Let me show you I'm staying."

The request was so simple and so impossible to refuse. "Okay."

"Okay." He smiled, and it transformed his entire face. "I'll see you tomorrow?"

"Yeah. Tomorrow."

Chapter 30

The stepladder wobbled under Lucy's weight as she stretched to hang another strand of silver garland across the community center's exposed beam, and Hallie gripped the aluminum frame with both hands while simultaneously monitoring all the activity unfolding across the large multipurpose room of the Community Center.

"A little more to the left," Hallie called up. "It needs to drape evenly with the one Taylor hung on the other side."

"Like this?" Lucy asked.

"Perfect. Now secure it and come down carefully."

Hallie released the ladder once Lucy had both feet planted firmly on the rungs, then turned her attention to the disaster unfolding near the stage. Two volunteers from the elementary school were attempting to hang the backdrop for tomorrow's children's play, but they'd somehow managed to get the support poles tangled in a way that defied both physics and common sense.

She pressed her fingers to her temples, took a breath, and headed in their direction. Around her, the community center buzzed with three dozen volunteers transforming the space from functional meeting hall into elegant gala venue. Tables waited in stacks against the far wall, ready to be arranged for tomorrow night's dinner. Boxes of center-pieces sat near the kitchen entrance, each one carefully assembled earlier this week. A Christmas tree occupied a prime position near the stage, its branches heavy with ornaments and lights.

"Mrs. Clark, Mr. Sanders," Hallie said as she approached the back-drop situation. "Let's try something different. If you lower the left pole completely and work from the center outward, I think we can untangle this without starting over."

Mrs. Clark, who taught second grade and had the patience of a saint, nodded with relief. "Thank you, Hallie. I was thinking we'd broken something."

"Not possible. These poles have survived years of elementary school plays. They're indestructible." Hallie helped them work through the tangle, her hands moving with practiced efficiency while her mind cataloged the seventeen other tasks that needed completion before they could call tonight's setup finished.

The sound system needed testing. Someone had to verify that the kitchen had received the final headcount for tomorrow's catered din-ner. The silent auction items waited in storage, ready to be arranged on display tables. Chairs needed positioning around tables. The dance floor area required marking off with decorative rope barriers.

And somewhere in the middle of all this, she needed to make sure the high school band and choir knew their setup locations for tomorrow, confirm the elementary school director understood the evening's timeline, and coordinate with Mayor Hayes about his wel-come speech.

"There." The backdrop poles finally cooperated, sliding into their proper configuration. "Now you can attach the painted canvas, and it should hang beautifully."

"You're a miracle worker," Mr. Sanders said, already reaching for the folded backdrop.

Hallie smiled and turned away, her gaze sweeping across the space to assess progress. Taylor and Sofia were hanging decorations near the refreshment tables. Nina stood near the entrance with a clipboard, checking off deliveries as they arrived and directing traffic with the efficiency of an air traffic controller.

The main doors opened, admitting a blast of frigid evening air along with four familiar figures.

Hallie's heart did something complicated as Chase walked in, followed by Aaron, Mark and Liz.

Chase's gaze found hers across the crowded room, and his face transformed with a smile that made her pulse skip. He raised one hand in greeting, then said something to his companions that made them all look in her direction.

They navigated through the volunteers and equipment with Chase leading the way.

"Put us to work," he said as they reached her.

Hallie looked at the four of them—Chase in jeans and a dark blue sweater that made his eyes even more striking, Aaron in casual clothes, Mark in his standard flannel and khakis, and Liz bundled in a thick cardigan with a lap blanket tucked around her legs.

"Silent auction setup," she said. "The display tables are already set up, and all the baskets are in the back room. They need to be arranged attractively, with the bid sheets positioned clearly, and everything has to be visible from multiple angles to encourage bidding."

"We can handle that," Liz said. "I've set up enough displays in the toy store to know what catches attention."

"The baskets are amazing this year," Hallie added, leading them toward the storage room. "Chase and I assembled most of them last night."

They reached the storage room, where Nina had organized everything earlier. Fifteen completed silent auction baskets lined the shelves, each one wrapped in cellophane and topped with elaborate bows.

"Wow... these are really nice," Aaron said, stepping closer to examine the outdoor adventure basket. "Someone put a lot of thought into these."

"That's all Hallie's doing," Chase said.

"The display tables should be set up by now," Hallie said, pulling herself back to practical matters. "Let me show you where everything goes."

They carried baskets out to the main hall, where three long tables had been positioned near the entrance, draped with white tablecloths that puddled elegantly on the floor. Liz immediately took charge and began directing placement of the items, offering suggestions about angles and groupings that consistently improved the overall presentation.

"That outdoor basket should be more centered," Liz said, studying the arrangement with narrowed eyes.

Aaron adjusted the position. "Like this?"

"Better. Now, if we move the spa basket to the left and bring the coffee collection forward slightly..."

Hallie watched, her role shifting from coordinator to observer as she realized she wasn't needed to micromanage this task. They had it under control.

"You know," Mark said, positioning the wine and cheese basket at a slight angle, "this reminds me of organizing donations for the church fundraiser last spring. Remember that, Liz? We had about this many items to display and half the volunteers."

"I remember you nearly dropping that antique vase someone donated," Liz replied. "My heart stopped."

"But I didn't drop it. That's what counts."

Chase caught Hallie's eye across the table and smiled. She smiled back, feeling the last remnants of her guard starting to drop away.

"Hallie?" Nina's voice cut through her thoughts. "Sorry to interrupt, but the catering company just called. They need to confirm the final headcount for tomorrow."

"I'll be right there." Hallie excused herself, leaving the group to their work.

The next hour passed as Hallie coordinated a dozen different moving pieces. She verified numbers with the caterer, helped position chairs for the children's program, tested the sound system with the AV volunteers, and confirmed timeline details with Mrs. Patterson, who was directing the elementary school play.

Each time she passed the silent auction area, she noticed progress. The tables were filled with beautifully arranged baskets, and someone had added small decorative elements—sprigs of holly, scattered gold stars, and LED tea lights that cast warm glows across the displays.

By eight-thirty, the community center had transformed completely. Tables arranged in precise rows awaited tomorrow's dinner service. The stage backdrop hung perfectly, ready for the children's play. Decorations caught light from every angle, turning the functional space into something magical. The Christmas tree presided over everything like a benevolent guardian, its ornaments glittering with promise.

And the silent auction display looked professional enough to grace any high-end fundraising event. Each basket was positioned to showcase its contents. Bid sheets clear and accessible. The entire arrangement was inviting and elegant.

Volunteers began gathering their belongings, calling goodbyes to each other as they headed out into the cold December evening. Hallie thanked each person personally, her gratitude genuine as she recognized how much they'd accomplished through collective effort.

Nina appeared at her elbow as the crowd thinned. "You did good, boss. This place looks amazing."

"We all did great." Hallie surveyed the transformed space with satisfaction. "Tomorrow night's going to be wonderful."

"Yes, it is." Nina's gaze traveled to where Chase stood with Aaron, Mark, and Liz near the exit. "I still think he's a keeper. In case you were still wondering."

"I wasn't wondering."

Nina squeezed her shoulder once, then headed out, leaving Hallie to do a last walk through. She checked all doors were locked except the main entrance, verified the heating system was set correctly for overnight, and made sure no equipment had been left in walkways where someone might trip.

When she finally made her way to the entrance, only Chase, Aaron, Mark, and Liz remained. They stood near the double doors, clearly waiting for her despite the late hour.

"All set?" Mark asked as she approached.

"All set. Tomorrow will be the easy part. The hard work's done now."

"You coordinated all this beautifully," Liz said. "Every year I'm amazed at how you pull off events like this."

"I have wonderful help." Hallie looked at Chase and found him already watching her.

She said hugged Mark and Liz before they headed out the door.

Chase pulled his truck keys from his pocket and held them out to Aaron. "Could you give us a few minutes?"

"Take your time." He accepted the keys and disappeared into the parking lot, leaving Chase and Hallie alone in the soft light of the decorated space.

Hallie's heart hammered against her ribs, and she couldn't quite make herself look directly at Chase even though she felt his attention on her like physical warmth.

"So," he said. "Are you still going to be my date tomorrow night?"

"I'll have to arrive a couple of hours early," she said, focusing on logistics because that felt safer than examining the emotions flooding through her chest. "The caterers need supervision setting up. The high school band and choir will need direction finding their spaces. I have to make sure the elementary school group understands how the evening flows, and Mayor Hayes wants to confirm his speech content beforehand. So I can't ride with you. I'll need to drive separately."

"That's fine," he said as he stepped closer. "I just need to know you'll be my date."

He reached for her hand, his fingers warm as they closed around hers. The contact sent electricity up her arm, and when he tugged gently, she stepped into the space between them without resistance.

His free hand came up to cup her face, his thumb brushing across her cheekbone with a tenderness that made her breath catch. Their eyes met and held, and he kissed her.

The kiss lasted only seconds—brief and tender and perfect—before he pulled back just enough to rest his forehead against hers. They stood like that, breathing the same air, neither one ready to break the connection completely.

His hand slipped from her face to tuck a strand of hair behind her ear, the gesture so sweet and careful that her eyes stung with unexpected emotion.

Chase drew back and laced his fingers through hers, and they walked together toward the exit.

Chapter 31

Chase had lost count of how many times Hallie had smiled in the past two hours, but he was certain he'd remember every single one.

She stood near the community center's kitchen entrance, speaking with the caterer while simultaneously gesturing to someone across the room about table arrangements. Her red dress caught the light. The color made her blonde hair seem brighter, her skin luminous, and when she turned slightly and the dress moved with her, Chase was mesmerized.

"Son, are you listening?"

Chase pulled his attention back to the table where he sat with his parents and Aaron. Their dinner plates had been cleared away minutes ago, the catered meal excellent but honestly unmemorable because Chase had spent most of it watching Hallie.

"Sorry, what?"

Mark's knowing smile suggested he understood exactly where Chase's attention had been. "I was saying the children's program was delightful. The twins... the ones you and Hallie helped practice their lines with a few weeks ago were wonderful."

"Mitchell and Maya," Chase said. "They were great. The entire program was great."

"The high school choir sounded amazing," Liz added, adjusting the wrap around her shoulders. "And Mayor Hayes kept his speech mercifully brief for once."

Around them, the community center buzzed with conversation and laughter. Well over two hundred people filled the space—families, couples, residents from the independent living facility, veterans, business owners, teachers, and city officials. Everyone dressed in their finest.

White tablecloths covered every surface. Centerpieces made from evergreen branches, red berries, and pillar candles created festive focal points. Christmas lights wrapped around exposed beams, and garland draped across doorways in loops that caught reflections from the ornaments on the massive tree.

The whole effect was beautiful, but Chase couldn't take his eyes off Hallie.

She finished with the caterer and moved toward their table, weaving between chairs and stopping twice to answer questions from people who flagged her down. When she finally reached them, she was still smiling despite the obvious exhaustion around her eyes.

"Everything going smoothly?" Liz asked as Hallie reclaimed her seat beside Chase.

"So far. The band will begin in a few minutes. The elementary school director confirmed all the children got home safely." Hallie picked up her water glass and took a long drink. "Mayor Hayes wants me to introduce the dancing portion of the evening and remind everyone about the silent auction deadline instead of him doing it.

Apparently, people respond better when I make announcements than when he does."

They talked easily—the five of them comfortable together in a way that felt natural despite the formal setting.

Through it all, Chase watched her, struck by how different she seemed from the woman who'd been pulling away just days ago. The careful distance was gone. The walls she'd built to protect herself had come down, and in their place was this—warmth and openness and a presence that came from someone who'd stopped being afraid.

The band tested microphones and adjusted instruments. A few children ran between tables, their parents calling half-hearted warnings about slowing down. The noise level rose as conversation shifted from dinner to anticipation of what came next.

Hallie glanced at her watch and stood. "I should get ready to make my announcement."

She excused herself and made her way toward the stage, stopping three times to speak with people who caught her attention. Chase tracked her progress across the room, noting how every interaction seemed to energize her despite the late hour and the stress of coordinating an event this size.

"You've got it bad," Aaron said quietly, his tone amused rather than mocking.

Chase turned to find all three of his companions watching him with identical knowing expressions.

"I'm not even going to pretend I don't know what you're talking about."

"Good," Liz said. "You've been staring at her all evening like she hung the moon."

"She might have," Chase muttered, earning laughs from the table.

"She's something special," Aaron said, his expression serious now. "The way she put together those baskets for us at the veterans' home. Personalized every single one based on who we are rather than just throwing random items together. That takes time and care most people don't give."

"She's always been like that," Mark added. "Even as a kid, she paid attention to what people needed. Remembered details. Made everyone around her feel important."

Chase knew all this. Had known it when they were teenagers, had recognized it again when he'd returned to Mistletoe Falls and discovered the woman she'd become. But hearing it from others reinforced what he already believed.

Hallie Dawson was extraordinary.

She stepped onto the stage with the microphone in hand. The room gradually quieted as people turned their attention toward her, conversations trailing off until the space held expectant silence.

She looked beautiful up there. Confident and poised, comfortable in front of two hundred plus people despite having admitted to Chase once that she hated public speaking. The red dress caught light from every angle, and her smile was genuine as she surveyed the crowd.

"Good evening, everyone," she began, her voice carrying clearly through the speakers. "I hope you all enjoyed dinner. Please give a round of applause to the catering team for tonight's wonderful meal."

Applause filled the room, and Hallie waited for it to fade before continuing.

"As most of you know, all proceeds from tonight's gala—including our silent auction—go directly to supporting the Mistletoe Falls Veterans Home. The facility provides housing, medical care, and community for veterans who've served our country with honor and distinction. Your attendance tonight, your generous bids on auction items, and your ongoing support throughout the year make their work possible."

"This community has always understood that service matters. That caring for those who've sacrificed for us isn't optional; it's essential. So thank you. Thank you for being here, for giving generously, and for proving that Mistletoe Falls takes care of its own."

More applause this time, sustained and heartfelt. Chase clapped along with everyone else, his chest tight with pride.

"Don't forget—we'll announce the silent auction winners at nine forty-five, fifteen minutes before we close at ten. So if you see something you want, make sure to get your final bids in. And please be generous. These items are incredible, and every dollar goes to a worthy cause."

"Now," Hallie said, her smile brightening, "it's time to enjoy the rest of our evening. The band has graciously offered to play for the next two hours, so I'm inviting everyone to the dance floor. Let's celebrate together and let's fill this space with joy."

Chase watched her descend the stage steps, watched Mrs. Phillips intercept her immediately with what looked like enthusiastic praise. Then Claire from the bakery stopped her. Then one of the city councilmen. Then a couple Chase didn't recognize.

The band started playing—something upbeat and energetic that had several couples moving toward the cleared area designated as the dance floor. Children ran to claim the space, spinning in circles with their arms out while their parents laughed and moved more sedately onto the floor.

Hallie kept trying to make her way back toward their table. Chase could see her politely extracting herself from conversations, smiling and nodding but clearly attempting to move. Yet every few steps, someone else stopped her.

Chase stood, straightening his shirt and buttoning his sport coat. He navigated through the crowd. He passed Mayor Hayes, who was in deep discussion with several business owners. He nodded to Sofia, who was dancing with her husband while their twins ran circles around them.

Hallie was currently cornered by Mrs. Davis from the public library and her husband, both of them talking animatedly about something that had Hallie nodding but also glancing past them toward where Chase had been sitting.

He came up beside the group with the politeness of someone who'd learned social navigation in military settings where rank and protocol mattered. "Excuse me, Mr. and Mrs. Davis. I hate to interrupt, but I believe it's Miss Dawson's turn to actually enjoy the evening."

Mrs. Davis's face lit with understanding. "Oh, of course! We've been monopolizing her."

"Thank you for coordinating everything tonight, dear," Mr. Davis added, stepping back to give them space. "The evening has been wonderful."

Hallie thanked them graciously, then turned to Chase with a smile that held equal parts relief and amusement. "My hero."

"You looked like you needed an exit strategy."

"Desperately." She glanced around at the crowd, the coordinator in her clearly checking that everything was running smoothly. "But I should probably—"

"No," Chase said as he held out his hand. "You did your job. The band is playing. People are dancing. For the next hour, you're not the coordinator."

"I'm not?"

"No, you're my date. And I'd very much like to dance with you."

She looked at his outstretched hand, then up at his face, and smiled. When she placed her palm in his, her fingers warm against his skin, Chase felt the rightness of it settle into his bones.

He led her onto the dance floor, navigating around spinning children and slower-moving couples until they found a space near the edge where the crowd was slightly less dense. The band was playing something with a steady rhythm—not slow, but not frenetic either. Something that allowed for conversation while they moved.

Chase pulled her into position with the natural confidence of someone who'd learned to dance young and had never forgotten. His right hand settled at the small of her back, feeling the soft fabric of her dress and the warmth of her beneath it. His left hand held hers at shoulder height.

Hallie followed his lead as if she'd been dancing with him for years.

They moved together, finding their rhythm. Her steps were sure, and her posture elegant. When he turned them, she expected the movement and flowed with it. When he adjusted their position, she matched him seamlessly.

"You're an excellent dancer," he said, guiding them around a couple who'd stopped moving to talk.

"So are you. Where did a Marine learn to dance like this?"

"My mother insisted. She said every man should know how to properly lady on a dance floor." Chase spun them gently, and Hallie's dress billowed out before settling back into place. "I complained constantly during the lessons, but I'm grateful now."

"I never knew that you had taken lessons... but I have to say, your mother's a wise woman."

"Don't tell her that. She's already insufferably smug about most things."

Hallie laughed, the sound bright even against the music and crowd noise.

They danced through the rest of the song, conversation pausing as they focused on movement and music. Chase was aware of everything—the way her hand rested on his shoulder, the subtle scent of her perfume, and the way her eyes held his without shyness or reservation.

The song ended and transitioned into something slower. Couples on the floor shifted, pulling closer as the tempo changed. Chase drew Hallie nearer. Her hand on his shoulder moved slightly, fingers pressing gently against the fabric of his sport coat.

"This has been a beautiful evening," she said quietly. "The program went perfectly. Dinner was delicious. The band is wonderful."

"You made it all happen."

"I had help. So much help." She tilted her head slightly to look up at him. "Your parents and Aaron were amazing last night setting up the silent auction. Nina and my team handled a dozen things I would have forgotten. This whole town showed up to support the veterans' home."

"Because you inspired them to." Chase guided them through a turn, moving them toward the center of the floor where there was more room. "That's your gift, Hallie. You make people want to be better, do more, and serve with purpose."

Color rose in her cheeks, visible even in the soft lighting. "That's too much credit."

"It's exactly the right amount of credit."

The song continued, and they moved with it, neither one speaking as the music wrapped around them.

When the next song started—still slow, still romantic—Hallie said, "So I've been thinking about your program idea. The Veterans Bridge

Program. I have some thoughts about the timeline, and I was wondering if you'd considered—"

Chase lifted his left hand from where it held hers and gently pressed his index finger against her lips, silencing her mid-sentence. Her eyes widened in surprise, and he smiled.

"No more work talk."

"But I just wanted to—"

He kept his finger there, gentle but firm. "Hallie. Tonight, you're not the coordinator. You're not the planner. You're not Operation Christmas Cheer founder or gala organizer or the woman who fixes everyone's problems."

"Then who am I?"

"You're mine. You're my date. The woman I've been trying to actually spend time with all evening while you've been managing every detail and talking to every person in this room. Can you just be here? With me? Nothing else for a little while?"

She reached up and took his hand from her lips, lacing their fingers together and bringing their joined hands down to rest against her shoulder instead of in proper dance position.

"I can do that."

They swayed together, the formal structure of their dance dissolving into something more intimate and less choreographed. She was close enough now that her forehead nearly touched his jaw. Close enough that he could feel her breathing, sense the way she'd relaxed completely into this moment with him.

"I'm scared," she said after a minute, her voice barely audible over the music.

"Of what?"

"That I'll wake up and this won't be real." She pulled back just enough to look at him. "I keep waiting for the other shoe to drop. For something to go wrong."

"Nothing's going to go wrong." He said it with absolute conviction. "I'm here. I'm staying. I want you in my life. In every part of it."

"You make it sound simple."

"It is simple. I care about you. You care about me. We're both done pretending otherwise or protecting ourselves from something good." Chase guided them through another turn, giving himself time to find the right words. "I'm not leaving. I'm not going to decide you're not enough and walk away."

"How can you be so sure?"

"Because I've spent the past month and a half getting to know you again. Watching you serve this community with such joy. Seeing you coordinate impossible logistics and make it look effortless. Working beside you and discovering that I like the person I am when I'm with you." He held her gaze, willing her to hear the truth in his words. "You make me want to be better. Build something meaningful. Create a life that matters beyond just getting through each day."

"Chase."

"I'm done being cautious about this. Done pretending friendship is enough when I want so much more. Done watching you pull away because you're scared."

She didn't respond in words. Instead, she stepped closer, eliminating the small distance between them, and rested her head against his chest. Her hand on his shoulder slid around to his back, holding him the way he held her—with certainty and intention.

They danced like that through the rest of the song and into the next one. Other couples moved around them, the floor growing more crowded as people finished conversations and joined the dancing.

Chase caught sight of his parents—his father guiding his mother's wheelchair near the edge of the floor, both of them watching him and Hallie and smiling.

The community center had transformed completely from the functional space it had been last night. The decorations and lighting created magic, but it was the people who made it special—neighbors and friends and strangers gathered to support veterans who'd given so much in service to their country.

And in the middle of it all, Chase held the woman he'd come home to find.

The song shifted again, tempo slowing further. The band's lead singer crooned something romantic about love and second chances, and Chase thought about how fitting that was. They'd both been given second chances—him to return to his hometown and discover purpose beyond military service, Hallie to risk her heart again after being hurt too many times.

"I'm all in," Hallie said suddenly, pulling back to look at him. "I'm done being scared of loving you."

Chase stopped dancing. They stood in the middle of the floor while couples moved around them, but he needed her to see his face, needed her to know how much her words meant.

"I'm in love with you," he said.

Tears spilled over now, tracking down her cheeks, and she made no move to wipe them away. "I love you. I've loved you since we were kids. Even when I was trying to push you away, I loved you."

People moved around them on the dance floor, the music continued, the evening progressed—but in this moment, nothing existed except the two of them and the truth they'd finally spoken aloud.

Chase cupped her face with both hands, his thumbs brushing away tears that kept falling despite her watery smile. Her hands came up to cover his, holding him there, and they stood like that—anchored to each other while the world spun around them.

Then he kissed her.

Not tentative or testing like their first kiss had been. Not brief and sweet like the one at the end of setup night. This kiss held certainty and promise and the weight of everything they'd just admitted to each other.

Hallie's hands tightened on his, her lips moving against his with the same sure confidence she brought to everything she did well. She wasn't pulling away or holding back. She was here, fully present, kissing him like she meant it.

When they finally pulled apart, Hallie's smile was radiant. "We just made a scene."

"I don't care."

"Your parents are watching."

"Don't care."

"Half the town probably saw that kiss."

"Good. Hope they enjoyed the show."

She laughed, the sound bright and unguarded, and rested her forehead against his as they started dancing again.

Chapter 32

The fire popped and hissed, sending sparks up the chimney while Mark reached for another wrapped package from beneath the Christmas tree. Wrapping paper littered the living room floor, ribbons curled between discarded bows, and empty boxes sat stacked near the hearth.

Hallie tucked her feet beneath her on the couch, the new snow globe from Mark and Liz in her hands. Inside the glass dome, a perfect miniature of Mistletoe Falls' town square caught the firelight, the tiny buildings so detailed she could make out individual windows. When she tipped it gently, glitter snow swirled around the scene like real snowflakes.

"This is so beautiful," she said for the third time, unable to stop looking at it. "I can't believe how much detail is in here."

Beside her on the couch, Chase shifted closer as he handed her another gift. The wrapping paper crinkled as Hallie accepted it. She opened the package to reveal a photograph in a simple wooden frame that nearly took her breath away.

It was from the gala. In the photo, Chase looked down at her with an expression so full of tenderness it made her chest ache, while she gazed up at him like he'd hung every star in the winter sky. The camera had captured the exact moment when everything else had fallen away. When the crowd and the music and the carefully planned event had faded into background noise, leaving only the two of them suspended in their own private world.

"Nina took that picture," Chase said.

Hallie couldn't speak past the lump in her throat. She traced the edge of the frame with one finger, studying their faces—the way they leaned toward each other, the way his hand rested at the small of her back, the way her fingers curled against his shoulder like she was holding onto something precious.

This was what love looked like. Not perfect or posed, but real and present and completely unguarded.

"I love it," she managed finally. "Thank you."

"You're welcome."

Mark cleared his throat and said, "Well, should we see what Hallie got for Chase?"

Hallie set the frame carefully on the coffee table and retrieved her gift from beside the couch where she'd tucked it earlier. The blue wrapping paper caught the firelight as she handed it to Chase.

He opened it with the same care she'd used, peeling back tape instead of tearing through paper, revealing the leather journal inside. His fingers traced his embossed initials on the cover.

"For all your ideas," Hallie said, watching his face. "And the challenges and the victories. So you can document everything as you build your program in the coming year."

Chase looked up at her, his blue eyes reflecting the Christmas tree lights in points of color. "This is—" His voice caught. "Thank you. Really. This is perfect."

"You're welcome."

He leaned over and kissed her temple, his lips warm against her skin.

Mark was already reaching beneath the tree, pulling out packages with the enthusiasm of someone who genuinely enjoyed gift-giving. "These are from your mother and me to both of you."

She and Chase opened matching boxes to find hand-knitted scarves in complementary colors—deep green for him, rich burgundy for her. The wool was soft and thick, clearly crafted with skill and patience.

"Mom, did you make these?" Chase held his scarf up to examine the intricate cable pattern running down its length.

"I did."

"They're beautiful." Hallie wrapped hers around her neck experimentally, and the wool felt like an embrace. "Thank you."

The last of the presents were distributed and opened—a cookbook for Liz, new work gloves for Mark, boxes of specialty coffee and tea, and chocolate that would probably be gone by New Year's. The pile of gifts beneath the tree dwindled, and the wrapping paper on the floor formed a colorful carpet of celebration.

Mark stretched and yawned. "All right, tradition time. Everyone ready?"

"Been ready," Chase said.

Mark stood and retrieved a worn book from the side table where he'd placed it earlier. The cover was faded, the binding cracked from decades of use, but Hallie could still make out the gold lettering: "The Night Before Christmas."

The room fell quiet except for the fire crackling and the wind outside pushing snow against the windows. Hallie leaned into Chase's side, and his arm came down from the couch back to wrap around her shoulders, holding her close.

Mark cleared his throat with theatrical ceremony. "'Twas the night before Christmas, when all through the house, not a creature was stirring, not even a mouse...'"

His voice filled the living room, painting pictures with words every child knew by heart. Hallie had heard this story a hundred times; her father used to read it to her.

She glanced up at Chase and found him watching his father with an expression she couldn't quite name. His jaw worked once, and she understood without words that this tradition meant more than just a story.

It meant home. It meant family.

Hallie reached for his free hand and laced their fingers together, squeezing gently. He squeezed back without looking away from his father, but his grip was firm and sure.

"The stockings were hung by the chimney with care, in hopes that St. Nicholas soon would be there...'"

Outside, the snow continued its gentle descent, coating Mistletoe Falls in fresh white.

"He sprang to his sleigh, to his team gave a whistle, and away they all flew like the down of a thistle. But I heard him exclaim as he drove out of sight—'Happy Christmas to all, and to all a good night.'"

Mark closed the book with a soft thump, and the room fell into the kind of peaceful silence that felt sacred. No one moved for a long moment. Then Liz reached over and squeezed Mark's hand, and he smiled at her with three decades of love written plainly on his face.

"Thank you for that, Dad." Chase's voice was rough around the edges. "It's good to be home."

"It's good to have you home." Mark set the book aside carefully. "Both of you."

Liz yawned delicately behind her hand. "I think that's my signal. We're not as young as we used to be, Mark. Let's call it a night."

"Speak for yourself." But Mark was already standing, stretching his back with an audible pop. "I could stay up all night."

"You say that all the time, and you fell asleep in your chair before ten-thirty."

Chase and Hallie rose from the couch, and the four of them moved through the familiar choreography of ending an evening. Hallie helped gather wrapping paper while Chase carried empty boxes to the recycling bin, and Mark and Liz supervised.

At the front door, Mark pulled Chase into a long hug. "Merry Christmas, son."

"Merry Christmas, Dad."

Then Liz was hugging them both—first Chase, then Hallie, holding on a moment longer than necessary and whispering, "Thank you for loving my boy."

Hallie's vision blurred. "Thank you for sharing him. And for this." She gestured vaguely at the house, the evening, the sense of family that had wrapped around her like those hand-knitted scarves. "For all of it."

Outside, the cold hit like a wall—sharp and clean, stealing breath and stinging exposed skin. Hallie gasped and pulled her new scarf tighter, grateful for the thick wool against her neck. Beside her, Chase was wrapping his own scarf more securely, his breath forming clouds in the space between them.

His truck sat in the driveway, dusted with fresh snow. The neighborhood was quiet except for the wind in the pine trees and the distant sound of church bells marking the hour.

Nine o'clock on Christmas Eve. Across town, other families would be finishing their own celebrations, tucking children into bed with promises of Santa's arrival, settling in for the quiet peace that came after excitement.

He opened the passenger-side truck door for her, then went around to the other side, got in and started the truck.

He turned toward her and said, "I love you."

"I love you too."

"Merry Christmas, Hallie."

"Merry Christmas, Chase."

Epilogue

The register drawer clicked shut with its familiar metallic snap, and Hallie pressed the last button to run the end-of-day report. The small printer beside the computer whirred to life, spitting out a receipt tape covered in numbers that would need reconciling.

Valentine's Day had been good for business. Better than good, actually. The shop had seen a steady stream of customers all day—husbands buying last-minute gifts, grandparents selecting special gifts for grandchildren, and tourists stopping in for souvenirs that captured the mountain town's perpetual Christmas charm.

Beside her at the counter, Nina sorted credit card receipts into neat stacks. Across the shop, Sofia straightened a display.

"I'm exhausted," she said, stepping back to survey her work. "My feet are killing me."

"That's what you get for wearing cute shoes instead of practical ones," Nina said without looking up from her receipts.

"These are practical. Practically adorable."

Hallie smiled at their familiar banter, her attention fixed on the computer screen where transaction totals scrolled past. The numbers were good. The day had been profitable. And she had dinner plans with Chase in forty-five minutes, which meant she needed to finish closing procedures and get upstairs to change.

Outside the large front windows, downtown Mistletoe Falls glowed with streetlights and the perpetual Christmas decorations that made the town famous. Even on Valentine's Day, garland wrapped around every lamppost, and wreaths hung on every storefront. February darkness had fallen early, and the snow that had started around three o'clock continued to dust the sidewalks in a gentle accumulation that would make the town look like a postcard by morning.

The door was already locked, the "CLOSED" sign visible to anyone passing by. Inside, warmth from the heating system and the soft glow of Christmas lights created the cozy atmosphere Hallie loved most about her shop after hours. This was when the space felt most like hers—when the customers had gone home and only the quiet remained, punctuated by Nina's occasional comment or Sofia's humming as she worked.

A knock on the door made all three women look up.

Chase stood outside, his breath forming clouds in the cold air. He wore dark jeans and a green flannel shirt under his winter coat.

Hallie moved automatically toward the door, already smiling. He was early.

Nina's hand closed around her wrist, stopping her mid-step.

Hallie turned to look at her friend, confused. "What—"

"Let Sofia get it."

Sofia was already moving past them, practically running to the door. She unlocked it with fingers that trembled, then pulled it open with a grin so wide it looked painful.

"Come in, come in!" Sofia stepped aside, and Chase entered on a gust of cold air.

Hallie stared at him, her brain trying to process what she was seeing. He held a thick stack of cards and envelopes bound together with a rubber band. And in his other hand, he carried a bouquet of a dozen red roses tied together with a gorgeous white satin ribbon.

Her heart started beating faster, a drum rhythm that echoed in her ears and made it difficult to hear anything else. Sofia closed and locked the door behind Chase.

"Hallie," Chase said, and his voice carried the same nervous determination she remembered from months ago when he'd first walked into her shop carrying these exact cards.

She couldn't move. Couldn't speak. Could barely breathe as he crossed the distance between them.

"I came to your shop last fall," Chase said, stopping a few feet away from her, "carrying these cards you'd sent me over twelve years to say thank you for never giving up on me."

"But I didn't understand then what I know now." Chase's blue eyes held hers with an intensity that made her knees feel weak. "That day changed my life."

She walked around the counter toward him as he held out the bouquet of roses, and Hallie's hands moved of their own accord to accept them. The flowers were perfect—deep red petals, stems cut in identical lengths, and the ribbon tied elaborately. She brought them to her nose, breathing in the sweet scent, and that's when she saw it.

Nestled among the roses, partially hidden by green leaves, sat a small white velvet jewelry box.

The shop tilted slightly, or maybe that was just her vision blurring. She looked up at Chase, unable to form words, unable to do anything except stand there holding flowers and trying to remember how to breathe.

Chase set the stack of cards on the nearby counter. Then he reached into the bouquet she held, his fingers gentle as he extracted the white velvet box from among the roses.

He dropped to one knee.

Behind her, Hallie heard Nina make a small sound—half gasp, half sob—but she couldn't look away from Chase's face. She couldn't process anything except the sight of him kneeling on the floor of her shop, holding a ring box, looking up at her with an expression so full of love it made her chest ache.

He opened the box.

The ring inside caught the light from a dozen Christmas displays, sending tiny rainbows across the walls. A vintage-style setting held a single diamond that looked like it belonged in a different era—elegant and timeless, with delicate metalwork that spoke of careful craftsman-ship.

"Hallie Rose Dawson," Chase said, his voice steady despite the emotion she could see in his eyes. "You kept believing in me even when I'd stopped believing in myself. You showed me what it means to come home—not just to a place, but to a person. To a future. You've spent your life wrapping gifts for everyone else in this shop, making Christmas magic for people who need it."

A tear slid down her cheek, hot against her cold skin. She didn't wipe it away. Couldn't move. Could barely stand as his words wrapped around her heart and squeezed.

"Tonight I'm giving you something you can't wrap—my whole heart, my whole life, everything I am and everything I hope to be. Let me spend forever making you as happy as you've made me."

Another tear fell, then another. The roses in her hands shook slightly, their petals trembling with the same tremor that had taken over her entire body.

"Will you marry me?"

She tried to speak, but her throat had closed around the words. Tried again, managing only a whisper that came out broken and thick with tears. "Yes."

Chase's face transformed, relief and joy flooding his features in equal measure.

"Yes," she said again, louder this time, her voice gaining strength. "Yes, of course, yes."

He stood in a fluid motion, taking her left hand and sliding the ring onto her finger. It fit perfectly, settling into place as if it had been made for her. Like it had been waiting for this exact moment to find its home.

Then his hands were framing her face, tilting it up toward his, and he was kissing her with a tenderness that made her forget about the roses still clutched in her other hand, forget about Nina and Sofia watching with their phones raised, forget about everything except the feel of his lips on hers and the solid reality of his love.

When they pulled apart, she was crying in earnest—happy tears that wouldn't stop falling no matter how many times she blinked. Chase's thumbs brushed them away, his own eyes suspiciously bright.

"Let me see!" Sofia rushed over, grabbing Hallie's left hand and holding it up to examine the ring. "Oh my word, Hallie, it's gorgeous!"

Nina appeared on her other side, wrapping her arms around both Hallie and Sofia in a group embrace. "I thought I was going to give it away when I wouldn't let you open the door!"

"You knew?" Hallie looked between her two friends, seeing confirmation in their matching grins. "You both knew?"

"Chase recruited us last week," Sofia admitted, finally releasing her death grip on Hallie's hand. "He needed someone to make sure you didn't leave early and to let him in after closing."

"And to take pictures." Nina held up her phone, where the screen showed Chase on one knee, the ring box open, Hallie's face a study in shock and joy. "I got the whole thing."

"Send those to me," Chase said, his arm coming around Hallie's waist and pulling her against his side. "My parents are going to want to see them."

"Your parents." Hallie turned to look at him. "Do they know?"

"Yes. I even asked your dad's permission first." His expression turned serious, then tender. "Metaphorically, I mean. I went to the cemetery last week and told him I was going to ask you to marry me. Told him I'd spend my life making you as happy."

Fresh tears spilled over, these carrying a different weight. Her father would have loved this and would have been so proud to see his daughter find this kind of love in the shop he'd built, surrounded by the Christmas magic he'd always believed in.

"This ring was my grandmother's—my dad's mother. I had it reset with a new diamond, but the setting is original. From 1952," he said.

Hallie looked down at the ring on her finger, seeing it with new understanding.

"It's perfect," she whispered. "All of it. It's perfect."

"We should probably let you two have a moment," Nina said, wiping her eyes with the back of her hand. "Sofia and I can finish closing up."

"Are you sure?" Hallie looked around at the shop that still needed attention—displays to straighten, receipts to file, doors to double-check.

"Positive. Go. Take your fiancé—oh my gosh, Hallie, you have a fiancé!—and go celebrate. We've got this."

Fiancé. The word settled into Hallie's consciousness with the weight of a vow. Chase was her fiancé. They were engaged. She was going to marry him.

"Thank you," Chase said to both women, his gratitude obvious in every word. "For helping with this, for being here and making this even more special and for being Hallie's people."

"Always," Nina said simply.

Sofia nodded, then made shooing motions with her hands. "Go on. We'll lock up when we're done. And Hallie? I'm so happy for you."

Chase picked up the stack of cards from the counter, tucking them under one arm. Then he took Hallie's free hand and laced their fingers together. The ring pressed against his skin, a tangible reminder of what had just happened, what they'd just promised each other.

They didn't leave, though. Not yet. Hallie needed this moment to last a little longer. Needed to stand in her father's shop wearing her future husband's grandmother's ring, surrounded by Christmas lights and the two women who'd been by her side through every hard season, and just breathe in the reality of answered prayers and second chances.

Chase seemed to understand without being told. He pulled her closer, both arms coming around her waist while she carefully held the roses to one side to keep from crushing them. His chin rested on top of her head, and she could feel his heartbeat against her cheek—steady and sure.

"I love you," he said. "I'm going to spend the rest of my life showing you how much."

She tilted her head back to look up at him, seeing her future reflected in his blue eyes.

"I love you too," she whispered. "Forever."

He kissed her again—soft and sweet, a sealing of vows not yet spoken but already written on their hearts. When he pulled back, his smile was bright enough to rival all the Christmas lights in the shop.

Around them, the store glowed with warmth and promise. Nina hummed "Here Comes the Bride" while she stacked receipts. Sofia's phone camera clicked repeatedly, capturing moments Hallie would treasure when she saw them later. Outside, snow continued to fall on Mistletoe Falls, blanketing the town in fresh white.

Hallie rested her head against Chase's chest again, listening to the steady rhythm of his heart and feeling the solid strength of his arms around her.

She'd spent years believing that home was this shop, this town, and the people she served so faithfully. But standing here in Chase's embrace, she finally understood.

Home wasn't a place at all.

Home was right here—in the arms of the man who'd crossed a covered bridge coming back home to Mistletoe Falls after twelve years of military service to find his way back to her, who'd knelt on the floor of her father's shop and promised forever, and who looked at her like she was every gift he'd ever wanted wrapped into one.

Home was wherever they'd be together, building a life one day at a time, one choice at a time, one moment of grace and love and laughter at a time.

Home was this.

And it was perfect.

Leave A Review

If you enjoyed this book, please consider leaving an honest review on Amazon

Visit Our Website:

www.tarabaisden.com

Visit Our Amazon Author Page HERE

Find Us On Social Media:

Facebook

Facebook Author Page

Instagram

Also by Tara Baisden

<u>**Laurel Ridge Series**</u>
#1. Season of Hope
#2. Finding Grace
#3. His Perfect Plan
#4. Love Redeemed
#5 Snowbound Blessings
#6 Sheltered Hearts
#7 Restoring Faith
#8 Love Rekindled
#9 Where She Belongs
#10 Shelter in His Arms
#11 Where Love Stands
#12 The Pieces We Mend
#13 Where Love Grows
#14 Where Hearts Heal
#15 Harvest of the Heart
#16 Heart of the Season

About The Author

Tara Baisden writes the kind of sweet, wholesome romances that feel cozy, comforting, and full of heart. She's the author of the beloved *Laurel Ridge* and *Riverbend Valley* inspirational series, as well as the *Mistletoe Falls* series, where Christmas magic and small-town charm are always on the menu.

A proud West Virginian, Tara makes her home on a peaceful stretch of mountain land where deer wander past her windows, the garden never quite weeds itself, and her pets supervise her writing schedule with great dedication. When she's not dreaming up stories of love, faith, and second chances, you'll likely find her quilting, digging in the dirt (sometimes successfully), hiking in the mountains, or curled up with a good book.

Family means everything to Tara, and some of her favorite moments are spent on the porch with loved ones—sharing stories, laughter, and maybe a slice of pie (because every good gathering needs pie). She also loves exploring the rich history of her home state and can't resist stopping at any bookstore she comes across.

TARA BAISDEN

Tara's readers often say her characters feel like family and her fictional towns like places they'd love to visit. Through every story, she hopes to inspire faith, celebrate love, and remind readers of the beauty found in life's simple joys.

You can connect with Tara at www.tarabaisden.com or follow her on social media for new releases, behind-the-scenes peeks, and the occasional glimpse of country life.

About Mistletoe Falls

Welcome to the fictional town of Mistletoe Falls, Tennessee!

Where Christmas Magic Lives Year-Round

*H*igh *in the Tennessee mountains, where winter lingers longer and Christmas spirit fills the air year-round, lies a town that feels almost too perfect to be real and looks like it stepped straight out of a holiday postcard.*

The winding mountain road to Mistletoe Falls tells you this isn't just any destination. Scenic Route 265 climbs higher into the Smoky Mountains with each breathtaking curve, past ancient trees heavy with snow that arch over the road like nature's own cathedral. But it's the final approach that steals your breath—crossing the enchanting Snowbell Covered Bridge, draped in evergreen garland and twinkling lights, as it spans the crystal waters of Mistletoe Creek below.

Beyond the bridge, the Welcome Pavilion greets every arrival with a hand-carved wooden sign: *"Welcome to Mistletoe Falls—Home of the Christmas Spirit."* The cheerful red pavilion, complete with candy cane striping and an archway of year-round twinkle lights, promises that something wonderful awaits just around the bend.

Mistletoe Falls (population 6,200) nestles in a perfect valley where the musical sound of cascading waterfalls mingles with church bells and children's laughter. The town spreads gracefully along Mistletoe Creek, whose series of waterfalls create the melodic backdrop to daily life.

This is Tennessee's beloved Christmas Town—because Christmas simply lives here. From the gas lamp streetlights wrapped in evergreen garland to the horse-drawn carriages clip-clopping down brick streets, every detail whispers of simpler times and sweeter moments.

The town square draws everyone like a magnet, centered around a Victorian gazebo where carols drift through the air and community life unfolds. Ancient oak trees frame the square, their branches creating natural shelter for the wooden benches below—each dedicated to a beloved neighbor who helped shape this special place. Thousands of lights transform the square into pure magic.

Mistletoe Lane curves gently around the town square before branching into charming side streets lined with century-old brick buildings. Each storefront tells a story through hand-carved details and cheerful striped awnings in hunter green, burgundy, and cream. Wide brick sidewalks invite leisurely strolls, while cozy benches appear just when you need them most.

The architecture whispers of careful love—original stonework preserved alongside modern conveniences, ensuring comfort while honoring the past. Three-story buildings house everything from the town bakery to the bookshop, with apartments above where business owners live.

From November through February, Mistletoe Falls transforms into a living snow globe. The special mountain microclimate ensures gentle snowfall that blankets everything in pristine white, while temperatures hover between 15 and 45 degrees—perfect for outdoor adventures and cozy indoor moments.

The partially frozen waterfalls become nature's chandeliers, catching winter light like thousands of diamonds. Snow-covered trails wind through frosted forests where the only sounds are your footsteps and the distant laughter from the town below. Long winter evenings mean crackling fireplaces, hot cider, and the kind of conversations that matter.

The Mistletoe Lodge stands as the town's crown jewel—a century-old mountain lodge with wraparound porches and stone fireplaces where love stories begin over morning coffee and evening wine. Its guest rooms blend historic charm with modern comfort, creating the perfect retreat for visitors who never quite want to leave.

The Snowbell Covered Bridge serves as more than transportation; it's where proposals happen and first kisses are shared, sheltered from mountain weather while framing perfect views of the approaching town.

The Mistletoe Christmas Tree Farm spreads across rolling hills on the town's outskirts, where families create memories among rows of Fraser firs and the air smells like pine and possibility.

What makes Mistletoe Falls magical isn't just its picture-perfect setting—it's the people who call it home. Three generations often work side by side in family businesses, while newcomers quickly discover they're not visitors but neighbors-in-waiting.

Local business owners coordinate holiday decorations and community events with the kind of collaboration that creates the seamless magic visitors remember long after they've returned home. This isn't performed charm—it's the real thing, preserved and protected by people who understand what they have.

In Mistletoe Falls, Christmas isn't a season—it's a way of life. The town square's gazebo hosts summer concerts alongside winter caroling. Local shops maintain touches of holiday magic through every season, because visitors quickly learn that any time is the right time to discover this special place.

The waterfalls provide cooling mists in summer and ice sculptures in winter. Mountain trails offer wildflower walks in spring and dramatic vistas in fall. But somehow, every season here feels like it's building toward December's grand celebration.

www.ingramcontent.com/pod-product-compliance
Lightning Source LLC
Chambersburg PA
CBHW011847300726
48970CB00009B/2686